BITTER PLAY

ALISON RHYMES

Dedicated to all the stupid men in the world who could learn a thing or two if they'd only pick up a romance novel.

PROLOGUE

"**H**ey, baby girl," I say, answering my phone. It's late for my sister, June, to be calling me. But then, Drew had a game tonight. She would have stayed up to watch it on television. She flies out to watch when she can, but it's less often these days since she's in her senior year of college. I still make it to most of his games, as I did today. Drew likes to have family in the stadium watching him.

He's not related by blood or name. We have been inseparable since we met at eight years old. His father is an asshole, has been for as long as I've known him. My family embraced him the first day I brought him home with me.

He's my chosen brother. Who just so happens to be one of the hottest young quarterbacks in the NFL.

"Reed." I make out through the sobs. They aren't my sister's cries, but it was her name on my screen. Her best friend must be calling me from June's phone.

"Leighton? Calm down, where's June?"

"H-hospital. He attacked her," she says before wailing again.

Fuck!

My sister has had a stalker for months. She's not told us the extent of it, or even the truth as to when it started. But it's escalated in the past few weeks. She's been in contact with the police over this guy, Jonas. There isn't a hell of a lot they'll do for her, though.

Obviously, not nearly enough.

"How bad?"

"Bad, but alive." Leighton's voice shatters over the three small words.

If I'd known it was to this point, I would have camped my ass in June's back pocket until she graduated.

"I'll be there as soon as I can. You do not put this phone down. Do you understand me, Love?"

"Yes. I'm sorry, Reed. I'm so sorry."

"Don't leave her side. I'll let you know when I land."

My hands shake as I call my parents. They're still shaking as I book two tickets on the next flight out of Green Bay to California. Drew exits the locker room as I'm finishing up.

"Hey, man. Sorry, that took so long," he says.

I look up from my phone, and his expression morphs to concern.

"It's June." My voice breaks apart on her name. On my sweet, innocent sister's name. "We have to go. Our flight leaves in forty-five minutes."

"What the fuck happened? Is she okay?"

I can only shake my head, afraid to speak. Afraid to lose it all together.

Crisis is a strange thing. Some come through with grace, others fall apart completely. I cannot fall apart right now. My sister needs me, my family needs me, Leighton needs me.

Breaking isn't a luxury I have just now.

"Reed, what the fuck is going on?" He's yelling now, panicked and scared. He's dropped his bag to the floor so he can pull at his hair.

"I don't know. He got to her, and she's in the hospital. Leighton is with her."

"Let's fucking go," he clips out. Leaving his bag, he marches straight out of the stadium.

It takes hours to get there, and I'm wrung out by the time we do. Drew has asked me, repeatedly, what exactly Leighton said. He's trying to glean information—I get it. I can't take it anymore, though. All I want to do is get to my baby sister. The plane ride was fucking brutal. I've been texting back and forth with Leighton; *Love* as my sister calls her. June is still in surgery, and nothing has changed. My parents are there now. That only makes me feel mildly better.

My sister's closest friend greets us at the hospital entrance when we arrive. Leighton Ward looks like a beautifully heartbroken angel. She's the most gorgeous woman I've ever laid eyes on, with long wavy strands of blonde hair that show a hint of strawberry in the right sunlight. Bright eyes, with a face peppered with light freckles I've often tried to count without notice. Even with her cheeks splotchy from crying, I can only stare at her in awe. I'm barely out of the car before she takes off running in my direction, nearly getting hit by a passing vehicle.

"Jesus," Drew curses beside me.

She collides into my chest the moment I open my arms for her. She shivers so violently, I'm afraid she will fall to pieces at my feet.

"I'm sorry. I told her to wait for me. I told her to wait."

"Take us to her," I tell her, brushing the wild hairs away as they stick to her tear-stained face.

Leighton grasps my hand tightly as she leads the way. I rub my thumb back and forth on her skin to calm her and myself. June didn't grow up with close girlfriends. Her time was spent reading books or hanging out with me and Drew. The girls that tried to befriend her typically only wanted to get to her hot brother and his even hotter friend.

It turned her untrusting of women in general.

Leighton has been good for her. She's honest, loyal, and cares about June in the same way we care about Drew. June and Leighton are like sisters, soulmates, kindred spirits, maybe. Whatever they are, they chose to be family.

I'll choose her, too. Someday. When the time is right.

Drew and I follow Leighton inside and up three floors where we find my parents. My dad is stoic and quiet, all while cuddling my mother, who is in much the same state as Leighton.

"Any news?"

"No, Drew. Nothing yet," my father answers him. "She's still in surgery."

He and I take turns wrapping our arms around my mother before we settle into the chairs of our own. Leighton takes the seat next to me. fidgeting with her hands. I reach over and steady them with my own.

"How did this happen?"

"She wanted to walk back to the dorms by herself," she answers, her voice clogged with the tears she's choking down. "I told her not to, to wait for me. Not even an hour later, I was on my way back when I saw the police and the ambulance. They already had her loaded, but I saw her face, her hair. I knew right away what happened."

"Where is he?" Drew growls.

"I don't know. I told the police what had been happening. There's an officer here somewhere. She's supposed to let us know when they have news," she says, her voice betraying how exhausted she is. "I'm sorry I couldn't stop her."

"Stop that, Love. It's not your fault," I tell her, wrapping my arm around her shoulders and pulling her in. She rests her head on my shoulder and closes her eyes.

Sleep doesn't come for either of us, though. I can't until I know June is okay. The way Leighton is twitching, I'd guess her mind isn't letting her forget what she's seen tonight.

The officer arrives before a doctor does.

"Miss Ward?" the woman asks, and I nudge Leighton to open her eyes. "Are Miss Turner's parents here?"

"That's us," my father says, and Leighton nods to the officer.

"Hello, Mr. Turner. Mrs. Turner." The officer shakes both of their hands. "We found your daughter's attacker. It appears he returned home and took his own life."

"Oh. Oh, thank you," my mother cries, turning into my father's chest. A huge sense of relief washes over me. As much as I'd love to see that sick fuck tortured by a prison sentence, this way saves my baby sister future turmoil. Plus, he'll never be able to hurt anyone again.

The officer speaks more with my parents. Something about waiting for news of June's condition before any final reports are filed. It's hard to pay attention between my own emotions swirling in my stomach and Leighton's hiccupping sobs at my side. She's got her hands on her face as she cries into them.

"Hey, Leighton," I say, moving to crouch in front of her. "Look at me, Love." I gently pry her hands away.

"She has to be okay, Reed. I don't know how to live without her."

She can barely speak the words through all the raw feelings. Leighton and June are everything to each other. Their bond is special. Much like mine and Drew's. Also, like him, Leighton has little family. Leighton's devotion to my sister only makes me want her more.

"She's going to be okay," I say, determined to believe it myself. "We're all going to be just fine. Okay?"

Her response is a silent, wide-eyed nod.

Hours and hours later, we're in June's room. She's out of the first round of surgery, the round that saved her life. But they've said more will be needed. She's stable though. She survived. And that's the most important thing. We'll get her through the rest, all of us.

I dozed off in the lounge chair a few feet away from her bed. My parents went to get some sleep at a hotel, as my mom was dead on her feet. Leighton is at my side, curled up and using my arm for a pillow.

Drew… Well, he is at my sister's side. He's pulled up a chair as close as he can get it; her hand tightly curled in both of his. All the while, he whispers the things he's always wanted to say to her but hasn't yet. He has his reasons, like I have mine with Leighton.

June almost died, changing his entire perspective. He tells her how much he loves her, how much he always has.

"When you wake up, Junie, things will be different. I'm not waiting anymore. As soon as you're out of here, baby. I just need you to wake up now. We have so much life to live, you and I, together."

Leighton sniffles, diverting my attention to her instead of the pleas I'm not meant to hear. She's awake, tears tracking down her cheeks as her heart breaks for my sister and for Drew. I palm her face, thumbing away the small pebbles of liquid. Her lips part. It's enough for me to know she's feeling the same thing I am.

The extraordinary connection always weighed heavy between us. Maybe it was love at first sight, if you believe in that sort of thing. I never did, though, June always swore it was real. Leighton makes me believe in something close to it.

So, I take the taste I've always denied us both. Closing the little distance between us, pressing my lips to hers. Letting her feel with me, through me.

We're going to be okay.

We'll get through this. All of us. Because we're a family, a strong one. Leighton included.

This is our first kiss. Emotional and traumatic as it is, it's special. *Meaningful.*

"Get some sleep, Love," I whisper against her mouth. She snuggles in, and within minutes, we're both napping again.

When I wake up, she's gone. June is still unconscious. The dim hospital room is quiet, save for the sounds of the medical equipment keeping track of her vitals. Drew sits beside her, guarding her dreams as much as her body.

Standing, I stretch out my muscles, trying to work out the kinks.

"Coffee?" I ask. He nods. He hasn't slept, but something tells me he won't. Not until she's awake anyway. The two have loved each other for more years than maybe even they realize. I saw it, my parents saw it. Neither of them has fought it, exactly. Rather, they've waited each other out. That wait is over and, frankly, it's about damn time.

As I make my way to the small coffee shop two floors down, I'm stopped in my tracks by the sight of Leighton, in the arms of some dude who's kissing the same lips mine had not so long ago. I hear him tell her to call if she needs anything as I turn the opposite direction to grab coffee.

Their kiss rankles me, but I brush it off. While I hate witnessing it, I know she dates. Actively. I'm only feeling the burn because I'm exhausted and worried more than I've ever been in my life.

June is the only thing I need to spend energy on right now. Since the day she was born, she's been the most important person in my life.

Besides, this is further proof that Leighton isn't ready for what I eventually plan to offer her.

We just shared our first kiss. It will be a while before we have another. Leighton has dreams, a life to settle into, young womanhood to explore, a career to obtain. I'll let her experience enough life without me to never have to wonder, or feel like she was tied down too young, too soon.

The wait isn't only for her; it's for me to live some life, too. I have a career as a graphic designer, it pays the bills, but I'm not where I want to be. More accurately, I don't know where I want to be. I only know who I eventually want to be with.

Except, Leighton isn't there yet. She's a free spirit, freer than anyone I've ever known. Her life right now is all about fun and exploration. I'll bide my time. Wait. Until she's over dating a new guy every week.

Until I know that she's in the same headspace that I am. The place that is certain once we commit to each other, it's the end game. Once she's there…

I'm coming for her.

There will be no one after her for me. There will be no one after me for her.

That was our first kiss. It means the world, but it's her last kiss I want most.

1

REED

"What can I get for you, Love?"

Ireland has been great, but if one more person calls any of us *love*, I'm going to lose my freaking mind. It reminds me of Leighton. Every. Single. Time.

As my sister's best friend, Leighton had been invited on this family vacation. This insanely lavish vacation. Thanks to my brother-in-law, Drew. He's normally frugal, especially for being one of the highest paid quarterbacks in the NFL. But Drew didn't skimp on this trip. It was a gift to my mother. A trip my father always planned on taking her on, but he died too soon.

None of us are flashy; he could have booked basic hotels and commercial trains. But that's not what he did. We've stayed in luxurious hotels and even one castle. And we have a private driver.

It's ridiculous.

We've experienced everything in a style none of us are accustomed to. I have to say, I've enjoyed it. Not that I care about polished luxury sedans and hotel rooms equipped with the best of the best. Ireland itself is what I've enjoyed. This is a special place, and I felt it as soon as we stepped off the plane. I've never been to another place like it. It's lively while still being inherently laid-back. And every touristy destination we've been to has blended seamlessly with its surroundings. Unlike in the US, where every landmark becomes a theme park. A return trip is high on my list of plans. I'd love to spend more time in Northern Ireland and Scotland. Both places are so rich in history, I could get lost in it too easily. Plus, the graffiti in Belfast—I could spend days and days there. But not with my entire family.

I'm an artist at heart. Something I've never been overly open about. Graphic design pays the bills, and while I enjoy it, it's not my passion. My family knows it. But other than my parents, June, and Drew, nobody has seen my paintings.

My mother has loved every minute of Ireland. She deserves it. Not only did she raise my bratty ass, she's also the reason my sister is the most caring woman to have ever lived. And she was a pivotal figure in Drew's life, as well.

My father, before his passing a few years back, had been planning this trip for some time. Mom always had the dream of coming here and he wanted to give her the opportunity. Drew is giving it to her instead, but it's no less special to her.

Leighton declined the invitation to vacation with us all. Because of that, I was looking forward to this trip. Not just in spending time with my family, but as a reprieve from all things Leighton. Or rather, all things Leighton and Connor, her boyfriend. That wasn't supposed to happen. Her being in anything remotely like a relationship with anyone but me. But she's been dating this guy for months now. On paper, they're a great couple; successful, good-looking, confident. Except, Connor Anders is nothing more than a placeholder, because Leighton Ward has always been mine.

Ireland has done nothing to quench my mind's thirst for her. She's taken up permanent residence there. Every blonde woman I see reminds me of her. Every new, gorgeous site we visit makes me wonder what she'd think of it. What she'd look like standing in grand ruins or along the Cliffs of Moher, her hair blowing in the wind as I'd wrap my arms around her to fight off the chill. So obsessed with her am I that every bedroom I step into at night creates an image of her spread out on the bed waiting for me.

It's a fucking problem.

My entire world purview has been reduced to Leighton Ward, and only Leighton Ward.

Even here, sitting in the busy hubbub of the Guinness Storehouse, surrounded by the chatter and laughter of hundreds of strangers. It's Leighton I hear asking me what I'd like for lunch, her hand softly touching my shoulder to gain my attention.

Our server looks nothing like Leighton, though. Perhaps the height is right, but that's where the similarities stop. She's not blonde, no. Instead, her red, curly hair is pulled into a messy topknot, exposing the fair skin of her neck dotted with freckles. Leighton's freckles lightly speck the apples of her cheeks, exactly where the hue deepens when I say the right thing or look at her a few beats too long.

Our server is pretty and has a comfortable ease about her that I like. Confidence is something I've always found sexy as hell. This waitress, Emma, as her nametag reads, has confidence in spades. And I'm frustrated enough to take her up on the flirtatious banter she's been throwing my way while taking our orders.

My head isn't interested in Emma. But my dick is.

I order fish and chips and watch her ass as she walks back to the kitchen.

"Drew, this has been the most amazing vacation. I could have never dreamed up everything you planned for us," Mom tells him, a smile brightening her face.

"But it's time to get home, huh?" He winks at her.

"Oh, dear, yes. I'm exhausted."

We're all wearing down with that homesickness that kicks in at the end of a long vacation. Drew and June need to head back to Seattle for training camp since the season starts soon. He's already pushed the date to make this trip. I'm sure his coach isn't pleased, but overall, the team has been supportive of him and June taking more time for their marriage.

June discovered last year that Drew had been cheating on her. It was a hard road for them both, and they've been through many, many therapy sessions. Both together and separately. Drew is a different man than before. Thankfully, because it's hard to hate your best friend, your brother. But I did during that time. I've always loved him, though, it's not impossible to feel both emotions simultaneously. It was hard on us all, my mother included, who sees Drew as more than a son by marriage. She helped raise him. We were livid at what he'd done, but supportive as he navigated his way to becoming a better man. It was difficult to help them while they worked through the issues that drove Drew to what he'd been doing.

It was a balancing act I never want to repeat. If he fucks up like that again, I'll murder him with my own hands. He's gotten a second chance from us all because we believe in his love for June. He won't get a third. But he knows that. He's very aware of how lucky he's been, and he's not taking it, or my sister, for granted any longer.

It says a lot about a man when everyone he knows stands behind him in the darkest times. Nobody condones what he did, by any means. But everyone gave him the chance to change. Drew's entire team has been overwhelmingly accommodating to his efforts. In return, he's ready to work harder than he ever has for them. He has big expectations for this season, and we all believe in him.

It will be a big year for me, as well.

I took a new job. A big one. While my sister and Drew will move back to Seattle for the next several months, I'll be relocating from there to where their second home is. New Orleans, Louisiana. And I'll be living right next door to the woman whom I see as both the love of my life and the current bane of my existence.

June has a love for real estate. Specifically, old houses that come with their own slew of ghosts. She's an adorable weirdo like that. Drew had been secretly buying them up all over the country. Likely to soothe his own guilt. Whatever the reason, he knew June would love the one in New Orleans most. It's a grand old thing and happened to be in the city where her best friend lived. Knowing June would want to spend a lot of time there, he bought the duplex next door, too. Half for me and my mom, half for Leighton and her dad.

Leighton moved in months ago, while my side sits empty.

That will change in a few weeks when I start my position with *Southern Lifestyle* magazine as the art director for their new publication. They've been around for years, but their subscriptions have been falling with the younger crowd. Looking to expand their demographic, they're revamping by adding a new online magazine geared toward the under-forty crowd.

That's where I come in. All I have left to do is pack up the few belongings I plan on taking with me, which isn't much. My clothes will come, although I won't need all the gear for colder, wetter days while living in the southern heat and humidity. Most of my furniture is staying too. Basically, if it doesn't fit into my SUV, it's not coming with me.

"Oh, that's pretty," June says absently, while looking at her phone.

"What is?" Mom asks.

"Lorelai posted a picture of the sample flower arrangement for the wedding."

"You follow her?" I ask, not a little astonished. June has empathy for days and days, but Lorelai is the woman Drew was involved with on the side. The one June caught him with.

She is also the woman marrying June's close friend and co-worker, Noah Anders. Noah, brother of Leighton's boyfriend, Connor. We could not be a more convoluted bunch if we tried.

It's a messy web.

Drew always insisted that Lorelai wasn't a bad person. Noah is even more adamant about it, and he's a hard man not to trust. I know little about the woman. What I do know is that it's twisted for my sister to be following her on Instagram.

"Yeah," she says with a shrug. "Morbid curiosity, I guess."

"Have you decided if you'll be going to the wedding?" Mom asks her. Noah and Lorelai invited June and Drew. I'm sure it was as to not seem rude, but I figure they don't expect them to attend.

June sighs heavily.

"We've been discussing it," Drew answers. "We can go to support Noah, but if either of us shows any discomfort... Well, that may ruin their day. So, maybe, it's better to skip it."

June stays quiet, still flipping through her phone.

"That's perfectly understandable. I'm sure Noah understands. If the tables were reversed, I imagine he'd do the same," Mom says. My sister doesn't look convinced. While I don't know Noah nearly as well as her, I'm not sure what Mom said is true. Noah Anders is unlike anyone I've ever met; it's probably why he and my sister get along so well. Because she is, too.

If ever there were two people who could stay friends after such a complicated situation, it's them.

"Maybe I'm overthinking it," June finally comments. "I mean, I know she's not trying to break up our marriage. It's clear how much she loves Noah, how happy she makes him. That should be enough for me. It's what's most important, after all."

"Sure, but that doesn't mean you're ready to celebrate with her. Noah wouldn't put those expectations on you, baby girl. Only do what you're comfortable with."

"Reed's right, Junie," Drew agrees. "Let's just see how you feel the closer it gets. There isn't any pressure to decide. Noah told us that himself."

"Do you want to go?" I ask him.

"The situation is different for me. Lorelai did plenty to piss me off, but I guess I understand her better. And let's be clear here, I'm the one that owed June more than I gave. Lorelai was a bystander, not an altogether innocent one, but still. I know that I had more power and responsibility in the situation than anyone else," he says, running his hands through his hair. A tell that he's uncomfortable. "I know firsthand how terrifying it is to lose the love of your life and not know if you can ever get them back. I'm honestly glad she and Noah have worked things out. I'm happy for them, and I want the best for their marriage."

"You've grown up a lot this past year, Drew," Mom says, reaching over to take his hand. He pulls it up to his mouth and kisses it.

Drew grew up with a dysfunctional father and no mother. When June left him, he was horrified that he'd not only put his marriage at risk, but that he might lose the only mother he'd ever known. He and my mom spoke often while he was going through therapy.

Emma comes back with our food and the subject changes to much less stressful topics. I notice the way she lingers at my side, touching my arm again after she sets my meal down.

"Let me know if I can help with anything else," she says, her meaning clear. Drew laughs and mumbles something under his breath.

"Seriously? That is like the tenth time some random woman has tried to flirt with you on this trip."

"What can I say, dear sister? I'm a fucking catch."

"Language, Reed," Mom scolds. "But you're right, of course. Any woman would be lucky to have you."

"You have to say that, Mom. He's your son."

"It's true, June. And I always said the same about you. Though it was clear from an early age, your heart was already taken."

"Ew, stop," I tease. "I don't need the reminder of their pining teenage years. It still gives me nightmares."

"Shut up, Reed," June says as Drew smacks my shoulder. Mom and I just laugh.

We call it an early night. There's time in the morning for breakfast before our flight, but it will be a long day and the rest will do Mom good. I have other plans.

In the form of one pretty, confident redhead who knocks on my hotel room door just after ten o'clock. June was right, plenty of women on this trip have shown me interest. This is the first time I've reciprocated. Emma came at the perfect time of my own self-pity.

I cure it with my dick in her mouth. It's not classy; it's cliché, even. Spending myself in some random woman as I pine for the one who isn't mine because I refused to stake a claim when I should have. I'm not proud of using her this way, but I don't stop either.

Emma knows the deal. This is just sex. Just one night. She's likely using me to forget someone else for a hot minute, too. By the look on her face, when I strip my clothes off, she's appreciative too. You don't grow up with a dedicated, elite athlete without learning how to take care of your body. I'm in excellent shape and I don't mind showing it off when the time is right. It doesn't happen often. My sex life is active enough, but I don't go out looking for it just for the sake of fucking.

I like sex. I like it more when there is some connection beyond mere mutual attraction. Lust is easy. Sex is easy.

I want more.

I want a challenge.

I want Leighton Marie Ward.

Despite not getting a full night's rest, thanks to Emma who left in the wee hours of the morning, I'm feeling better the following morning. Slightly less in my head. More present and alert. Maybe I needed a good release.

I meet the family in the dining area of the Bed and Breakfast Drew bought out for our stay here in Dublin. I'm the last one, but it doesn't look like they've been here long. Taking a seat, I grab the carafe of coffee from the center of the table.

The owners of the B&B bring out too much food for us. Scones, boxty, oatmeal, porridge. I forgo the black pudding but add several pieces of sausage to my plate.

"Good morning, son."

"Morning," I say before taking a bite of my scone.

"Sleep well, dude?" Drew asks, a smirk taking up half of his face. He knows me too well.

"Sure did."

"Gross," June says, so I shoot her a big grin. Her phone rings, and after a peek at the caller, she gets up and steps away from the table to take the call.

"I hope you were safe, Reed."

"Mother." I sigh.

"I'm just saying," she says, holding her hands up. "The last thing you need is an STD or a woman pregnant halfway around the world."

"Jesus," I mutter while Drew laughs loudly. "I was safe. Would you like the details, or can you just trust me?"

"Reed," she admonishes. Drew laughs even louder.

After several moments, June returns to the table, looking more somber than she did when she received the phone call.

"Everything okay, baby?" Drew asks.

"It was Love," she says, shaking her head. "Connor is moving to Thailand and asked her to go with him."

My heart almost stops beating, and the edges of my vision blur. Anxiety is never something I've struggled with; panic attacks aren't anything I've ever worried about. But I'm sure I'm about to be swallowed up by one as the voices around me sound farther and farther away. My focus narrows into tunnel vision on one single thought.

I will murder that man if he takes Leighton to Thailand.

She's mine; I'm sure of it. Gut-clenching guilt wracks me at the idea that I've missed my opportunity to make it clear to her. To the world.

Something June says breaks through the thick fog in my head.

"No, they broke up."

"Say that again," I nearly growl.

"Say what?"

"Say it again, June. The whole thing. Say it again," I grind out.

"Connor asked Leighton to move to Thailand with him, but she said no. They broke up."

Oh, thank fuck.

"She's sure?"

June looks at me like I'm asking the dumbest question on the planet. I just want clarification. Or reassurance.

"Obviously."

The blood rushes back through my limbs, tingling the tips of my fingers.

"Don't fuck this up, buddy," Drew whispers to me.

I have no intention to, either.

I'm coming for Leighton. She better be ready.

2

LEIGHTON

I wonder what age it is, specifically, that we stop learning new technology. Whatever it is, apparently, I've hit it. Navigating these dating apps is a nightmare. Why are there so many? Trying to figure out which ones cater to booty calls as opposed to which ones seem to attract people looking for real relationships was enough of a struggle. You discover quickly by the caliber of messages that hit your direct messages.

The number of unsolicited dick pics I've received is unbelievable.

I don't know why I'm even trying so soon. Connor has been gone for a few days now. He literally moved two days after asking me to go with him. Who does that?

In the ten months we dated, there had been no discussion of a future, or of any longevity for our relationship. There weren't labels to what we were; we were more like each other's perpetual plus one than two people exclusively dating. We were casual, but it was still the most meaningful relationship I've ever been in with a man. And we had a bond, an easiness with one another. I'd hoped it could grow, and that someday, Connor and I would see each other as more, and passion would spark.

Love never entered my thoughts where Connor was concerned, but attachment sure did. Affection was there. I *cared* about a man who spent weeks in a hiring process for a job on the other side of the world and he never said a single word to me about it.

Maybe he didn't owe me that, as we hadn't defined our relationship in strict terms. But we were exclusive for almost a year. I can't help but feel as if it's a slap in the face. Or that I wasted nearly a year nurturing a relationship I thought was full of respect, even if love didn't live there yet.

There were moments these past few months when I was sure Connor appraised me with an affection he hadn't shown before. As if he was seeing me as more than someone to pass time with. Maybe that was his guilt eating away at him.

I want what most women want. A man that supports us in our endeavors and ambitions, who takes care of us when we need it and stays out of the way when we don't, who loves us without fail, and fucks us like he hates us.

Connor was fun, nice to look at, easy to talk to, and good in bed. It hurts that he left. That there wasn't more discussion, that he wasn't sad at my decision of not moving with him. There was never that tingle with Connor. The feeling that flutters in your toes and tummy when a man touches you.

Those things have only happened once. Exactly, one time in my life. The only time Reed kissed me. Then shortly after, he turned cold. And while I tried to continually place myself in his way, he ignored me with a steady pace. Now? Well, now, he's become downright rude.

So, screw Grumpy Reed Turner. Screw Connor Anders, too. There's a big sea to dive into and my fish is out there, waiting for me to reel him in.

Hence, these damn dating apps.

After all, the best way to get over a man is to get under a new one.

Ugh, did I just think that?

I've never been one to believe in the fable of a woman's biological clock. Until now. There's this innate need for something different. A change. Or, just *more*. The next step, a commitment. I don't know, maybe a family. Not necessarily a brood of kids, but people I can call mine.

My mom disappeared when I was young. I remember very little about her. According to my dad, she struggled with addiction shortly after I was born. He looks back on it now and believes postpartum depression spiraled out of control. There was only so much he could do, and he tried everything to help her. She eventually ran off with her drug dealer. I was three then. We never heard from her again.

Technically, my dad is still married to her.

My dad, Larry, is my world. He's been nothing but loving and supportive. June is my soul, the best friend anyone could ask for. It was fate being paired with her as a roommate in college.

I have friends, sure. But people I know I can rely on for anything and everything? Just those two. I'm realizing now that I want to expand my small circle. Maybe that's why I kept going out with Connor.

Which is a depressing thought. Choosing a man in my life should depend on much more than just convenience and need. Until recently, if someone asked me who I'd choose for a life partner, my answer would have been swift and confident.

Reed.

That's not such an easy answer anymore.

The first time I met Reed, I was entranced. I'd flown with June to California for one of Drew's games. It was my first time meeting both men and June's parents. Reed was the best-looking guy I'd ever seen up close and personal. He's tall, fit but lean, and his hair, which is perpetually too long on top, is the most unique color of bourbon. His defined jaw and dark eyes only add to his sexy good looks.

It was like a teenage crush, the way I wanted to follow him around like a puppy. He never reciprocated the attention, and I eventually gave up. Until June ended up in the hospital. Reed and I were joined at the hip then. Joined in our worry. Looking back, I understand that when he kissed me, it had much more to do with the situation we were all in. Far less to do with me.

Which explained how he took several steps back from me after that. His concern for my well-being was still evident, but there was no longer any cuddling as we slept in that stark hospital room, hoping for June to wake up. Reed must not have wanted me to get the wrong impression.

It hasn't stopped me from trying to gain his attention at every chance I've gotten, hoping someday he'd notice. He does. I know he does. I see him watching me sometimes. But he refuses to act.

BEN

Tomorrow. Bar Tonique. 6PM?

ME

Sounds good. See you then.

This guy, Ben, and I matched on one of these apps. He looks dark and handsome in his picture, but it also looks filtered to within an inch of its life. I hope this one goes better than the last blind date I went on, before I met Connor. I should have known better than to go out with a guy named Chad. He wanted to meet at the park for a coffee. Sounded easy, comfortable, most importantly, safe. Except, Chad brought his five chihuahuas with him.

I do like dogs well enough. But my idea of a first date does not include five hyper ones that acted as if they hadn't seen daylight in months.

I left the 'date' after ten minutes and blocked Chad on all platforms while I walked home. He wasn't the worst of the worst I've conversed with. But he was the worst I met in person. It would be silly for me to think there won't be more horrible experiences to follow.

I may be on the wild side, but silly, I am not. So, I'm prepared for a wild dating ride while I search for my future husband.

Who is decidedly not Connor Anders or Reed Turner.

Checking the clock, I decide it's time to call it a night. I need to be up early tomorrow for an interview. I love being a journalist, but being a beat reporter for the local news station is wearing me down. There isn't a set schedule; it's a lot like being on call twenty-four-seven. A national publication based here in New Orleans is hiring for writers. Both the schedule and the salary appealed to me, and I was lucky enough to get an interview.

As I'm climbing into bed, I hear a banging sound next door. June hasn't said anything about Reed coming to town. And since June and Drew are in Seattle, there's even less reason for him to be here. As he's never too far away from them.

Peeking out my bedroom window, I see it is Reed, and he's grabbing a box from the back of his Jeep.

What the hell?

Rushing downstairs and out the front door, I catch him as he walks out his door, heading back to his vehicle.

"What are you doing?"

He stops, pinning me in place with the intensity of his stare. It drags down my body, slowly enough for me to know every body part he's looking at as he does it. A shiver runs up my spine at his assessment.

"You're cold," he says, roughly.

"What?"

"Go back inside, Love. I'll come see you in a minute."

"What?" I ask again, confused that he's here, and a little annoyed that two seconds into our meeting and he's already being bossy. And why is he calling me love? He hasn't done that in years. It affects me more than I'd like to admit.

Reed's strong jaw tightens in what I guess is frustration. *But, like, join the club, buddy.*

"You're practically naked. Go back inside. When I unload the last of this, I'll come over."

"I can help."

"No."

"No?"

"I don't need your help, and you aren't dressed to be out here anyhow. Inside." He gestures with a nod behind me. "Now."

He speaks quietly but with an authority I've never heard from him before. I'm so dumbfounded by the past minute that I go along with what he said and retreat into my house. Though, I leave the front door open and stand where I can watch him make a few more trips from his car to his house. Apparently, he's moving in, but I'm certain June would have told me that.

ME

Why is Reed here?

She doesn't answer me right away. Instead, I hear Reed's phone ring as he walks back inside with another arm full of boxes. I pace around, waiting for a response or for him to come over. Eventually, he walks back outside, and my phone chimes.

What the hell?

I turn from the door and start furiously typing back to June. Rambling messages, really. I'm not sure what I'm saying. All I know is that I am unprepared for Reed to be living next door.

My front door slams, making me jump.

"Don't walk out front looking like that anymore."

Looking down at what I'm wearing, I pause. Because, yeah, it's skimpy and light, but all my bits are covered. *Mostly.* It's a silk camisole that dips low, with matching shorts that, at least, cover my ass cheeks.

"You don't make rules for me, Reed," I say, spinning toward him. A half smile stretches across his. "What are you doing here?"

"Moving in," he answers, taking a step closer.

"At ten o'clock at night?"

"What's wrong with that?"

"It's creepy. It's when axe murderers or covens of witches move in."

Reed laughs. "You have an overactive imagination, Love."

"Why are you calling me that?" I ask, narrowing my eyes.

"I drove for three days. Hardly slept," he says, taking a few more steps closer, until we're only inches apart. "I'm exhausted. Can you just give me a goodnight hug without a fight?"

"You want a hug?"

He nods, that same half-smile lighting up his face.

"Um, okay," I mumble and put my arms around his waist. Reed wraps me up in his presence, cocooning me in his scent that is unique to him. I've smelled it before, many times, and never been able to place it. It's just *him.*

He bends at the knees, lowering his face into the crook of my neck, then takes a deep inhale.

"Did you just smell me?"

"Yes," he says quietly, humor lacing the word.

"Why?"

"Didn't we just establish that I'm creepy?"

I can't help the burst of laughter; his arms tighten around me. Then he steps away. There's a brief stare down, where I try to detangle how he's acting. Except, how good he looks gets in the way. He doesn't look haggard from driving across the country. He looks more relaxed than I've seen him in ages.

The darkness he's carried the last few times I've seen him has faded. His high cheekbones carry a happy hue. It looks damn good on him. Pangs of the unrequited crush I held on to for far too long poke at my insides. If I couldn't shake it easily before, it will be even harder now that he'll be a bigger part of my world here in New Orleans.

But I'll figure it out. Somewhere, a man exists that will pine for me when I'm not around. I won't settle for anything less.

"Goodnight, I'll see you tomorrow," he says and walks to the door. "Lock this up. And know that the next time you walk out this front door with your nipples pitching tents like that, you'll answer to me."

Asshole.

3

LEIGHTON

ME

I got the job!

JUNE

Congratulations! They're lucky to have you.

ME

I'll call you after I get back home.

Miss you, love you!

JUNE

Miss you, love you!

My entire body tingles with excitement. The publication, *Southern Lifestyle,* has been around for decades as a guide to Southern living for an older or more affluent crowd. But their new publication, *Moxy,* is for the twenty- and thirty-somethings. We'll be focused on singles, young families, and activities for both. To top it off, they're hiring me as one of their lead journalists. Which means more freedom on the stories I write, and I'll only answer to the editor-in-chief.

My salary will be nearly double to what I was making at the station, but the biggest bonus is that I'll make my own schedule, revolving around whatever piece I'll be writing.

I hadn't realized what a weight my crazy schedule was until the moment I realized it was almost gone. There won't even be a reason to be camera ready either, because I'll never have to be on camera for this job.

Strange how accustomed you get to the way your life is that you don't expect it to ever change.

I call my dad on the way to the station to turn in my two-week notice. Dad, as always, is proud and supportive of my decision to take the new job. He's always been my biggest cheerleader. We're close, and always have been, born from the fact that we only had each other to rely on for so many years. Dad was in the Army, and we moved around a lot. He was my only constant in life. Until college. Until June. Then she became a constant, too.

Heading straight to Brad's office after arriving at the station, I wave hello to a few co-workers. I'll miss a few but see no reason we can't keep up a casual friendship after I'm gone. Bradley Newton has been my boss since I took this job several years ago. He's pompous as all fuck, but decent enough to work for.

"Do you have a minute, Brad?" I ask, knocking on the frame of his office door.

"Sure," he says, glancing up. "Whatcha got for me?"

After shutting the door behind me, I take a seat across the desk from him.

"I accepted a new position today. I need to give my two weeks' notice."

"Damnit, really?"

"Yep, it's a great offer. I can't pass it up."

"Anything I can do to talk you out of it?" he asks.

"Highly doubtful, Brad. But I appreciate that you'd try."

"You've been fun to have around, Ward. We'll miss you. And I can't promise I'll take it easy on you for your last two weeks."

I groan but smile. "You've been a good boss, Brad. No need to screw that up now."

He laughs as I walk out and I'm thankful the conversation didn't last longer. My mind is made up, and I'm happy with my decision. It would have been an awkward waste of our time if he'd made any real effort to talk me out of it.

And another unnoticed weight falls from my shoulders.

As soon as I get home, I call June and place her on speakerphone while I get ready for my date with Mr. Too Many Filters aka Ben.

"Hi, Love," she answers after the second ring.

"Hey, how's my second favorite city treating you?"

"Good so far. It hasn't started raining yet so I've been able to get the flowerbeds cleaned up."

June and Drew spent most of the off season down here in New Orleans instead of sticking to Seattle. Well, June spent more time down here because she left Drew, but when they reconciled, he followed her here and stayed put. And while they have more money than they know what to do with, neither is the type to hire someone to take care of the things they can do themselves. Like yardwork, apparently.

"Ah, I miss trees. I think there's enough room in the backyard here. We should plant a magnolia."

"We? You going to consult Reed, or just do what you want?"

"Your brother would probably say no just to spite me," I retort, and June snickers, knowing it would be like him.

"Did you talk to him after he got in last night?"

"Briefly. He shooed me inside after I offered to help him unload, then he came over to say goodnight."

"Did he tell you about the job?"

"No. What is it?" I ask.

"I don't know. He was very short with me when I called to find out why he was there. It's bizarre—why would he rush out of here just as we move back home? And not tell us about it."

That is weird behavior for Reed. He never strays too far from his sister or his best friend.

"When I meet him next, I'll see if I can pry anything out of him. But you know how that goes," I say, my meaning clear. He's been rude and abrupt with me the past few times we've been in each other's vicinity.

"Yeah." June sighs. "Enough about him. Tell me about this job and this date."

I fill her in on *Moxy*, and predictably, she is enthusiastic about the position.

"Love, that's going to be amazing for you. I know you hate the schedule of nightly news. And you'll be working for Fran, which will be such a great experience. I'm jealous."

Fran Carmichael will be Moxy's editor. She's a huge personality with a long history in the industry. June's right; it will be a great experience being under her tutelage.

"And the date?" June asks.

"Ben is his name. We're only meeting for a drink. He looks yummy, but pictures can be so deceiving on these dating apps. I don't want to get my hopes up. He was very nice and polite with his messages, though."

"No dick pic?"

"Thankfully." I laugh. "I mean, if a guy had something to work with, I'd be happy to assess it, maybe give him a rating. Unfortunately, the only dudes who send them unsolicited seem to be borderline micro-dicks."

"Oh my god! That bad?"

"Either that, or they're oddly shaped. Do you remember when Favre's dick ended up all over the media? No way he could lie to his wife that it wasn't his. It was distinctive. And not in a good way. The head was weird, like it was wearing a little umbrella hat. Well, that's the kind of shit guys send me."

"Oof."

"Right? Just once I'd like someone to show me something impressive."

"Maybe you'll get your wish tonight, if this Ben works out."

"One can hope." Though, honestly, I'm not looking for that. But I've never set rules on my sexual activity. I do what feels right for me. I'm not stupid about it, but I don't deny myself pleasure just because I'm a woman. Purity was never a virtue I coveted. Never mind that my father taught me that anything a man can do, I can do too, and better.

Like casual sex.

"What are you going to wear?"

"The Alice and Olivia baby doll you gave me, I think." June always gives me the best clothes for holidays, and often just because. In return, when she and Drew were struggling, I spent the better part of my savings on sexy underthings and playthings for her. She needed the confidence boost and the dick-on-demand vibrators.

Her marriage therapist had prescribed her pornography. June and I are a lot alike, but not in that respect. I watch porn; I masturbate—I've never found any issue with either, in moderation. June had never explored either. When she needed them, I made sure she had the tools necessary.

"Good choice, those colors look great on you," June says.

"Thanks, Love," I say. "I should get going. I'll let you know how it goes."

"Okay, be safe."

"Always."

After hanging up, I dress and put on the finishing touches. Keeping things casual, I lightly curl my hair but leave it down. Then I throw on some simple flats, because I don't know how tall Ben is and I don't want to tower over him in heels.

With that, I'm ready and heading for my door. I open it to Reed, who looks like he was about to knock. There's a smile on his face, but it falls slightly after a quick perusal of me.

"Hi," I say.

"I was going to see if you wanted to grab some dinner." There's a tightness around his mouth, and he squeezes his words, making them come out strained. As always, I'm so confused by this man.

"Oh. I, um, I have a date."

"I thought you and Connor broke up," he states, finally looking from my body to my face.

"We did. This is a new guy. First date," I stammer, flummoxed by how intently he's looking at me.

"What's his name?"

"Ben," I answer.

"Last name?"

"I don't know yet. We're only on a first-name basis."

"Except that you're a local public figure with an unusual first name, so he probably knows plenty about you already." He rolls his eyes to emphasize his displeasure of the situation. *The situation that has nothing at all to do with him.*

"It's possible," I admit. It's likely, even.

"Where?"

"Where what?"

"Where is the fucking date at?"

"Calm down, Growly. It's at Bar Tonique."

He takes a full step closer, his eyes bearing down on me.

"You're meeting him there?"

I nod.

"Be safe, or so help me, someone dies tonight," he says, taking yet another step closer. "And do not go back to his house. Or bring him back here."

"You don't make rules for me, Reed."

"Fucking watch me, Blondie," Reed speaks quietly, but I feel the authority of it like I feel his sweet breath hit my lips. Before I can react, he walks back toward his side of our building.

Oh! He's infuriating.

My mind rages horrible thoughts about Grumpy Reed the whole way to the bar. So much so that I have to take a few minutes to calm myself before walking inside. How dare he show up at my door and spew commands as if he owns me!

I shake it off and walk into the bar, scanning the place for a man that resembles the pictures on the app. When I don't see him, I find a few empty stools at the bar and perch there to wait. Sitting at the bar is my favorite spot for first dates. Firstly, because watching the drink making is a good way to entertain yourself during lulls in conversation. Secondly and more importantly, I find bartenders are tuned in to conversations happening close to them. If my date takes a wrong turn, the men tend to be slightly more contained if they know someone might be listening in.

The bartender, a younger brunette woman with arms covered in colorful tattoos, comes by to take my order. Ben arrives as my Pimm's Cup is placed in front of me.

"Leeton?" he asks, pulling the stool out from next to me.

"It's pronounced Lay-ton. Hi, you must be Ben?"

"Oh, I assumed by the way it was spelled," he says, but something about it doesn't sound sincere. As if he knew exactly how it was pronounced and instead found the spelling ridiculous. It's a family name, from my father's maternal side. I love it, regardless of how many people mispronounce it. It wouldn't raise my hackles if I thought he was being truthful.

Strike one.

"Mmm, I can see how that could happen," I reply, blandly. "It's nice to meet you."

"Nice to meet you, too," Ben says, then orders a drink for himself. He turns to the bartender to order his drink, his gaze lingering on her longer than it should for a guy on a date. When she steps away, he turns back. "I like your dress."

"Thank you," I reply. "Tell me about yourself, Ben. Where did you grow up?"

"Miami born and bred."

"What brought you to New Orleans?"

"Work. But the inhibition and decadence of this place made me stay." He grins, but it's more sinister than charming. Plus, he doesn't elaborate on his work. He doesn't elaborate on anything, just waits for another prompt from me.

I get the feeling he would be a selfish partner and an even more selfish lover. He's the type that would always expect a woman to be on top and do all the work. There wouldn't be time for him to explore what gets her off; he'd ask her to hurry herself up so he can come when he wants.

When you interview and analyze people for a living, you get a good sense of people's character. Florida Man here is a Me Monster. I'd bet on it.

"And what is your work?"

"Mortgage broker," he says almost dismissively, as if it's a fact I should already know. "What do you do for a living?"

Not answering right away, I take in his look. Admittedly, he's better-looking in person and I wonder why his pictures were all so overworked. He's not too tall but would still stand a couple inches above me. His dark, wavy hair is curled over one side of his brow stylishly. He's dressed impeccably. Almost as well as Connor's brother, Noah, who

I'm not sure leaves the house in anything less than a suit. The most stunning of his features are his bright blue eyes.

"I'm a journalist. Currently with Channel 5." He doesn't look surprised. Again, he knows this.

Strike two.

"Do you do the weather?" A condescending smile spreads on his face.

Oh, fuck this guy. *Strike three.*

"No, I don't. Not that there would be anything wrong with that. Regardless of how much guys like you love to have some cute piece of ass telling them when it's going to rain, there is more to that job. And meteorologists aren't all vapid and stupid. But you know that, don't you? Just like you knew what I do for a living and how to pronounce my name. Why did you even ask me out, anyway?"

"You looked like you'd be fun," he says, shrugging and holding up his hands.

"In bed, you mean."

Another shrug.

"And you thought being an asshole would get you there?"

"I'm just being me," he says, defensively.

"Clearly why you're still single," I say. When I make eye contact with the bartender, she steps over. "He's paying for my drink. This is for you, because I doubt he's much of a tipper."

Palming a twenty-dollar bill to her, I then leave Ben and the bar behind. It's always amazing how many men, and I use the word loosely here, think they can do whatever they want, and women will just fall at their feet.

I'm home in about fifteen minutes, not long enough for my sour mood to subside. Still so in my own head about a shitty date, I fail to notice the man sitting on the other side of our shared stoop.

"That was quick."

Huffing a breath, I turn toward Reed casually lounging on his front step.

"He was an asshole," I say.

"How?" He rises, his entire demeanor changing in an instant as he goes from relaxed and amused to puffed up and pissed off.

"In the typical way pretty men often are. Rude and condescending, skating by on good looks alone. You should understand that well," I say, hands going to my hips.

"Should I?"

"Isn't that what you do?"

"You think I'm rude and condescending?"

"You've rarely been anything else to me, Reed. So, yeah, that's what I think." Turning to my front door, I punch the code into the lock and open it up.

"You also think I'm pretty," I hear him say as I walk in.

What a dick.

4

REED

Leighton has ignored me for several days now. I've only allowed her to because I've been busy getting settled into my new home, which has taken all my time. Each side of this duplex has two bedrooms. The second room on my side was meant for my mother, but June and Drew have added a suite in their home next door for her. Leaving me a spare room to do whatever I want with. I've turned it into a studio; it's the first time I've had a dedicated place to paint.

The rest of the place is now furnished as well. June will probably come through and fine-tune the decorating. I'm more focused on practicality. Everywhere, except my studio, anyway. It's loaded to the gills with more canvas, paint, and tools than I know what to do with. The windows allow so much daylight to stream through that it's the perfect space.

Just stepping into the room excites the fuck out of me.

My position with *Moxy* doesn't start for two weeks, so I have nothing but time to dedicate to my favorite pasttime. And so, I immerse myself in it. In every soft drag of my brush, the rub of my thumb against my pallet knife. This part of my art was not taught, it was learned. From a pure desire to get the images out of my head before I choke on them. Before they consume me whole. A critic might call them immaturely made; they lack technical skill. But my art, or this part of my art, has no patience for technicalities. That's saved for my day job.

Painting this way is dirty, raw, messy. It's like sex, instinct, and passion mixing to create whatever movement feels right and good. Inside this room, it's all passion bleeding onto canvas. No technical skills can replace the emotion I feed my art.

At some point, I strip off my clothes. I don't recall when. So lost to the image growing on the canvas before me. My favorite subject. It's always this these days. Always her.

She ignores me in the way she believes I've always ignored her. That's not the case, however. I'm never free of thoughts of her. I couldn't ignore her if I tried. Which I don't. Seeming indifferent to her is easy enough, but I'm nothing of the sort.

By the time the image is complete in front of me, I'm full of tension and adrenaline. Something she always does to me, like a drug. Leighton Ward is my own personal addiction. Though she doesn't know it.

One of the first things I did after moving in was set up a water trough pool in the backyard. It needs a deck built around it, maybe a gazebo, with lighting and plants. But it's functioning in a rudimentary way already. Basically, a tub full of cooled water, but just what I could use right now. I like the idea of bathing outside, so much so that I'm considering an outdoor shower as well. Hard and covered in paint splotches, as I am, a bath is just what I need right now.

Leighton isn't home as I walk out back, dropping the rest of my clothes as I go. But I hear her car pull up as I step in the tub. I always know if she's here. Sometimes, I know exactly where she is in her home, because she tends to be noisy. There's always music playing, while she sings along with that sultry voice of hers. But I stay quiet. The only noise for me are the ones playing out in my own mind.

Stepping into the water, I sink to my waist and stretch my arms out along the edge. It's cold, though not nearly cold enough to assuage me of the raging stiff dick painting Leighton always causes. Tilting my head up to the rays of the warm afternoon sun, I bask in what's left of the dim light. Growing up in Arizona, I never hated the sun until I moved to Seattle and realized what a joy temperate weather could be. It will be yet another change here to deal with the hot humidity of the summer months. An easy price to pay for living in this city. New Orleans is a gem with its history, food, music, and art scene. It's more alive than most places I've visited in the States.

That's one of the things I loved most about Ireland. They play hard and love life. New Orleans feels similar.

"What kind of hillbilly shit did you set up out here?" Leighton calls as she steps out of her backdoor. Our yard isn't separated; we share one decently large patch of grass. A six-foot fence surrounds it, giving us privacy from all but one neighbor, or them from us. *Whichever.*

"It's an outdoor tub, and it's glorious. You're welcome to join," I tease her as she slowly approaches like a skittish animal, not sure if it's nearing friend or foe.

"What is all over you? Paint?"

I nod and drop one hand into the water. My erection is throbbing now, especially since the object of its desire is standing right in front of us looking as beautiful as ever. Her blonde hair is plaited today, up and off her shoulders, leaving her neck bare above a simple cornflower blue dress that sways lightly in the gentle breeze. The color is the same shade as her eyes.

It's my favorite color.

"*Why* are you covered in paint?"

"Why don't you hop in?"

Leighton has the sexiest blush I've ever witnessed. It colors the globes of her cheeks in the perfect shade of coral. If she blushed always, she'd never feel the desire to wear makeup. She doesn't need it, anyway.

"You're dirty," she says, face scrunching up in something like disgust.

"You have no idea."

"Eww, not what I meant," she protests, and her cheek color deepens a shade. I raise an eyebrow at her. "Oh my god, are you naked in there?"

"It's a bath. Of course I am." Her face is still screwed up, but she steps forward, regardless. Moving my hand up and down my erection, I watch as she follows the movement. "Come in and get dirty with me, Love."

She blinks a few times to steady herself.

"Why now?" The two small words come out just loud enough for me to hear.

"Now is as good a time as any. Isn't it?"

Her gaze slumps back to my hand working myself up, then quickly snaps back to my face.

"No, Reed. It's not. You've been nothing but an asshole to me, and I'm done with assholes. You're too late. You should have hit me up a year or two ago when I was far less discerning about the men I fuck," she huffs, turning to walk back toward her door. I stare at her back so hard, I know she feels it. The connection between us is too intense to be one-sided.

Standing, I never avert my eyes off her back. Exactly as I expect her to, she spins to face me before sliding her back door shut with a heavy thud.

A noise I ignore completely and instead focus on the equally heavy lust that shrouds her as she takes me in. Every long, hard inch that I move my hand up and down on.

Maybe I should feel guilty for never making my intentions known before this. Or for how I lick my lips while she watches me edge near my release from the opposite side of the glass. But I don't. I can't feel guilty for making decisions I am certain were right. And for sure not for the one I'm making now. I'll bombard her senses until she sees sense. Until she knowingly admits, with the same certainty that I do, we're meant to be.

The Leighton I know wouldn't pass up a chance like this. But that woman is hiding out, for whatever reason. Maybe it has something to do with Connor. Perhaps she enjoyed the stability he gave. I don't know. I don't care about the why, I care about getting her past it. I care about making her mine.

It takes a few moments, but eventually I see her shadow move away from where she had perched to watch me. Uncomfortably, I climb out of the tub and head inside to the shower, letting the steam work its way into my skin as I dream of my fist twisting around blonde hair. As I fuck my hand while I pretend it is her tight cunt. I imagine how amazing it will feel, all while knowing my mind can't conjure the pleasure of finally being inside her with her legs wrapped around me, her heels digging into my ass, her screams and sighs.

Fuck.

I explode all over the shower wall, shaking with my release. Damn, I want her. I knew she wouldn't make it easy on me. Too stubborn to give in only because I show up. We're a lot alike that way. Fighting for her isn't a problem, I'll put in the work. Even make her think she's giving me a battle bigger than what it is, if that's what convinces her.

I'm all in.

After a few hours of puttering around, unpacking and organizing more shit, I send her a text.

ME
Did you eat?

LOVE
No.

ME
Do you have a date?

LOVE
How's that your business?

ME
Yes or no.

LOVE
sigh

Laughter rumbles out of me. She amuses me greatly. It's another thing I've never shown her, though it's been a struggle.

ME
I'm coming over. I have pizza.

LOVE
Sausage and olive?

ME
What else?

It's her favorite. She and June lived off it in college.

I'll take it.

Grabbing both the pizza and a six pack of beer, I head over to her side of the house. She must be waiting by the door, because I don't even knock before it opens. Leighton is still dressed in the blue sundress. The thin straps show off her shoulders and a collarbone, tempting me to lick every inch.

"Hey," I say, leaning in to give her a kiss on the cheek.

"Hi?" she stammers, not understanding my sudden show of flirtation and affection. "Thanks for this. I was about to order something myself."

"No worries."

Leighton doesn't cook. She always says it's not because she can't cook, but that she had her fill cooking for her dad growing up and she's over it. It's not something she's ever enjoyed, so she rarely does it. I like cooking, but also seldom find the time. Because when I do it, I go big with some ridiculously elaborate recipe or meal. It's the artistry of it that appeals, more than the food itself.

Following her back to the kitchen, I take in what she's done with the place. Drew gave us blank pallets to work with. Leighton's filled it with furniture that fits her personality perfectly. Colorful and eclectic, some new, some obvious antiques. Tidy, but not pristine, it feels comfortable and lived in.

Leighton grabs two plates and sets them on the table, while I pop open the pizza box and two bottles of beer. She pulls a piece onto her plate and eats, not saying anything or even making eye contact with me. I'm not letting her off that easily.

"How's work been?"

"Fine. Next week is my last week. I accepted another position."

I know this already. Partly, because the editor in chief of *Moxy* has kept me abreast of key positions. Partly, because June told me. Neither June nor Leighton knows I'll be working there as well. There's a small voice in my head that says if Leighton knew, she wouldn't have accepted the job. So, I stay quiet. I'd quit before I let her quit, but my intention is that it not come to that.

"Good for you," I say. "I like what you've done in here. It's nice. Comfortable."

"Thanks," she says, that blush creeping up again. "How's it going next door?"

"I've got the basics covered. The rest will come."

"And work?"

"It's good, not very busy yet, but that will get there, too."

Silence blankets us, and she picks at another slice of pizza, removing the olives one by one before taking a bite.

"How's it been without Connor?"

Her eyes narrow on me as she tries to suss out where I'm headed with this line of questioning.

"Fine."

"Lonely?"

"Not particularly."

"Then why the date the other night?"

"Why not? It's a natural part of life. To seek a partner to spend it with. To have someone to depend on. It's not strange for me to want that. It doesn't mean I'm lonely, per se. I just want more."

So do I.

"I can understand that," I tell her. "But if you're determined to date, we're going to need some rules."

"It's not determination. It's desire. And as I've said, you don't make rules for me." She tosses the half-eaten piece of pizza back to her plate, perturbed.

"Don't get grumpy. Finish your dinner."

"Like a good little woman?" she asks, snidely. "One that obeys your commands while you beat off in the backyard."

"Yes, baby, like that." Leighton flinches back at the endearment, surprised. "Have I ever told you how much I like it when you blush?"

"I don't," she says; a hand going to her cheek.

"You don't with anyone else that I've ever seen. But with me, it's often."

"Make your point, Turner," she bites out, embarrassed and frustrated now, but at least she's no longer about to bite my head off for the display I put on earlier.

"My point, Ward, is that I'm here. *Really* here. Understand? I'm ready whenever you are."

"Ready for what, exactly?" she asks around a bite. I smile at her crudeness. The important thing is she's eating.

"I'm ready for the beginning of us. Whatever that looks like to you. You want to take it slow? We can do that. Jump right in? We can do that, too. If you want to keep dating strange assholes, we'll draw up some parameters that fit the both of us."

I watch as she quietly stands and paces the small kitchen. Her temper rises in increments as she squints, sets her jaw, clenches her fists.

Moving to stand toe-to-toe with her, I cup her heated cheeks in my palms.

"Calm down."

"No, I will not calm down. You don't get to come in here and boss me around."

"I'm trying to negotiate," I tell her.

"Negotiate my dating life?" She almost growls it out. I've rarely seen her temper, but it's fucking hot. I'm half hard from her glaring at me like she wants to murder me.

"Yes. Because whether you want to admit it or not, we're destined to end up together," I say, making eye contact and rubbing my thumb over her tight jaw. "I get that you need time to wrap your hot head around that. I'll give it to you, but only if you understand a few key things."

"Like what?"

"Every date should occur in crowded, public, safe places. You have fun, but you make no long-term commitments. Most importantly, you don't share this gorgeous body with any of those men, Leighton. You need to get fucked after a date, you come home to me."

"And you'll fuck me?"

"Better than you've ever had, Love."

Her eyes drift close and her body slumps in my hands, for the briefest moment. Then she straightens, and when her eyes open back up, they're glowing mad.

"Get the fuck out of my house, Reed."

5

LEIGHTON

I'm no less pissed off the following day. Not lying to myself, I know a good deal of my anger is because I *want* to take him up on his offer. There isn't a man on Earth I'd rather fuck than Reed Turner. But I think he knows it and is using that knowledge to fuck with me; I'm sure of it.

So, I will fuck with him right back.

As soon as I figure out how. Games aren't my specialty. But if he wants to play, I'm up for the task.

Today is a day off for me and I'd scheduled the afternoon at the salon for a refresher. I've kept my look basic. Although sad, I find people take my reporting less seriously the more done up I am. As if all pretty women can't be smart as well. I played into that for a career. But that's no longer something I need to appease. So maybe it's time to ramp up my look.

And maybe make Reed eat his heart out.

ME

Have a good game tonight, buddy.

I send the text to Drew before I leave the house for the day. It's NFL opening night or whatever they call it, the first game of the season. My best friend's husband is a fancy big-time quarterback with big goals of getting to the Super Bowl this year. I'm sure that's the goal every season, but he's extra determined to prove himself this year. Probably because of all the bad press his cheating gifted him. Drew's a good man at heart, I'll say that. He was a colossal fuck up when he cheated on June, but he's regretful and repentant, and most importantly, he's consistently working on being a better man.

He also bought me this house. The least I can do is wish him well on big game days.

DREW

Thanks, Leighton. Maybe we can get you out to one of the games soon. Junie would love it.

ME

Definitely! I'll let you know what works with my schedule.

DREW

You do that. And keep an eye out on Reed, would you? He's acting strange.

Don't I fucking know it.

ME

Will do.

Reed acting weird with Drew and June is bizarre. The three are so close, I've often felt like a third wheel when around them. Not because they ignore me, well, Reed always does unless he's giving me shit. It's that they've been so inseparable since a very young age. They know everything about one another. I don't get all the inside jokes like they do.

Switching on the television, I put on an episode of *Killing Eve* while I enjoy my cup of coffee and toast. If I was a horrible person, I'd strive to be Villanelle.

Whoo, boy, that sounds bad.

Not because I want to be a ruthless assassin. She's just so resourceful and creative. And funny. Jodie Comer plays the perfect psychopath. And Villanelle's sense of fashion is top notch. I have a closet full of clothes. All cute, but mostly practical for my job. That's at the top of my to-do list today. Find a few items that are fun and all me.

Reed's comment about how I made this place my home rings in my ears. Shedding the television job is an opportunity for me to become the woman I've always seen myself as. A woman with more of an eclectic style, a fun outer shell that matches my personality more.

A knock sounds on my door, and I groan. It can only be one person and I'm not ready to face him yet. But I can't hide out from him, either.

"Good morning," Reed says when I open the door. He's holding a bag out to me I recognize from District Donut and Sliders.

"Oh my god," I say as I snatch the bag. "I can smell it from here."

Reed follows me in as I open my goodie bag and take a big whiff of the cinnamon roll.

"How did you know?" I'm not sure he can understand me since my mouth is full of the first delicious, gooey bite. These damn things are my favorite.

"Lucky guess," he lies. "We need to talk."

"No, we don't." I lick each sticky finger, slowly and thoroughly, letting my tongue trail the icing. Reed watches with hungry eyes, making my heart flutter. "You said enough last night when you offered up your bullshit post-date booty call rules."

"Leighton," he warns, as if I'm saying something offensive.

"Reed," I parrot, deepening my voice to mimic his. "Thanks for the breakfast. I have a busy day, so you're dismissed." I gesture to the door behind him.

"This isn't over," he says before turning to leave. His ass looks amazing today. Too bad, it comes attached to a mouth that says so much stupid shit.

I spend the rest of my morning rummaging through vintage shops and ignoring the text messages I've been receiving from Connor.

CONNOR

I tried to call you last night.

Yeah, I know, I ignored you.

Who knows?

June must have told Noah and Noah must have relayed that to Connor. Sweet of him to message me, but I'm still pissy about how we ended.

He gives up after the third one and I head to Briana's salon for my appointment with something of a heavy heart and a deep need for some change.

"Hey, lady. How are you?"

"Good, good. How are you, Briana?"

"Fantastic," she says, wrapping a cape around me. "Are we just trimming you up?"

"Nope. I'm switching jobs, so I think it's time to put a little more personality into my hair. Maybe add a little color for fun."

"Ooh, I have the perfect idea. Do you trust me?" she asks with a huge grin.

"You know I do."

"Awesome! I'll mix the color, then you can tell me all about this new job."

A few hours later, I have the subtlest pink highlights woven through my gentle wavy hair. Briana has done an amazing job making it look almost natural, as if I was born with bolder strawberry lemonade locks than what I actually was. People say getting a haircut can be a stress reliever. I've never wanted short hair, and this is the most dramatic thing I've ever done. But it does feel like a relief. Like shedding another brick I didn't know I was holding.

To top off my day, I set up another date. Tonight, it's Lucas, a forty-something doctor. Tall, dark, and handsome, according to his pictures. Can't help but wonder what's wrong with him that makes him still single. Which is dumb to think because it's probably what men think when they see my profile, too.

I found an amazing dress at a shop today. It gives off great Marilyn Monroe in *Bus Stop* vibes. With a green and black embroidered bodice and a slinky black skirt, complete with a long slit up one leg. Embracing the feel, I pair it with a tight fishnet stocking and simple, strappy black heels.

Lucas is meeting me at Mr. John's Steakhouse, which is only a few blocks from home. I can make the trek even in my heels, but it's on the streetcar line if my feet hurt.

Like the black cloud he is, Reed steps out of his house at the same time I do. Barely sparing him a glance, I don't see how quickly he moves down his stoop and up mine, until he's standing inches away from me. His eyes are studying every inch of my body.

"Fuck, Love. You look amazing," he murmurs. The heat of his words skate down my spine and pool in my skimpy lace panties. If he always said sweet things like this, maybe at least we could be friends again. But then he goes and fucks it up. "Where the hell are you off to looking like that?"

Sigh.

"Date."

"With who?"

"His name is Lucas and he's a doctor at Tulane Medical Center. I don't even know why I'm telling you this. It's not your business," I grit out.

"This will go easier the sooner you realize you are my business," he says to my rolling eyes. "Where are you going?"

"The steakhouse down the street, *Mom.*"

"Are you taking the trolley?" he asks.

"It's a streetcar, and probably on the way back," I answer as I step around him. "I'll be late. Goodbye, Reed."

"Have a good dinner, Leighton. I hope you warm up on your walk over."

"What? Why?" I turn back to him, trying to understand his meaning. He gestures to my chest with a nod of his head. Looking down, I see that my nipples are hard under my dress that doesn't afford me a bra unless it's strapless. And, well, fuck those.

Damn him for causing this and noticing it. I let out a tiny growl of frustration and huff off toward the restaurant.

Lucas is waiting for me at the door when I arrive, thankfully, without hard tits.

"Leighton, hi." Lucas reaches a hand to shake mine. It's cordial but he doesn't grip my hand like I'm porcelain, nor does he squeeze it like he's attempting a show of dominance. "It's nice to meet you."

"Nice to meet you, too, Lucas."

"I hope my choice of dining is okay. After a long week at the hospital, I'm usually ravenous. This place has great portion sizes." There's almost a bashfulness to him; it's endearing, really.

"It's great. I have a healthy appetite myself."

"Great," he says, opening the door for me. I follow him in, and we're quickly seated by the hostess that seems to recognize him as a regular. We settle on a bottle of wine and fried green tomatoes to start. "So, I know you're a reporter. I've seen you. But what else can you tell me about yourself?"

"I only have a week left at the station. Then I'll be moving on to a new online magazine," I tell Lucas.

"That's great. Are you excited?"

"I am. I won't have to report on every tragic story in this city, and I won't have to be in front of the camera all the time. It feels like a big win."

"Well, the camera will miss you. You're the best-looking thing in front of it. But I can understand."

I smile at the compliment and evaluate the lack of heat on my cheeks. Reed was right. I don't blush with other people. Chastising myself for thinking about my next-door brute, I tune back into my date.

"What's your favorite here?" I ask.

"The cowboy steak," he says with that same bashfulness. "Mac and cheese, and garlic mash."

"So, the fattiest cut with a side of carbs and extra carbs?" I laugh.

"Exactly."

"Just what sort of doctor are you?"

"Cardiologist."

"Oh my god." I laugh harder.

"You can't tell anyone." He grins. "Every time I come here I worry I'm going to have a run-in with a patient who I just lectured about the importance of a heart healthy diet."

"If you see any of them tonight, you can blame the side dishes on me. You're on your own with that steak though."

"Yeah? What are you ordering?"

"Fish. But only because I'm eyeing that bread pudding for dessert, and I need to save room."

"Solid choice, it's delicious."

"You eat dessert, too? How are you so fit?" I ask.

"I hit the gym a few times a week. That, plus long, busy days at the hospital make it easy to burn off the occasional indulgence," he says, laughing when I screw up my face at the word gym. "You don't work out?"

"Not like that," I say with some flirtation, making him laugh more. We pause conversation to place our orders, but when the server walks off, Lucas starts back up.

"You seem great, Leighton. Why the dating app?"

"I think I've exhausted the men I can meet within my current circle of friends. I want love; it just hasn't found me yet," I say, shrugging. "What about you?"

"Much the same." He takes a drink of the pinot, savoring it some before continuing. "Mostly, I meet women in the medical field. To some, it would make sense to get involved with someone who would understand my life. But, for me, that only makes it more difficult. I've dated other doctors and nurses; it was near impossible to find time to spend with each other."

"And you thought a journalist would have a calmer schedule?"

"No. But if I'm being honest, I remember when you started reporting here. I noticed you. It felt, I don't know, like luck that you showed up as a possible match."

"Are you saying I'm pretty?" I tease.

"I'm saying you're fucking gorgeous. But it's your personality that screams through the screen."

Honestly, I don't know how I'm not blushing. But...I'm not.

"You get a gold star for thinking you're the lucky one on this date, when I'm the one sitting here with someone who's spent years in college so he could learn how to save lives," I say.

"It was a calling," he says. "My mother died young of a rare heart condition. Losing your mother early tends to change your character."

"Something we have in common. Though mine ran off, so not quite the same."

"Maybe it's worse when done by choice," he ponders.

Maybe.

The conversation continues easily throughout dinner and dessert. There aren't holes or awkward pauses, and we find we have more in common than just growing up motherless. Lucas is also close to his father, who retired in Florida. And, like me, he's moved around a lot as a child. His father was a nuclear engineer, so they went where he was most needed. While I moved around the States, Lucas is much more worldly, having lived in China, South Korea, and Ukraine at some point.

We've discussed families. Both my lack of one and Lucas's small one due to his father eventually remarrying and having two daughters much younger than himself.

By the time we're ready to leave, I'm more confused by how this man is single. He seems too good to be true.

"I'd offer to walk you home, but I understand that's probably outside of your comfort zone since you don't really know me yet. Will you get home safely?" Lucas asks after we exit the restaurant.

"I'll make sure she does," a deep voice says behind me.

Reed.

6

REED

"Excuse me?" Leighton's date asks. He does his best to puff up in a protective way. It doesn't work, though. It's hard to look tough in pressed khaki pants.

"It's fine. I'm family," I say at the same time Leighton lets out a slow sigh.

"Lucas, this is Reed, my neighbor and the brother of my best friend."

"June's brother?" he asks, as if he knows my sister.

"Yep, that's me. June's brother." I reach to shake his hand. They're soft and that makes me smile. "Say your goodbyes. I'll wait over here."

I step away, but only a few feet. Leighton narrows her eyes at me before turning her back completely. I'll give the man credit for respecting the privacy of her home, but that's all this fucker is getting from me. His pretty boy looks give me bad vibes. Clean-cut and put together much the same way her ex, Connor Anders, was.

The doctor is her type. Or what she thinks is her type. They aren't though, because I am her type. Her only type.

It's not surprising that she's fighting me on that. I brushed her off far too many times. The last was when June showed us the duplex Drew had bought for us. Leighton asked me to kiss her, point-blank. I rejected her and have regretted it every day since. Refusing her that day went against every physical instinct I had, but I did it anyway.

It wasn't long after that she was regularly on Connor's arm. Had I kissed her that day, told her how I feel about her, how I've always felt, the situation would be different today.

She's so like my sister, I thought I knew what was best for her. I still think I do. Which is why I'm not letting a stranger walk her home. If it was up to me, his lips wouldn't be pressing a kiss to her cheek either.

"Goodnight, Leighton. I'll call you," he says, flashing me a side-eye as I unfold my arms crossed over my chest while I waited.

She watches him walk away, and I step up behind her.

"Did you have a nice dinner?" I say softly in her ear, and her hair rustles at my words.

Leighton spins around, and I get up close and personal with the most beautiful glare she's ever leveled on me. I shift my stance because the erection it causes gets uncomfortable.

"What the hell are you doing here, Reed?"

"Making sure you get home safely."

"I don't need your help with that. I'm a grown woman who's lived on her own for quite some time."

"And yet anything can happen at any time. I'm erring on the side of caution."

"You're erring on the side of a psychotic stalker," she huffs.

"It's hardly stalking when you tell me where you're going."

"I didn't though, did I? And I certainly didn't invite you to tag along," she says, but doesn't protest when I place my hand to the small of her back and guide her back toward home. Leighton has much more bravado than my sister ever has, but in most ways, they're alike. To the point of always putting others in their lives ahead of themselves. She's more discriminate about that than June, though. It takes more than casual acquaintance to get a top spot in Leighton Ward's life.

She doesn't need to be nice. I don't need her to put me first in our twisted relationship. It's far more pleasurable when she pushes back at me. Because it's truer. Her anger, her frustration, the latent feelings she tries to hide under a thick skin… that's real, that's her. That's the woman I love.

"You're acting like I crashed your date." I move my hand a little lower on her back, and she doesn't resist.

"You did."

"No, I didn't. I patiently waited outside for you to finish so I could walk you home safely."

"How long were you waiting?" She stops abruptly and turns. "Did you follow me there?"

"Of course not. I'm *not* a stalker. I was across the street getting my own dinner and I saw you."

She studies me for a moment, trying to work out if I can be trusted. I can't. But this isn't a lie. While she glares at me, I peruse her right back, and watch the flush rise on her chest and cheeks. It's hot today, or rather hotter than I'm accustomed to. I unbutton my shirt sleeves and slowly roll them up, enjoying how she still has not moved or uttered a word.

Also enjoyable are those nipples once again pebbling under her dress.

"Did khakis cause this type of reaction during dinner?"

Leighton blinks rapidly at my question, remembering herself.

"Fuck you, Reed." She stomps off in her high heels.

I follow, liking how she looks as she walks away, but not letting her gain too much distance. Leighton is hot as fuck when there's a little anger lighting her up. Maybe I should feel guilty for purposely pushing her buttons the way I do.

Nah, fuck that.

I know from nearly a decade worth of experience that she enjoys these games as much as I do. If ever I go too long in her presence without giving her the proper attention, she instigates a reaction from me. It's what we do, who we are.

Only now I want more.

We've made it the few blocks back home when I finally move to catch up to her. As she stands at her front door, punching in the code on her digital lock, I slide up right behind her. Barely an inch separates us. Her sugary scent floats around me. I imagine she tastes the same.

Leighton tries to ignore me behind her, but I see how her body reacts, and the slow step she takes inside leaves me time to follow her. Follow, I do, kicking the door shut behind as I reach around to palm her stomach. She stills, all but the flutter of her heart under my hand.

"Was the good doctor polite?"

"Yes."

"Charming?"

"I guess, yes. He was bashful and sweet."

Because you are so far out of his league.

Dragging the hand on her stomach to her hip, I place my opposite hand to her other side, pulling her.

"Did he turn you on, Love?"

"Some," she whispers.

"Did you want him to kiss you?"

Leighton shakes her head.

"No?"

"No, I wanted to kiss him."

Brat.

"Did you hope he'd touch you?"

Her body slumps in a sigh.

"No," she admits, so much emotion in such a little word. As if she'd hoped she would be turned on by him and is so disappointed that she wasn't.

My hands grip at her skirt, fingers moving to crumple it up inch by inch, baring her long legs for me. Leighton hates to work out, but if she can walk somewhere instead of driving, she does. It's a habit that's left her legs toned in a subtle way that makes me want to lick every inch of them.

"Did I tell you how fucking luscious you look tonight?"

"Yeah… yes."

"I didn't. Not really," I whisper in her ear. "Take a few steps forward, hands on the back of the sofa. I'm about to tell you the right way."

"Reed," she says, quiet and needy.

"You can say no, tell me to stop, and I will. Otherwise, my name is the only thing I want to hear spilling over those pretty lips of yours."

"Oh my god," she says as she takes position.

"That works, too."

Laughter bubbles out of her until I have her skirt pushed up far enough to bare her fishnet encased ass. I've seen her in bikinis, so I knew she has a great ass, but damn, it makes all the difference being able to touch it. Round, full, so fucking bitable.

She's only wearing a thin scrap of lace for panties under them. They're a pale color almost the same tone as her skin. Pale enough that as I spread her legs and easily rip apart her stockings, I can see the barest stain of fluid on them.

"What's happening right now?" she asks, confused or shocked. Turned on like I've never witnessed her.

"You're wet for me."

"How do you know it's not for Lucas?"

"Because I'm not stupid. Because your tits didn't have sweet little erections until he was gone, and you were alone with me."

"Asshole," she mutters and shifts as if she's going to stand up.

"No, it's your pussy I want this time." And I dive forward before she can get away. I suck, panties and all, right where her heat was making itself known. As expected, she tastes as good as she smells.

So damned sweet.

Just like the small gasp that escapes her.

I pull away only long enough to drag the lace down the long lines of her legs, guiding her feet out of them. They're mine now, so I tuck them away in my pocket. A souvenir, a trophy to commemorate the first orgasm I give her. It won't be the last. I aim to die with my tongue in this woman's cunt.

Pulling apart her cheeks, I go back in to feast on both her flavor and the sounds of approval she makes. Leighton is vocal enough that I quickly learn what she likes; my tongue thrusting deep and swirling inside. She even grunts when I move away to catch a breath, so I don't do that often. I'll forgo breathing to get her off. It's the least I can do.

She edges closer and closer, her muscles tightening as she rises bit by bit onto her toes. I place my fore and index fingers to her clit and keep a rhythm while I tongue-fuck her until she explodes.

"Fuck, Reed!"

It's the best thing I've ever heard.

Her legs shake and her head falls to rest on her hands that still grip the backrest of her couch. But I don't move away; instead, I lap at every inch of her. As long as there are still remnants of her release, I'll stay right here on my knees cleaning it up with my mouth. Minutes pass, as I still drag over her soft skin, while she quietly chases after her racing heart.

"What are you doing?" she finally asks me in a feathery voice.

"Savoring."

"Just how creepy are you, Turner?"

For that, I bite her ass. I wanted to anyway, but at least she gave me reason.

"Ouch," she squeals, though I know it didn't hurt her. I press a kiss on the spot before rising to my feet and pulling her to stand with me. Her skirt is still bunched at her waist, and I pull at it until it falls around her once again. "You bit me."

"Don't count on it being the last time," I say as I turn her to face me. "For the record, I'm dirty. Maybe even depraved or deviant. I'm *not* creepy."

"Noted." Her eyebrow rises as though she doesn't believe me in the least. "What's happening here, Reed?"

"The natural order of things, Leighton." I lean in, run the tip of my nose up the side of hers.

"What does that mean?"

"You and me."

"There is no you and me."

"It sure felt like there was when you were fucking my mouth," I say, feigning indignation. She's acting as I expected she would. Leighton's not ready to give in to us. That's fine. I've given her so much time already, I can suffer a little more. It's the space I'm taking back. There will be no more circumstance of geography.

"Ah, honey. One orgasm does not make a relationship," Leighton snipes, and I fight the smile from taking over my face. Fuck, I love her bullshit.

"I see how it is," I say, trailing a finger along her jaw, then down the line of her neck. "You keep dating men that don't make you wet. I'll keep giving you orgasms in their place. When I've tallied enough of them that your body no longer recognizes the existence of other men, you let me know and we'll make this official."

"Ooh, official? Like, on Facebook? Or are we going to make a blood pact?"

"Blood play isn't off the table, if that's what you want."

"I knew you were a creeper." Her nose scrunches up in adorable disgust.

"No blood," I say. "Noted."

"You don't need to note anything, Reed. We're not negotiating, because we aren't in a relationship."

"But you're going to let me keep giving you orgasms," I state. *I'm not asking.*

"You weren't half bad and you are conveniently located, so yes."

Laughter almost spills out of my chest, but I swallow it down.

"You can lie to yourself, Love. But I know how hard you came. I swallowed it all down, remember?"

And there it is, that blush I adore so much.

"Sleep well, Leighton," I tell her before I head to the door. "Sweet dreams."

7

LEIGHTON

I did not have sweet dreams. They were so, so filthy. Reed was a vampire, sexy with an edge of danger, who bit more than my ass. And now I fear I will always look at him with a weird longing for him to grow fangs and suck the blood out of my thigh while his head is buried there.

New Orleans is to blame, with all its gothic charm and love for Anne Rice. It has an aesthetic, a vibe, that sinks into the very depths of your soul. People speak of cities being alive with different feelings or energies. But New Orleans is special; it contains an existence all its own. You feel it when you walk the streets and the shadows dance to the lively music with you, ghosts of the long dead desperately holding on to life.

Living anywhere else isn't an option for me anymore. I fell in love with the Crescent City as soon as I arrived, and a little more with each day I have spent here.

While I miss so much about living in The Quarter, the garden district has a calmer pace and is much quieter. Except today as I wake to banging sounds coming from the backyard. Sneaking a look out my window, I spy Reed. With so much bare skin and lumber that, damnit, I can only imagine what my dreams will be tonight. He'll be a sexy lumberjack and I'll be a damsel in distress with her pussy stuck in a tree.

Damn him for being so sexy. And so amazing with his mouth. Last night, he made me come harder and faster than I'd ever had before. When he left, I tried to sleep, but all I could manage was wonder what happened and why I so easily succumbed to him. He told me to bend over, and I was like, *yes, sir, how far?*

Ugh, it would be pathetic if he wasn't so mind-numbingly good. It took all of about two minutes and I couldn't feel my legs. I've never been quick to orgasm, and I don't come on demand. It takes work. Admittedly, Connor did a better job than most. I'll miss that about him.

Well, unless I let Reed keep picking up the slack.

Oh God. I can't do that. *Can I?* My mental debate ping-pongs around my sleepy brain while I head out to the backyard to see what Mr. Grumpy Pants is up to today. I've mostly decided that what happened last night can't happen again, until I step outside into the yard and get a good look at the man making all the ruckus. Reed is dressed in only cut-off black sweat shorts, his chest as bare as his feet. His skin shines with beads of sweat as he swings a hammer, and I can't divert my attention from the sinewy muscles of his arm and shoulder.

How is he so fit?

Reed turns around, stepping toward me and away from the fence he was banging on.

"My best friend is an NFL quarterback. I know how to work out."

"Did I say that out loud?"

His eyebrow raises to affirm that yes, yes, I said it aloud.

"What are you doing?" I ask to divert away from my blunder.

"Where are your clothes?"

I'm wearing a short kimono wrap that I pull tighter to cover up the silk pajamas I'm wearing beneath it.

"Inside," I say with a shrug. "Where are your shoes? You could step on a nail."

"You know that house over there." He gestures with his head to the property line we don't share with the McKennas. "They can see directly into our backyard from their balcony. You're probably giving them quite a show right now."

"Yeah, but they're much more likely to peer out to look at you than they are me."

"Why?"

"Because that is the home of Ivy and Olive Broussard. Sisters who are in their sixties, both widowed before the age of thirty. Under mysterious circumstances, I might add. Their family has owned that house since the dawn of time, they're filthy rich, and those women are two of the city's most notorious cougars."

"Huh," he says, leaning to the side to get a better look at their house.

"You interested, Turner?"

"Intrigued, I'd call it," he says with a shrug of his own. "Breakfast is over there by the tub."

"Breakfast?" I question but beeline for it because I'm starving. I'm almost always hungry, a horrible trait when you don't cook. I spy it right away—another cinnamon roll. "Are you trying to fatten me up? This tub of yours is really a stew pot to cook me up in, isn't it?"

"Love, I don't care what you weigh. I'll fuck you blind if you're one thirty-five or two thirty-five, and everything in between."

Even if I hadn't taken an extra-large bite of the breakfast cake, his comment would have shocked me. But because I did, I choke a little as I try to swallow it down. Reed's there instantly, a hand patting my back, the other gently soothing away the hair from my face.

"I'm okay," I tell him after I take a moment to gain my composure and pick my jaw up off the floor.

Reed and I have always lived on the periphery of flirting. This new, direct, banter is throwing me off balance.

"You sure? Here, take a sip of coffee. It's hot, so be careful," he warns as he hands me his mug.

I take a few sips without taking my eyes off his face so full of concern. I've seen him look at June this way but never me. He's standing close, with all that bare skin and muscle, and it's overwhelming all my senses. My fingers want to drag over his rippled abdominals and my mouth wants to taste his. I lick my lips and my eyelids flutter as I think, *just kiss me, Reed.*

But he doesn't. Instead, he steps back abruptly.

"What's on your plate today," he asks after clearing his throat as if I've made him uncomfortable. When clearly, he's started this whole awkward situation.

"It's my last day at the news station." I set the coffee down and pick another piece of cinnamon roll. "What about you? Don't you have a job?"

"I do, but it doesn't pick up for a couple more days. I thought I'd get some stuff done around here."

"What are you doing, anyway?"

"This section of fence was leaning in; I'm shoring it up. Then I'm going to finish my tub and clean up the landscaping," he says.

"I was thinking I should plant a magnolia tree over in that corner," I say, pointing to the area.

"Good idea, but then Ivy and Olive won't be able to watch me take my baths."

"You like to be watched, eh?"

"Depends on who's doing the watching. You interested, Leighton?"

"Hard pass, Turner." I grab the rest of my breakfast and retreat inside. Because, yes, I am interested, but damnit, he doesn't need to know that.

As soon as I get to the station, I'm sent out with a crew to report on a community art center in the Ninth Ward that's been hit with vandalism. I meet with Irma, a woman in her early seventies, who has donated both her land and time to supply her neighborhood with a safe space for people to create, to gather, and to learn from each other. It's a noble endeavor, but someone has come by and ravaged most of her supplies, including the kiln. The front door was kicked in and several windows were shattered. It's likely the kids, malicious but not fueled by hate of the program itself.

Not that any of that makes it easier for Irma to handle. Her hands are clammy from being in gloves all day while she scrubbed at the graffiti on the walls, inside and out.

"Would it be okay if I come back on Sunday to help?" I ask her after we finish the interview. "I'm pretty good with a broom and a mop."

"Oh, aren't you a sweetheart. That would be lovely, dear. We've got a lot to do." She wrings her hands together in worry.

"I'll be here to help. And, hopefully, the story will generate some assistance."

"I hope you're right. Thank you for coming out, Ms. Ward. I'm all about expression, but this just wasn't the way. If they'd have asked, I would have found them a wall to tag."

"You're doing a good thing, Irma. We'll get you back up and running."

It weighs on me the rest of the day. Raised by a busy single father, I spent a good amount of time in daycares, community centers, afterschool programs. They're a lifeline for both children and parents. I hate to think of how many kids won't be able to go to Irma's until it's back up and running.

I carry sadness with me for longer than I should. Dad once said he thought it was because my mom left. That I wasn't this way before that. But after she left us, small things that made me sad lingered with me for longer and longer. When I was six, we watched the movie *E.T.*, and I cried myself to sleep every night for a month. Maybe that's not so strange, it is a sad movie, but Dad thought it was extreme behavior for me. And it didn't stop.

My first pet was a goldfish when I was thirteen. We never had one before because of our busy schedule and moving around as often as we did. But Dad gave in and let me get Frank the fish under the condition I understood fish didn't tend to live long. I swore up and down I understood, and I could handle it when he'd die.

That turned out to be false.

Frank died within six months, and I was hysterical for three days. Refusing to go to school or even eat, until my dad had his own panic attack about my behavior. That scared the shit out of me, and we agreed that I needed to be in counseling. Again, something difficult due to moving around. It was tricky getting comfortable with a new counselor every year or two. At least I learned coping mechanisms. I've never had another pet, so I don't know how I'd handle that. But I can watch a sad movie and get over it after a day or two.

Few people know that about me. Only Dad and June, really. Basically, I'm full of shit. Happy, outgoing, carefree. I am those things, sure, but not always. Sometimes I'm just blue, and sometimes the reason is small.

Other times, they aren't. Connor's departure wasn't easy. I shut down for a solid day, didn't answer calls or respond to texts. Until Dad called three times straight. I knew he wouldn't let up and I finally answered.

"Connor wasn't your person, sweet girl. That man is still out there waiting for you."

I've clung to those words. My man is still out there waiting. I only need to find him. It doesn't stop the hurt, though. Rejection is a hard pill to swallow. Especially when you've spent the majority of your life carefully avoiding situations that could lead to it. Which I have, because the harder pill to swallow is abandonment. And Connor leaving the way he did teeters somewhere in the in-between.

In my efforts to move forward, I set up a second date with Lucas when he texted me earlier. We're having dinner again tomorrow night, and we'll see if it sparks something… more. Perhaps I need to get to know him better, let the feelings grow, ferment into more than passing appreciation of his good looks and noble career.

The phone buzzing on the coffee table in front of me brings me out of my swirling thoughts. Leaning forward on the couch, I answer it.

"Hey, Love."

"Hi," June says with exasperation.

"Oh, no. What's wrong?"

"I need to let Noah know if we're coming to the wedding or not." Noah is one of June's closest friends. I'd say he's only second. But he's marrying the woman June's husband had an affair with. It's a long, complicated history between the four, and June tries to navigate it all with a graceful strength that I'm not sure many are possible of having.

My BFF is an amazing woman.

"Without overanalyzing it all, answer this one question. Gut reactions only. You ready?"

"Yeah, shoot."

"Do you want to be at Noah's one and probably only wedding?"

"Fuck. Yeah, I do."

"Well, then I think you have your answer, babe. Nothing says you have to stay if it's uncomfortable. Hang out long enough for the ceremony and then bail if you need to."

"Right, right. I know I'm overthinking the whole thing. It makes me nervous because I know the ceremony is going to be small and private. What if I have some kind of emotion that I can't hide? I don't want to ruin his day," she says with all sincerity.

"June, you could never ruin his day. They wouldn't have invited you if they thought that was an issue. I'm not trying to talk you into doing something you don't want to do. But I do know you well enough to say that if you don't go, you're going to be upset at yourself."

"God, I really will."

"Like you've said, you're never going to be friends with Lorelai. But if you want Noah in your life, you're going to have to make uncomfortable concessions." Connor told me that Lorelai is cautious about doing things that would make June uncomfortable. She doesn't want to do anything that would jeopardize the friendship Noah has with June. I can't help but respect that. I'll never like the woman, but I don't hate her with such a passion that I don't want her to have a happy life.

Everything I know about her is second-hand, but she doesn't sound all bad. Just someone who's made a lot of mistakes and is trying to take responsibility. I can't hate on that. Even if I don't want her around my best friend more than necessary. June does not hate Lorelai. Truly, I think it's just easier to forgive the people you love and not forgive the ones you never knew or cared about.

She didn't know Lorelai as anything more than a passing acquaintance. Drew, she knew her whole life. Lorelai would carry more of June's ire. It's human nature.

"You're right. Rebecca even alluded to the same thing. Maybe it will be cathartic for me." Rebecca is June's therapist. Has been for years and years. June puts a ton of trust in her, and I think it's paid off.

"So, what are you going to tell Noah?"

"I'm going to tell him we'll be there. And then I'm not going to be critical of myself if I must leave right after the ceremony."

"That's my girl."

"Thank you, Leighton. I always know you won't lie to me or placate me. You know I appreciate you, right?"

"Of course, I know that." I laugh. "I treat you the way you treat me. No lies, Love."

"No lies," she repeats. "How's my brother? He's still being weird. Have you seen much of him?"

Have I ever.

"I can't say he's acting quite himself. But he seems good. He's getting some stuff done around here before work gets busy for him."

"That's the thing! He hasn't even said what his new job is."

"What? Why wouldn't he tell you that?"

"I don't know! You'd think it was top secret or some shit."

"Maybe he's a secret agent. A spy! Ooh, or an assassin."

"Oh my god." She giggles. "You've been watching *Killing Eve* again, haven't you?"

"Yes. It's fucking amazing."

"Even the fourth time around?"

"Familiarity only makes it even better."

We chat a little longer, then I go rummaging in the kitchen for something to eat. My detest for cooking means I keep my place stocked with snack items, mostly. It's not all unhealthy options; there is plenty of fruit and I almost always have carrot sticks prepped as a go-to. Beyond that, it's a bleak situation.

It's not even that I can't cook, honestly, I'm not that bad. But I was the main meal maker my entire childhood because Dad worked so much. I'm bitter it fell on me at such an early age. Not that he expected it of me when I was young, but I wasn't blind to his hard work and sacrifices. We were a team, and I pulled the weight.

It's a ridiculous rebellion that I don't cook now. A rebellion that only has consequences for my own self.

Healthy snacks aren't what grabs my attention tonight, though. My conversation with June helped my sullen mood in some ways. In others, not as much. She's like a sister to me. When she worries, I worry too.

I want cake. Chocolate lava cake, or maybe turtle pie. Maybe my period is coming, I'm not sure as it hasn't been predictable in years, but I know the apple in my hand doesn't look appealing. I'm about to go grab my phone to order something when a knock sounds at my front door.

What does he want now?

When I open the door, I find Reed, holding out a takeout bag toward me.

"Hungry?"

"Always," I answer, and his sexy mouth that always spits rudeness at me curves into a genuine smile. "Turkey and the Wolf?" I ask as I dig into the bag.

"Collard green melt."

"And cabbage salad? Have you had this before?"

"Nope."

"You are in for a treat, it's one of the best things you can put in your mouth." Reed doesn't have to point out my blush this time. I feel the heat of it as his smile grows into something more… sinister.

"One of them maybe, definitely not the best." His eyes trail down me and land at my core. To that place his mouth savored not so long ago.

"Whatever you're doing right now… stop it."

"Anything you want, Love. Let's eat and you can put one of those serial killer shows on that you like so much."

"You want to watch television with me?" Reed never wants to be near me, let alone hang out alone with me. This is uncharted waters, and I'm afraid of drowning in the attention Reed is showing me.

"Yes, Leighton. That's why I said it."

"You're so condescending," I tell him and punctuate it with an eyeroll.

"You wouldn't love me any other way."

"I would… What?" I don't. I do not. I love what your mouth did to me."

Great save, Leighton.

"Wait until you see what my cock can do."

"Hard pass," I say, but oh my god, that's such a lie.

He steps closer, and I freeze instinctively, my heart taking several hard beats. So accustomed to him being snappy with me, I'm uncertain if that's what I'll get or this new sexual version of him.

"You let me know when you change your mind, okay?" he asks, and I nod, baffled. "Now let's get some food in you.

8

REED

Leighton has another date tonight with Khaki Pants. Despite having a nice night with her last night, she's still looking for someone else. Someone who hasn't played the games I have for so long. I get it, I do. I've been heavy-handed, rude, standoffish.

That doesn't mean I am not head over heels for her. I think it just makes me a dumbass. Admitting it is half the battle, I hope. The other half will convince Leighton I'm done with the stupid shit I've been playing at. Taking it all back isn't an option, not that I would anyway. I believe that she needed the time to grow into herself. The way I went about it all was stupid as hell, though.

And now I'm paying for it by watching her date other men, and watching her phone blow up with calls from her ex-boyfriend.

After we ate dinner last night, we relaxed on her bright peacock blue velvet sofa and watched her favorite television show. It is exactly how I want to spend every night with her. Chilling out after a long day, sharing in something one or the other of us enjoys. Only I wouldn't be walking next door to an empty bed after.

Perhaps things would have progressed differently last night if Connor hadn't called and texted her relentlessly for twenty minutes straight. She went from happy and languid to rigid and tense in that time span.

I went from happy to aggravated at both him and me. Him for not getting the message she didn't want to talk; at myself for ever letting her get into the situation with another man. I should have explained my intentions long ago.

Hindsight is a bitch.

There is some good that has come out of my emotional state; I've been working like a madman in the backyard all day while Leighton's been out doing whatever it is she's doing. The decking around my little pool is done and only needs good staining. I even have a pergola built above it so we can grow some vine type flora on it for living shade. But the best thing is the fence. What was a sun-faded wood fence has now been brought to life with a mural of muted, yet still vibrant colors. I painted a landscape of lush foliage, and with a few more touches, some comfortable furniture and dim lighting, this will be an oasis like no other.

It's also been a workout for me with all the squatting and stretching so I could reach every space I wanted. Besides all the lumber hauling and lifting over the past couple of days.

It's a small backyard, but now it's full of personality.

"How did you get all that done in a day, mon cheri?"

A raspy voice calls from above, full of sultry curiosity. Looking up, I get the first glimpse at one of the infamous Broussard sisters. She leans carelessly over her balcony, swirling a glass of dark liquor in one hand as her deep mahogany curls trail over her shoulder. Leighton said they were in their sixties, but you wouldn't be able to tell. I'd guess late forties, if I didn't know differently.

"Pure determination," I say with a grin. "Which are you, Ivy or Olive?"

"Oh, our reputation precedes us, I see. But I never give my name to a man until I know his name first. Especially the handsome ones." She leans forward an inch or two more and the silk dress she has on gapes open to reveal a light lacy bra that nearly glows in the afternoon sun. I know it's a calculated move, aimed to highlight her ample cleavage. I can appreciate it without shame.

"Reed Turner, at your service."

"A charmer, to boot. I'm Ivy, amou," she purrs. I don't know how else to describe the soft, sexy way she calls out the endearment. "Olive is the prettier one of us, but much softer. She'd have lurked up here all day and watched you work without ever uttering a word."

"Well, what a shame that would have been. It's nice to get to know my new neighbors."

"So, you aren't just the hired hand for Miss Leighton?"

"No, ma'am. This is my home."

"You're that sweet lady's brother. June, the one that's fixing up that old pile of bones on the other side of you?"

"Affirmative. She's the prettier one of us, but much softer."

Ivy laughs, throaty and deep. This woman exudes a natural sensuality like none I've seen before. If I wasn't so focused on Leighton, I'd be eager to see what Ivy is capable of in bed. I'm sure she'd be able to teach me a few things. But my dick only stirs for one woman these days, and it's relentless about it. I sat next to her last night with a constant need to adjust because hearing her breathe, smelling her, listening to her excited laughter… all makes me hungry for her.

I stopped by an art supply store yesterday, and the salesclerk was pretty and showed interest. Yet, I had none in return. Being this close to Leighton, having my hands and mouth on her, has ruined me for all other women.

I only want her, and I'll be damned if we fuck it up again this time.

"Touche, amou," Ivy says. "If you're done for the day, you should come over for a drink. You can get a view of your amazing work from here."

"You know what? That sounds like the perfect way to end this day."

"Front door is open, mon cheri. Follow the stairs up and listen for the music. You'll find me easy enough."

Brave damn woman.

"I'll be right over."

Two hours later, I've had a full tour of the Broussards' palatial home that feels more like an eclectic Antebellum Museum than it does a home. Though, it fits the women to the core, as they, too, are eccentric. Both full of Southern charm, humor that straddles the line of classy and crass, and personalities that could swallow a room on their own. Together, they're irresistible. They command attention and you don't mind because they're just that captivating.

Olive isn't any more handsome than Ivy, only younger by a few years. And perhaps she has more regality to her. She sits more elegantly, while Ivy seems perpetually relaxed, as if she's always near to napping or fucking. Ivy is forward, where Olive is all-silent smolder.

I'm not an easily overwhelmed man, but these women make me feel some way.

Their home is amazing as well. Every trinket and piece of art has a story to tell, and the sisters happily recount each one. After the tour, we moved to the back balcony that overlooks the yard I share with Leighton. Three whiskey sours in and I'm having a great time getting to know the two.

Both are enamored with what I've done to our yard, and they've not so subtly hinted at commissioning me to paint a mural in their powder room. I've never sold my art in that way but I'm finding it an intriguing prospect. Maybe it's the warmth of the booze in my veins, or maybe it's the influence of the sisters; I can't say.

We heard Leighton come home not so long ago, but she's only now coming out to investigate. The sound of her back door opening grabs all our attention.

"Her reaction makes you nervous, amou," Ivy says, picking up on the tension that has set in. I'm unsure of what her reaction will be. She could love it. Or she could hate that I made such an impact without discussing it with her beforehand.

"Because he's in love," whispers Olive, soft enough so Leighton won't hear. I shoot her a quick, affirming grin before focusing back.

"Oh my god," Leighton says, her hands coming up to her face as she slowly surveys the change.

"I think that's my cue, ladies." I rise to exit. "Thank you for the neighborly welcome, but I think I should go say hi to my *amou*." Ivy uses the Creole word for love or lover as if it's everyone's name. I like it; it reminds me of Leighton and June.

"We may have to watch." Ivy winks.

"Feel free. I'm not afraid of an audience."

Olive smiles brightly and nods goodbye as I pass by to find my way back down to the entrance of their home. Leighton is still in the backyard, tentatively touching the fence, when I arrive.

"It should be dry there, but if not, I know how to fix it."

"You did all this?" she asks, spinning toward me.

"Sure," I answer with a shrug. She may not know my talents, but this didn't take much effort. Just time.

"Reed, this is amazing. It's like our own little paradise back here."

"I'm glad you like it." I step closer to her, run a hand down her arm until our fingers entwine and I can tug her to the other side of the small yard. "I was thinking we could get one of those double chaise lounge chairs over. It'd be good for stargazing. Over there, we could put a table. String up some festoon lighting, if you'd like."

I look at her to gauge her reaction, but her eyes are on our hands, on her trembling fingers.

"That sounds nice." Her lips waver, too.

"What's wrong, Love?"

"You're staying, aren't you?"

There's no accusation in the way she asks. It's desperate. Needy. Afraid.

It makes my heart break for her.

Cupping both hands around her face, I make sure she's watching me as I answer. "Yes, Leighton. I'm here, and I'm not leaving. Do you believe me?"

"I want to."

"You can," I tell her and her eyes flutter as her mouth parts just slightly. I know she wants me to kiss her. We've been here before. More than once. I pull her in for a hug instead, knowing she doesn't like it or understand it. Yet she lets me cradle her in my arms while I tell her why I painted the things I did. What each flower means. The bleeding hearts because they were my grandmother's favorite. Lily of the Valley for June's birth month. Snowdrops for her birth flower. She shivers when I tell her that one, and her eyes dart to all the spaces on the fence filled with them.

Leighton says little, but I see the emotion play out on her face and in the way she calms in my arms. It's a much different version of the woman most see. She rarely shows a vulnerable side.

"Do you like it?"

"I love it, Reed. It feels bigger out here, somehow. I didn't know you could do all this. It's beautiful."

"You're beautiful. The yard is pretty."

Her face turns up to look at me, and I want to kiss her more than I've ever wanted to do anything. Ever.

"Why are you being so nice?"

"You don't know?"

"It's confusing," she starts when we hear a knock coming from her front door. "Shit! My date."

Leighton jerks from my arms and rushes inside. I follow. *Of course* I follow.

"He's here?"

"Yes, he's picking me up," she calls over her shoulder before opening the door to Khaki Pants. "Lucas, hi. I'm so sorry, I'm running late. Can you give me ten minutes?"

"Yeah, absolutely," Lucas says.

She shows him in, all while side-eying me. I don't move. I don't leave. There is zero chance I'm walking out with this stranger here alone with her. Zero.

Leighton mouths a silent, *Be nice,* before rushing up the stairs.

"Hi. You're June's brother, right? I'm sorry, I don't remember if I caught your name the other night."

"Reed Turner. I know I didn't catch your name," I say as I make myself comfortable by leaning against the banister, a living barrier between him and Leighton.

"Lucas Brown," he says, reaching his hand out to shake. I cross my arms instead.

"You be charming tonight, Lucas. Treat her with care, like she's the most precious thing you've ever known. Because she fucking is. You understand?"

"I… I mean, yeah. Of course," Lucas stumbles over his words, obvious in his discomfort. I couldn't give a shit. I want him to be uncomfortable. Scared, even. Terrified to hurt her.

"Good. If she has even a single second of wariness tonight, I'm coming to find you."

"Understood. She's lucky to have such a staunch protector."

"I'm the lucky one."

He balks, probably because he thought Leighton and I have a relationship more like a brother and a sister. Now, he's not so sure.

She eventually makes her way back down, now wearing a much smaller and tighter dress.

"Sorry again, Lucas. I'm ready," she says as she moves toward the door. He follows, but I step between them, standing close enough to gain the reaction I'm so accustomed to from Leighton. Heat on her cheeks, deep breaths, hooded eyes. It's sexy as sin, and I hate this tool will get any benefit from it tonight.

I bury a hand in the nape of her neck, guiding her face up to mine.

"Have a nice time. Be safe, and I'll see you when you get home, Love."

All she can do is blink. I know I'm overwhelming her, but it's her own fault she's so confused right now. My intentions have been laid out clearly. And as far as what Lucas thinks of all this… I give no fucks.

9

LEIGHTON

What a disaster.

I don't invite Lucas in when I exit his sleek sedan. The date started out nice enough. Lucas drove us to a fancier restaurant in the Quarter, complete with candlelight dining and stiff drinks. He was adorably bashful, once again. Only tonight, every time he could manage, he steered the conversation back to Reed.

Seven times.

I counted.

Seven damn times, he fished for clarification about the strange man who lives next door.

And what could I say? He's the guy I fancied myself in love with when I thought my best friend might die. Or he's the man that had his tongue buried in my pussy a few nights ago. An experience I'm still not sure I've convinced myself happened anywhere but in my lurid fantasies.

This is Reed's fault, but Lucas was obnoxious about it, too. However, this is only our second date, so I don't owe him any more explanation than Reed is protective of me because I'm considered family. I explained my nickname, and that it's one adopted by the Turners and Drew because it's what June calls me nearly exclusively. Lucas made it clear that he wasn't buying that.

I'm certain that was Reed's intention.

He's lounging on my couch when I storm into my house.

"What the hell are you doing here?"

"Waiting for you," he says casually as he sits forward to grab the television remote and presses the power to shut off whatever he'd been watching.

"I don't need a babysitter."

"No, but I'll sleep better knowing you're home safely."

Again, what am I supposed to say? Sweet Reed is as impossible to deal with as Grumpy Reed.

"You ruined my date."

"How? I wasn't on it," he says with a healthy amount of indignation.

"Lucas focused on you all night, wanting all sorts of details about who you are to me," I say.

"And what did you tell him?" Reed stalks until he's in my personal bubble.

My brain fizzles when he's so near, towering over me and looking at me like I'm his next meal. It takes me a few moments to remember he asked me a question. The quirk of his lips tells me he knows I'm stumbling.

"That you're protective because I'm family."

"Brotherly protection?" He laughs.

"This isn't funny, Reed. He's nice, has a stable career, and as a bonus, is handsome. That's almost a unicorn in the single market."

"Those are the three qualifiers?"

"Yes," I huff.

"How many of those do I have?"

"One."

"Only one?"

"You aren't nice, and I don't even know if you have a job. All I've seen is you puttering around here for two weeks."

Reed places a finger under my chin, lifting my face to his. His thumb teases my lips, and I part them slightly.

"But I have the bonus of being handsome."

"You have the bonus of being a pain in my ass."

His eyes dance with humor and heat, as if he's saying *not yet*. I can almost hear the words.

"Did he manage to turn you on tonight?"

"That's not your business," I snap.

"That's a no."

"Go away."

Reed laughs again, deep and pealing, and the sound tickles my pussy.

"Whatever you want, Love," he says, then presses a kiss to the top of my head. "Sleep well."

When Reed tells me to sleep well, I'm sure he's saying it as a curse. Again, I had spicy dreams about his smart mouth doing dirty things. My sleeping brain is as obsessed with Reed as Lucas was at dinner last night.

I'm getting ready to head to the community center in the ninth ward when my phone rings. Connor again, and I suppose it's time I stopped ignoring them.

"Hello, Connor."

"Hi. I didn't think you'd answer."

"Well, I did."

"Do you have a minute to talk?" he asks. I have some time, but honestly… why?

"What's left to say?"

"Don't be like that, Leighton. It was a big opportunity for me. I had to give the job a try."

"That was never the problem, and you know it. All you had to do was talk to me throughout the process. Instead, you kept quiet until days before you left. It was shitty and you know it."

"I know it was. Again, I apologize. I didn't think I'd get the position at all."

Understandable that he didn't believe he'd get such a prestigious position across the world. But still, we could have had a conversation.

"What do you want, Connor?"

"I'm coming back for Christmas, and again in February for Noah's wedding."

"Okay."

"I'd love it if you'd accompany me to the wedding. Of course, I understand if you don't want to."

"I'll consider it." What a strange tangle we've all become. If Connor and I had worked out, I could have become sister-in-law to the woman that had sex with my best friend's husband. *Yikes.*

"Maybe I could stay with you when I'm home in December?"

Oh.

"How long will you be here?"

"Two weeks. I can get a hotel, if it's uncomfortable for you. I'd understand, of course. But I'd like to spend time with you. I do miss you, Leighton."

"I'll consider that, too." I'm not sure what else to say. Do I miss Connor? Yes. Am I heartbroken by his absence? No. I'm sad, but I'm not wholeheartedly distraught over his leaving. I can't deny that my heart flutters, knowing he misses me and that I could see him again soon.

"Okay, that's all I ask. And maybe, don't shut me out? I care about you. That didn't stop when I moved."

Care. Not love. Connor cares about me, just not enough to be upfront with me.

"I'll try, Connor," I promise.

"Thank you, Leighton."

With little left to say, the conversation dies a quick death and I return to getting ready for my day. Excitement surges through me as I pull up to the center. I don't have much opportunity to get my hands dirty. Today, I get to do that and help a woman with a big heart so she can pass that help on to others.

It feels good. With all the relationship turmoil of my own and my friends over the past year... good feels nice. Spending the day doing something that benefits others is enjoyable for me. I like giving back however I can.

By the time I get to Irma's, I'm ready for a day of hard work, only to find Reed Turner already there.

"Ms. Ward," Irma calls as I enter the front door. Reed spins around at the sound of my name, halting the task he was completing. He's painting a mural on the far wall, and I'm once again awestruck at the talent I didn't realize he had.

"Call me Leighton, please. Hi, Irma." I speak to her, but my eyes don't leave Reed. "Where do you need me?"

"Oh, dear. We have had so much help since you ran the story. We're down to the details now. Just clean up and beautify. Could you help Mr. Turner? That's him over there." Irma points, and Reed grins like a fool.

"It so happens that I'm acquainted with Mr. Turner. I'll go see what he needs from me." I leave her to the other volunteers and head over to Reed. "How are you here?"

"I saw your story," he says with a one-shoulder shrug. "Thought I could lend a hand."

He's drawn out a city skyline at one end of the wall that morphs into a forest by the time it reaches the other side of the wall. On the urban end are children playing in the shadows of the building and in the forest, it's woodland animals.

"How long have you been here?"

"I was waiting in my car when Irma got here at six this morning."

It's not even noon now. It's unbelievable how much he's gotten done. The wall isn't huge, but still.

"Are you some kind of savant?"

"Am I a creeper, a serial killer, or a savant?"

"Are they mutually exclusive?" I ask.

Reed laughs that deep, throaty laugh that he rarely shares with me and makes me a gooey mess. My lips travel into the beginning of a smile, but I fight it.

"Grab a brush, Ward. Start filling in the lines."

"What color goes where?"

"There are no rules, just do what feels right." He says it as if he's talking about something else.

I've learned not to trust my feelings with Reed though. Since before I was even at a legal drinking age, I had a crush on him. Every time I thought he was returning an interest, it proved to be wrong. Now, with him living next door, we should have a friendship where my unrequited bullshit doesn't get in the way.

Even if he gave me a fantastic orgasm. Even if he does that again. It's just sex. Lust. An itch we both need to scratch.

It's probably all a horrible idea and I'll be the first to admit that I am not thinking these days when romance is involved.

I grab a brush and pick a small container of a russet color and feather it on the tree trunks. Reed and I don't speak much while we work, unless I have a question, in which he patiently answers and offers skillful instruction. Irma comes to check on us here and there, always with a huge smile on her face. After a couple hours, a few more volunteers who have finished other tasks join us.

It turns out to be a long day, but we get it done, and it's a colorful scene full of joy by the time it's complete.

Emotion and exhaustion hit me at once. Reed's arm falls across my shoulders, and he pulls me to his side as we say a tearful goodbye to Irma. She's overjoyed with not only the repairs but also the improvements. The community came through for her program this week, and the children in the area will benefit greatly.

"Head home, Love. I'll grab some dinner and meet you back there," Reed says, dropping a kiss to the top of my head. It's comforting, knowing I don't have to go home and sit with all my varying feelings alone tonight. I nod up to him and follow him out.

1 0

REED

Yesterday was one of the best days of my life. Spending the day with Leighton while creating art, especially for a good cause, put me in such a calming mood. Coming home afterward to her waiting for me made it even better. The cherry on top was her letting me get my mouth on her again.

I had stopped at her favorite deli, ordered two of her favorite sandwiches, and came back to feed her. As always, she seemed surprised by my food choice. She's surprised I know so much about her, but I don't think I've ever forgotten a word she's said. Even the ones that weren't said to me. She'd call it creepy, but yeah, I eavesdrop on her and June's conversations every chance I get.

Leighton's voice is my vice.

After we ate, we watched another episode of the silly assassin show she watches repeatedly. The lazier she got, the cuddlier she became. I used it to my advantage, pulling her down to lay atop me on her sofa. My hands ran over her body, massaging her limbs until she was languid and pliable. Until there was only enthusiasm at me pulling her t-shirt over her head and removing her bra. She almost fed me her fucking spectacular breasts, and I could have feasted on them for days while she fucked the hand I had shoved down her pants.

It was glorious, the hottest thing I've ever seen. I came twice in the shower before I passed out in my own bed wondering how long we will play this game before she admits to feeling the same way about me that I feel about her.

Absolutely obsessed. Destined. Fated.

Though, today might set us back. Because today, she'll discover that we'll be working together, and that for whatever stupid reason, I haven't told her.

Fran Carmichael, Moxy's editor in chief, is already in the conference room when I arrive at the office. We'll be spending a good part of the morning there, getting to know the team and discussing the vision of the online magazine. It's a small team, meant to grow with the publication. When I interviewed with Fran and the parent publication company, she said it was her goal to make the Moxy staff a family, one that worked for the community in the Southern states it would focus on. She may have been blowing smoke up my ass, but I hope not. I'm keen on immersing myself in something more than a typical corporate job.

"Good morning, Reed," Fran greets as I enter the room with two large coffees in hand. One Americano for me, one oat milk latte for Leighton. It's not much of a peacemaker, but it's a start.

"Morning, Fran. You ready?"

"Yes. Excited, even. I've been in this business a long time, and worked my ass off for an opportunity like this."

She has, too. Fran's been in the business for over forty years and has worked for some of the best lifestyle magazines in the world. There's a lot to learn from her.

"You've earned it, Fran."

"Thank you. You needing the extra caffeine today?" she asks, nodding to the second cup I've set beside me on the table.

"Nah, I'm feeling fresh today. This is for a *friend* who was also hired here."

"Oh, it's like that, is it?" she says with a smile.

"She's important to me. I assume that won't be a problem."

"No, Reed. If you know anything about me, which I'm sure you do, you know I married my editor," she says as she moves around the room, needlessly straightening up chairs already straight. "You do your jobs, and we'll have no issues."

I know this about her. Fran was a lower-level editor when she married her wife, who was also her boss. It was scandalous, but that was a long time ago now. Things have changed, maybe not enough, but Fran gets to make her own rules here.

"It won't interfere."

"Good. Which one is it?"

"Leighton Ward, my sister's best friend."

"Oh, that's cute," she teases.

"Yeah, yeah." I laugh as more people file into the room.

I see Leighton before she sees me. Always beautiful, but today, she's more than that. Her excitement and confidence bring out an ethereal glow about her. She's dressed in colors that bring out the new rose tones in her hair that is so like the bashful hue her cheeks carry so often around me. There's a wide smile on her face as she chats with another woman, until she sees me, and it falters.

Nodding to the chair next to mine, I point at the coffee I've brought for her. She might be caught off guard, but she never refuses gifts of the edible version. She flashes a small wave to Fran as she makes her way around the table.

"Why are you here?" Leighton asks defensively as she sits next to me.

"I work here. Oat milk latte," I say, gesturing to the paper cup.

"Thank you," she says before remembering she's annoyed. "Explain."

"They were hiring, I applied, interviewed, and was hired."

"Cute, Turner." She rolls her eyes at me, and I don't even want to know what it says about me that it makes my dick twitch with desire. "When did you get hired?"

"The week before I moved down here."

Her lips pull tight, and she pushes the coffee away, a clear sign she's pissed.

"Good morning, everyone," Fran says from the far end of the large oval table. "Welcome to the Moxy team. The twelve of us in this room are the lifeblood of this rag, and we'll be working very closely together each month. We'll be adding to the support team over the next few weeks, but us." She gestures around the room. "We're the spine of Moxy. The word moxie means force of character or nerve. That's my vision for Moxy, to have the determination to dig into the Southern community, find all the aspects that don't get seen, and shine a light on them. It's a lifestyle magazine, yes, but not dedicated to just fluff. I want grit, the taboo, *and* all the bright, pretty places as well. No pitch is off limits unless the story doesn't fall in Louisiana, Mississippi, Alabama, Georgia, Arkansas, or Tennessee. I may make exceptions for Eastern Texas and the Florida panhandle, but they better be damn good stories. Understood?"

Everyone gives a form of agreement while I take quick study of Leighton. She's shifted in her chair to turn her back toward me, but I can still glimpse her face and she's lit up again like she was when she first entered this room. She loves her work and I've noted all the times she's felt disgruntled at not being able to report on things she's passionate about. She's ecstatic at the opportunity, and I couldn't be more pleased for her.

I want her to have everything she's ever dreamed of. It's all I've ever wanted for her.

Fran speaks for a few more minutes before working around the table and introducing everyone. Leighton's shoulders stiffen when I'm named Art Director, and I smile when she's named Lead Journalist. Kenneth, a young yet talented photographer, turns his attention to Leighton throughout most of the morning, and my hackles rise. His groomed good looks, paired with dark and expensively 'edgy' clothes, are like a billboard reading douchebag player.

Clara, Fran's assistant, gives me similar attention. I'm not interested, but I do notice. She's hard to miss being all tall and gorgeous. Her hazel eyes defined by dark eyebrows and a mass of natural black curls fall around her shoulders.

I prefer strawberry blonde. Or rose gold. Hell, Leighton could dye her hair emerald green, and it wouldn't matter a fucking bit. Her looks weren't what attracted me; they're just the icing.

Leighton continues ignoring me, mostly. She's at least polite about it. Occasionally, she forgets herself and takes a drink of the coffee she's trying not to enjoy since it came from me... the grumpy man that plays all the games and keeps her running in circles. That's not what I'm trying to do anymore, but she doesn't see that yet.

There's no rush, though. I'm not going anywhere.

The rest of the morning moves quickly as we all find our desks within the office and settle in. Our space is bright with floor-to-ceiling windows. Most of the interior walls are glass too, allowing for natural light to illuminate the entire place. My office, much to my delight, opens across the common space to Leighton's. I'll be able to look at her all day.

Creepy? Whatever, I don't care.

Clara steps into my office with a quick knock to the door jamb and another woman in tow. This one younger; I'd say, fresh out of college.

"Reed, this is your assistant, Holly Stoops. Holly, this is Reed Turner," Clara says, gesturing between us.

"Nice to meet you, Holly," I say, standing and offering a hand to shake.

"Nice to meet you too, Mr. Turner."

"Reed, please," I say to her, then turn to Clara. "Thank you, Clara. I've got it from here."

"Of course," she replies, patting a hand to my shoulder on her way out the door.

"Okay, fill me in on your skills. This isn't a test, so there is no right or wrong answer. I just want a feel for what I can let you run with and what we'll need to work up to." I gesture for her to take a seat opposite me after taking my own.

"I have a B.F.A. from Savannah College of Art and Design. I'm proficient with Office applications, great with all Adobe programs, and a talented illustrator as well. I pride myself on being a quick study and a creative thinker." She rubs her thighs as she speaks, reminding me of one of my sister's nervous gestures.

"Those are great credentials, Holly, and that's an amazing school," I tell her with honesty. "I'd love to see some of your art. I paint myself."

"You do?"

"I do. It's my passion and a stress reliever."

"Same for my drawing," she says, her shoulders sagging.

"Good, then I'll know if I catch you doodling, you need help with something. Like Fran said, we're a team here. But more importantly, you and I are a team. I'm not the type to be an asshole boss. I'll never ask for anything unreasonable, and I want you to be honest with me. Always. It's important that you feel comfortable here."

"Thank you, Reed. I appreciate that."

"You're welcome, Holly," I tell her, sincerely. "The rest of the department will be in the office tomorrow; we have four more on our team. We'll have a meeting first thing, then we'll get them started on mockups right away. We're six weeks out from going live, but Fran wants options to approve or reject within two weeks. The earlier, the better, in case she hates them all."

"Understood," she says with a nod.

"Meanwhile, I'd like you to set up a shared calendar. My items will be shared with you only, but share department items with the entire team."

We discuss more action items, then Holly leaves to start her tasks, leaving me with a clear vision into Leighton's office across the way. She has a young woman in her office too, and Leighton speaks to her with so much animation I can't help but grin. I move to my open office door to get a better glimpse. Her excitement is infectious.

Until I hear a hushed voice to my side.

"She's more fuckable in person than she was on television."

Peering next to me, I find exactly who I expect. Kenneth.

"Come inside, Kenneth. Let's get to know one another," I say, and he follows me into the office. The door gets shut firmly before I take a seat behind my desk. "Fran showed me your portfolio before hiring you. It's quite impressive."

"Thanks, man."

"It wasn't so impressive that I won't obliterate you if I ever hear you speak of fucking Ms. Ward, or any other woman that works here, ever again."

The congenial smile he wore seconds ago slides away to a frown as my own features tighten into barely controlled rage.

"Come on, man. She's fucking gorgeous."

"She is," I clip out as I stand, palms stretching out on my desk. "She's also a talented journalist who has earned the respect this position affords her. Which does not come with lustful comments being made by and to her coworkers. Treat her properly. Treat her and all other women here like a man should. Not a shithead boy that just learned boobies give him an erection. Do that and we won't have any problems. Understood?"

"Yeah, Mr. Turner," he says, fidgeting uncomfortably. "Understood. I didn't mean any harm."

"I get it, you have a crush. But keep that shit to yourself. That old school water cooler talk bullshit doesn't happen in this office."

"Got it," he says, clearly admonished from my dressing down of him. He took it better than I expected, and I respect that he sees the error in judgment. If he fucks his second chance up, I'll end the little twat.

1 1

LEIGHTON

"June didn't know he was working there?"

"No, Dad. I don't think he told anyone," I answer him. I called June on my lunch break today, one I hurriedly ran out of the office for, not wanting Reed to follow. She said she had no clue that he had taken the position at Moxy. Drew seemed as surprised.

But why wouldn't he tell anyone? Unless it's because he got me the job there and didn't want to say. I'm hardheaded enough that I wouldn't have even shown up for the interview if it was one that I had only gotten because Reed called in a favor. Stupid as that may be.

The timing of it all is suspicious as hell, though. He could have done what I fear. It was my first thought when I saw him sitting in the conference room. I want to have earned this.

"You should just talk to him, sweetheart."

"Eww, so he can lie to me?"

"He won't." My dad laughs at my dramatic behavior. "You and Reed have a... different relationship, but I don't believe he's the type of man to lie to you if you ask him a question outright."

"No." I sigh. He wouldn't lie, but he may dance around the answer. Reed's very good at that.

He's also very good at giving me orgasms. The second one proved that. He works me over as if he designed my body with his own skillful hands.

I hate how much I love it. And how much I crave it when he's near, which is all the damn time lately. It's only going to get worse working with him every day. I'll need to take spare underwear with me to work because all it takes to soak them is for me to notice him looking at me. He did that a lot today. Reed doesn't even try to hide it or look away when I catch him. Instead, his smolder deepens like he, too, is thinking about how easily I fall apart for him.

"So, talk to him. You're probably just jumping to conclusions, which isn't like you at all."

"You're right, Dad. He just drives me crazy."

"I know." There's a bit of playfulness in his voice. "I've watched you two push each other's buttons for years. Now, go deal with it so it doesn't fester. I'll see you next week for Thanksgiving."

"Okay, love you."

"Love you, too, sweetheart."

Ending the call perfectly timed as I pull up at home. Reed's SUV is already parked, so I figure he's home now too. I take my time and change clothes before going to find him, since it gives me a chance to calm down. My father is right; I don't jump to conclusions often. I'd suck at my job if I did. Reed rattles my nerves.

Peeking out the window on the way upstairs to my bedroom, I see he's already soaking in his new tub out back. An idea niggles its way into my mind, and I run with it. A few minutes later, I step out into our shared yard and enjoy the sight of Reed being the one uncomfortable for a change. He shifts, abruptly sitting up as I walk toward him wearing an incredibly see-through cover up. Which I shed as if I'm not nude underneath and climb up the stairs to the small pool.

It's not a balmy night, yet this pool isn't heated by anything except the sun which has already disappeared, but I ignore the chill, focusing instead on the heat in Reed's eyes. It's enough to warm me from the inside.

"We need to talk," I say, using my foot to gently push his legs out of the way so I can sink into the water. I do it slowly, giving him time to drag his eyes all over me. While mine can't move away from the magnificent cock proudly showing itself in front of me. I always suspected Reed's dick would be amazing, but this is beyond imagination. My pulse quickens, pounding so loudly in my ears I almost can't hear his response.

"Is that what you want to do? Talk?"

"Yes," I say. "You need to explain to me how I ended up with the job at Moxy."

Reed's brow furrows in confusion.

"What do you mean?"

"Did you ask Fran to interview me?"

"No," he says, quickly. Sitting up further, his hands wrap under my knees, and he pulls me closer. "You think I had a hand in getting you the job?"

"Yes." I shrug. "It's suspicious, don't you think? You didn't tell anyone you had the job. A fantastic job, at that. You admitted that you'd been hired before they even interviewed me."

"Love, sometimes it's as if you don't know me at all." Something close to hurt sounds in his words, and Dad was right. That I have it all wrong. But...

"Why the secrecy, Reed?"

"After Fran hired me, we had a long discussion about the team she wanted to build. That included her rattling off names of people she was hoping to hire. She mentioned that you'd applied, and she was excited to talk to you because you'd done several pieces about local homeless youth, and she admired you for it. I didn't admit to knowing you; I kept my mouth shut," he says. His eyes squint at me as if he is trying to read my reaction. "Do you have any idea why I would do that?"

"No," I admit freely.

"Because if you got the job, Leighton," he says, moving his hands farther up my legs. "If you won the position, I wanted you to know you won it on your own merit. And if you wanted the job, I didn't want you not to take it because of me."

"Oh."

"Yeah, oh. So maybe you can quit being mad at me now? Or should I give you an orgasm or two before I feed you dinner, so you know I have your best interests at heart?"

Holy fuck.

"You're feeding me dinner?" I stammer out the words when really, I want to scream, *please give me all the orgasms.*

"There is lasagna baking in my oven right now. Larry's recipe."

"You have my dad's recipe?"

"Yes," he says with a nod.

"How?"

"I asked."

"I didn't even know you and my dad talked," I say, and Reed brings a hand up to rub a thumb along my cheekbone.

"I've known Larry almost as long as I've known you. Of course, we speak on occasion."

"Why haven't either of you ever mentioned it?" I ask, though it's hard to focus because Reed's other hand, the one still underwater moves to play with my inner thigh. My brain function stalls altogether.

Reed stills, looking at me with amusement.

"You let me know when you figure it all out, Love."

Then his thumb is at my lips, parting them before breaching and thrusting it in for me to suck. Simultaneously, two fingers tease at the opening below. Arching my chest out of the water at the sensation, I gently bite down with a pleasurable sigh.

"You're always so responsive for me," Reed says. His voice sounds like my body feels. Needy, greedy, and so fucking ready. "Barely a touch and you're ready to explode. I've felt you on my fingers, tasted you on my tongue. Are you going to let me fuck you this time, Leighton?"

"I… I don't know."

His head drops down on to my chest, his next words sending shivers straight to my nipples.

"You're not ready for that yet. I'm patient, I'll wait," he says, then runs his tongue around the underside of my breast. "Do you know how amazing it's going to feel? I do. I've dreamed about it for so long."

He has?

"You have?"

"Fuck, yes. It's all I dream about. How your cunt is going to hug my cock. How it will tighten up every time I pull out, fighting to keep it inside you forever. How goddamned fantastic it will feel to fill you up with my cum until it's seeping back out and slicking your thighs with"—he takes a quick nip at my tit—"me."

I reach down, wrapping a hand around his girth. He's slick and soft in my hand as I begin a slow, steady rhythm, one that matches the pace of the fingers he's working inside me.

"Reed," I cry out louder than I expected, but he makes me feel so much.

"Shh," he says, his thumb going back to my mouth. "I'm sure we're being watched by at least one of the sisters. Maybe both."

I smile and push my hips forward, allowing his fingers deeper entry.

"You like the thought of them watching us? Do you want them to see how hard I make you come?"

"I want them to see how hard I make you come."

"Fuck, Love. I want to see that, too."

"I owe you a couple, don't I?"

"Look at me," he demands as he stills. "Is that what you think?"

"I've yet to reciprocate."

"Sure, but you don't owe me that. I'll come in you or on you, whenever you want. But you never owe me, we don't keep tally because this isn't tit for tat. I give you orgasms because I love to, not because I expect to get one in return. Understand me?"

"Yes," I answer, then lean forward and lick a line from the dip at the base of his neck all the way up his throat. He pulls back to look at me before I can get to his mouth. "Can I make you come now? I need to know how much I'm going to love it."

"I'm at your disposal."

"Fuck my hands, Reed," I whisper an inch from his mouth. Expecting him to take my lips with his, I'm surprised when he doesn't, and instead he lands at my ear, tugging at the lobe.

Regardless, he does what I told him to. The hand not currently still performing magic on my pussy thuds on the edge of the tub at my shoulder and his hips start a smooth, even motion.

"When I'm finally doing this to your cunt, it's going to last hours. Then I'm going to spend all my free time fucking you. Whatever you want. *However* you want it. You bring me to my knees with only your hands, so just imagine what your pussy is going to do to me."

Reed pushes faster and harder, and I feel every ridge of every vein, the lip of his head. The slightly sticky threads of precum wash away too quickly in the cool water. What if it could be like this always? Neither of us at each other's throats. No more sniping but flirty jest. He says he wants that, but I can't trust that.

I can't trust that he'll stay. Others haven't.

"Damn, Love," Reed says, pulling me back to the moment and to his face. He's so beautiful it's almost painful to look at him without the certainty that he's mine. "Fuck my hand, baby. Try to come, do it with me."

I don't look away and neither does he as we edge closer and closer. Together we rise, together we crumble apart. Together, we call out each other's names.

Reed Turner came in my hands, and if I died, right now, I'd do it as a content woman.

His forehead rests on mine while our bodies settle down. Reed's arms wrap around me, and he shifts us until I'm cradled on his lap.

"I like this, Leighton."

"Orgasms?"

Reed's laugh sends the water surrounding us into tiny rippling waves, matching the thoughts in my head. Each is foggier than the next.

"Yes, but not just the orgasms. This, Love. You… draped all over me." I hum in agreement; it is nice, even if I'm not sure about what's happening. "We should do it more often. As soon as you quit dating other men."

Well, shit.

"I have another date this Friday," I hedge.

"Are you fucking kidding me?"

"No."

"Khaki Pants again?"

"No."

"Someone new?"

"Yes. We chatted a couple times. He has some charity thing to go to and needs a plus one."

"Fucking hell, you'll be the death of me," he says, once again bundling me up into his arms. This time, he hauls me out of the tub with him and places me on my feet. "Go dry off and open a bottle of wine. I'll bring the lasagna over."

"Okay," I say on a tremble as a small breeze blows through the backyard.

"Go, before you catch your death, or I get another erection from you standing there looking like you do."

"How do I look?"

"Like the only meal I'll ever need. Now, go."

But I can't go. Not right away, because it feels imperative standing here and staring at the water droplets trailing down Reed's chiseled chest, then his abdomen, and farther.

Damn, he's perfect.

"Go," he barks.

Right.

I rush to the other side of the yard, to my backdoor.

"Have a wonderful night, my darlings," calls Ivy's smokey voice from the balcony next door.

12

LEIGHTON

I had a nice night with Max. The charity event we went to was raising money for an organization that goes around to local schools and teaches youth about philanthropy. Max is on the board of directors for the organization and is also the coach of one of the local high school football teams.

I figured my connection to both Drew, a current NFL quarterback, and Noah, who is retired, is the reason he asked me out. I'm a great connection for someone like Max. Knowing that when I said yes, I'm not bothered he focused so much of the conversation on football.

Otherwise, it was a great night, and I was happy to be involved. But I'm exhausted walking through my front door at the end of the night. It was a big week. A great one, but full of changes and meeting so many new people at Moxy. Tomorrow, I don't want to do anything that requires wearing pants or getting off my couch.

Which is where I find Reed when I enter my home. When Max came by to pick me up, Reed was waiting on the stoop to give him the third degree. It was as annoying as it was adorable in his own overbearing way. I distinctly remember locking my front door behind me when I left.

Reed stirs from his nap when I walk in, looking ridiculously sexy in his sleepy state.

"Breaking and entering now, Turner?"

"You make it easy when you never changed the code to the front door," he says on a stretch. "How was your night?"

"Nice," I say, taking a seat on the spot of the couch his feet vacated.

"Just nice?"

"Yeah, it was a good cause. Met some wonderful people. Raised a nice amount of money."

He sits up further, more alert now.

"How did he treat you?"

"Fine. Though I think he was more interested in my famous and wealthy football connections than anything else."

Reed's eyes squint, clearly not liking that answer.

"Did he tell you how beautiful you are?"

Come to think of it… "No."

"Then he's an asshole and you don't need to attempt a second date with him, because you look fucking fabulous tonight and that should have been the only thing on his mind."

"Thank you," I say, wishing I didn't feel the heat of a blush coming on. I don't know how he does that. A few days ago, I wasn't feeling shy when I stripped down naked and joined him in the backyard. So why am I now?

"Come here," he mumbles, pulling me onto him until I'm tucked in front of him in a position that allows us both to watch the television. He's been watching that British baking show that people love, and it makes me giggle. "What's so funny?"

"I'm imagining you in an apron making elaborately decorated tiny desserts."

"Don't make fun or I won't make you come."

"Your impressive rhyming skills are panty-wetting, Turner. But I have plenty of toys that can make me come just as easily as you do."

Bold-faced. Lie.

"Care to test that theory?" he asks as his hand slides down, only to drag my dress up.

"What do you have in mind?"

"Let's go find your toys and figure it out?"

As much as the idea intrigues and excites me, there's something else I'd rather do.

"Can we try something else?"

"Whatever you want, Love." His eyes dance with anticipation.

I wiggle out of his hold and stand, turning my back to him. "Will you unzip me?" He, too, stands. The space between me and the couch leaves little room and his breath tickles at the nape of my neck. I wore my hair up today, so it's exposed. Reed presses a kiss to the spot, then follows the path of the zipper as he pulls it down slower than I'd have thought was humanly possible.

"I've waited many years to get my lips on you."

After he's finished with the zipper, he fingers the thin straps off my shoulders, letting me shimmy it over my bare breasts and hips until it's on the floor and I can step out of it.

"Why don't you kiss me?" I ask after I turn back to him. There have been many times I know he wanted to, several times I thought he was close to giving in to it. But he never does. Not since that first time so long ago.

"Who says I want to?" The smile gives him away. That, and the way he rubs his nose against mine as he asks the question.

"I know there have been a few times you've wanted to. I could see it."

"You don't know me as well as you think you do," he says, and I frown. "Because there hasn't been a time that I haven't wanted to kiss you. Since before June's attack. For years and years, Love."

"Then why don't you?" I can't keep the hurt away; it seeps into every word. "Why haven't you?"

"The first time I kissed you; you were the only light in the darkest time of my life. I had an incredible infatuation with you already, but the way you loved my sister? That cemented it into something else. I kissed you that night because I couldn't not kiss you. It felt more right than anything else in my life ever has," he says, wiping away the dewdrop of moisture at the corner of my eye. "When I woke up, you weren't in my arms, and I thought maybe I'd dreamed it. I could still taste you, like a ghost on my lips. I went looking to find coffee and found you in the arms of some guy with his mouth on yours."

What?

"Who?"

"How should I know who the guy was?" He laughs. "Were there so many you can't keep track?"

"Are you slut-shaming me?" I snap.

"Jesus, you really don't know me at all if you think your body count matters to me. At all."

"It doesn't?"

"Not even a little."

If I didn't already love him… Wait, no, no, no. I don't love him. Infatuated, flustered, lustful… all proper descriptors for how I feel for Reed.

"Reed, I'm standing here in some of my sexiest panties, waiting to give you the best blow job of your life if we could only get past this bullshit. Why won't you kiss me?"

"Damn, baby. Is that what the plan is?" I nod at him while I pull off my underwear. "I don't know who the guy was; I assumed it was someone you were dating at the time. A random guy stopping to check in on you and June. I didn't resent him. Or you. But I did promise myself that the next time I kissed you, it would be because I knew I'd be the last man you kiss."

Oh. My heart can't take sweet Reed Turner. It's clueless on how to defend against him. No point in fighting it here and now, when instead, I can unbutton his jeans. Reach a hand in to find no other barrier between me and his hard, fat cock.

"I vaguely remember Joel Lydell, a guy who I had one coffee date with, coming by the hospital. He brought a box of chocolates like it was Valentine's Day instead of the worst time in my life. When he moved in for what I thought was a hug, he kissed me. Briefly, before I shrugged him off," I tell him as I gently run my fingers down to cup his balls. "If you'd stayed a minute longer or asked me about it, I'd have explained. I'd have told you that when you kissed me, I believed everything was going to be okay. I had been terrified beyond words for days until that kiss."

Reed unbuttons his shirt, then shucks it off altogether. Desperately wanting him bare, I push his jeans over his hips and drag them down as I lower myself in front of him. He's barefoot and even his feet are sexy.

Would it be considered a foot fetish if I become obsessed with just one man's feet?

"It wasn't really about the guy, Love," he says. "It was about timing. Like how right now, it's time for me to fuck that mouth of yours."

"Don't take it easy on me, Turner."

"Do you know what you're asking me, Ward?"

"I'm asking you to take as good as you give."

Reed rubs a finger down the bridge of my nose, then across my lips. "Do you like the way I make you come, Leighton?"

"I don't like it, Reed. I love it. I'm beginning to crave it, even."

"Show me your tongue," he commands in a raspy voice. Between his dark tone, hard dick, and the slight twitch in his abdomen, I know he's as turned on as I am. I open my mouth and push my tongue out for him. "It's a pretty pink right now, but before too long, it's going to be all white. I want you to show me before you swallow it all down."

"It will be my pleasure," I purr. Not breaking eye contact, I shove a hand in my pussy so I can coat a few fingers in my own wetness. Then I use it to coat the base of Reed's cock, giving my palm the slickness it needs to pump him up and down. Then squat and mirror the movement with my mouth. Reed groans as I cradle his dick with my tongue.

I continue to work him for a few moments, attuned to each move he makes. Every sound he utters and demand he barks while in the throes of arousal; I take it all in and commit it to memory. The uncertainty of what Reed and I are will not stop me from enjoying this experience and remembering it forever. I want this to look back on if ever there's a time that I don't have this same access to him.

What a sad day that would be without his gorgeous body on display in front of me. He's built like a professional athlete, which I suppose makes sense since he has regularly worked out with one for most of his life. He's leaner but no less sculpted. His dick is the star of the show, though. If I were a man and had a dick like this… well, people would know. I'd make it known. I'd show that fucker off.

"You're exquisite with my cock between your lips," Reed says, making my eyes snap up to his which are lit up with a fire I've never seen on him. One of his hands cups my cheek; the other buries itself in my hair so he can maneuver me exactly where he wants me. The long strokes of his hips gain speed and depth, so I have to focus more on relaxing my throat to accommodate him as he takes control.

I let it go happily, enjoying the view of Reed taking what he wants and how his body responds. A flush of his own creeps onto his skin, beads of sweat pebbling along his pecs, and I have to touch it. Touch him, drag my fingers over his tensing muscles. I grip his ass with one palm, while the other stays on his chest, and I tease his nipple with my finger. It's hotter than anything I've ever experienced. I sway on my knees, needing some friction and finding none.

Reed needs to come so I can, because I can't stop touching him. I physically cannot stop touching him. So instead, I move my hands from spot to spot, studying how each touch sparks a new reaction in him. He likes it when I squeeze his hip almost as much as he likes it when I play with his perineum; that's the spot that takes him over the edge.

"Fuck, Love. Right there," he says with some urgency. His thighs tense, tightening as he rises ever so higher on his toes. I taste the beads of precum. It spurs my need for him and my desire to see him come apart. For me. "Fuck. Tongue, Love. Let me see it, give it to me."

I do, as he stares at my mouth while giving me all he has. He does his best to keep it on my tongue but fails as some hits my upper lip and cheek. There's so much and I feel some drip down to land on my nipple.

Regardless, I don't close my eyes or blink. When he's spent, his gaze moves to my face, and I nearly choke. Not on the cum; I haven't yet tried to swallow that down, still letting it sit on my tongue for him to see. No, I choke on the pure lust he wears… for me.

"You're better than anything I've conjured in my imagination," he muses. Two of his fingers settle on my tongue. "Suck them, Love. Swallow it down. Are you on some sort of birth control?"

I am—*IUD sucks*—so I nod. He squats in front of me, removes his fingers from my mouth and inserts them in my cunt instead. All it takes is a handful of strokes and his head bending down to draw a nipple between his lips, then I'm gone. I'm dying a million tiny deaths and floating through space as I lose all brain function to another fantastic orgasm at the hands of Reed Turner.

13

REED

I almost came as soon as her mouth engulfed my dick. Like a boy with his first glimpse of porn. Thank fuck I didn't; how embarrassing that would have been. Leighton on her knees with her tongue hanging out for me was not what I was expecting tonight.

And now, spent like she is after her own orgasm… well, it's sexy as hell and I want more.

"The next time you come like that, it's going to be around my cock."

"Okay," she pants with a sated smile. She's still breathing hard as I pick her up and carry her up to her bedroom. Leighton doesn't fight me. There isn't even a smart remark. While that's a nice change, it doesn't seem right. It's not us. We play, we bicker, we tease. Leighton, limp in my arms as her lips kiss and nip my neck, is new. I could easily get used to it.

Pushing her bedroom door open with my foot, I freeze with only a step inside.

"Um, baby?"

"Mmhm?"

"You're messy."

"What?" she asks, popping her head up from my shoulder. After a quick glance around at the clothes strewn over every surface, she giggles. "I tried on an array of outfits before I settled on what I wore tonight."

I call bullshit. There are at least twenty dresses lying about. No way had she tried them all on. Right? Luckily, the bed is mostly clear for me to toss her onto it.

"Do you have any idea how many things I want to do with you?" I ask. She bites her bottom lip and gives me a flirty nod. "I'm not sure you do."

"I bet I do, considering how many I want to do with you."

"Yeah? Tell me some." It's a dare, and I smile as her cheeks pinken. But she's not shy, so it isn't unexpected when she climbs up to her knees so she can get closer to my eye level as I stand next to the bed.

"In all my twenty-eight years, Reed, I've come across very few hard limits when it comes to sex. I'm not going to let anyone defecate on me, but barring that sort of extreme, I'm game for almost anything. You want fuck my mouth, my cunt, my ass? I'm in. You want to fill me up with gags and dildos *while* you fuck my ass? Go for it, I'll love it. Hold me down, tie me up, spank me, choke me—I'll reciprocate in kind if you want. I don't care where you come on me as long as you're coming for me." She punctuates her words with a long lick up the column of my throat. If her words hadn't made me hard again, that move would have.

"How much of that have you tried?"

"Most of it."

"Bondage?"

"Not so much. Mostly, I have been cuffed to the bed a few times."

"That's not my kink, but I'd go there if you wanted." She smiles, but I can tell it's not a big interest of hers either. "Have you had multiple partners?"

"A few years ago, I went on a few dates with a guy who would only have sex if there were multiple partners. Once, we had a threesome with another woman. Once, it was with another man," she says cautiously. She thinks this will be a deal breaker for me. Further proof that she doesn't know me nearly as well as I want her to.

"I meant what I said earlier. I don't care how many people you've had sex with, so quit with that fear seeping into your voice. I consider myself lucky to have a woman with enough experience to know what she likes and what she wants. Understand?" I ask, and she nods. "Which threesome did you like better?"

I gently push her shoulders until she falls back on the bed, then I climb up after her. Positioning myself, I pull her arms over her head with my thighs on either side of her chest so I can nestle my cock between her ample tits.

"I loved two dicks at once. But there was something incredibly sexy about him fucking another woman while his eyes and mouth were focused on me. What about you? Have you had a threesome or more?"

"I've had plenty of threesomes, and a couple times, there was a fourth. Always women." I move my hips back and forth, slowly building friction.

"It doesn't intrigue you? Another man working over a woman with you. Your dicks sliding against each other inside her while she loses her mind?"

Fuck.

The way she talks about it and how her eyes slightly glaze over with lust makes it more intriguing.

"It never did until you just described it."

"Happy to be of assistance."

"Anything you want to discuss before I shove my cock in you?"

"One thing."

"What?"

"This means something to me, Reed," she says. The lustful fire in her eyes a moment ago changes into something sad. An emotion I've never liked seeing in her. "I don't fully understand why you won't kiss me, but I don't want you to think this is frivolous to me. It's not. *You* are not."

"I know that, Love," I tell her, placing my palm over her heart. "I often think I know you better than you know yourself." My dick hits where my hand is resting, so I give it a few strokes and see the passion return to her eyes.

"Then fuck me, Reed. Fuck me how you know I'll like it."

There it is, the snipe, the tease. Damn, it turns me on.

"Flip over on your hands and knees," I tell her as I climb back off her. "Good, Love. I can't promise this won't be quick, since you've starred in every fantasy I've had for as long as I've known you."

I move behind her, part her ass with forceful fingers. Leighton is slender but has healthy curves everywhere I like them to be.

"Every single one?" she asks.

"Every damn one. You're a distraction." Dipping a finger in her pussy, I gauge how ready she is, before sliding it up her crease and watching her shake with need. "You are my sole obsession."

I thrust my cock without warning, and her moan indicates she doesn't mind. But I have to hold for a minute to regain my senses because I'm finally inside the only woman I have ever loved, and it feels more than I could have ever expected.

"Reed," she gasps. "It feels so…"

"I know, Love. I know." Reaching under her, I slide a hand up to her throat as I push in and out of her. Hard. Punishing thrusts. Punishment for making me wait so long. Which is fucking stupid since that's as much, or more, my fault.

Whatever the reason, I want her to feel it too; this knowledge that we could have had this for years if we'd only been less ridiculous and more communicative. We will be from now on. Tonight was a start—she gave me a lot and I'll give her everything.

My life, my name, a ring, my whole heart. Anything she wants.

But first, my seed.

"How's the pressure? Too much?" I don't want to choke her, just enhance the feeling.

"More."

She arches her back, and I slide my other hand to her ribs, pulling her back up to my chest. Both her hands reach up to tangle in my hair. I thrust hard and fast until it's too much for either of us to maintain the position. Our bodies are slick with perspiration, our muscles twitching with fatigue.

"Come on my cock, Love," I whisper at the shell of her ear. "Coat me with it."

"Oh God," she cries when I play with her clit in the way I've learned she loves. She won't last long now. "Reed."

"Give it to me."

Her fingers tighten in my hair, pulling to the point of pain that only takes me over the edge with her. Surprisingly, another rope of my come slides inside her, astounding me, considering how little time has passed since I exploded inside her mouth. It's her though; she's got some mystical power over me, and I'll never complain about it. I'm entranced.

When we're both coming down, I shift so I can lie back with her sprawled on top of me. After my dick calms, it eases out of her and the soft trickle of fluid follows. I rub it in to the skin around my cock, then dip into her for more and rub that into the sensitive skin at her inner thigh.

"What are you doing?" Leighton asks, turning her head on my shoulder to see my face.

"I don't know exactly. Painting us, staining us, marking this moment in some way."

She blinks a few times before she speaks again.

"I want nothing more than to kiss you right now."

And fuck, I want that too. So much. I'm not a jealous man by any stretch, but I will lose my shit completely if I ever have to see her kiss another man after me again. I've built that small, stupid detail up so much over the past seven years that it's become more important than it should. It carries too much weight now that I think if I let it go, I'll float away with it.

Ridiculous, but it is what it is.

"Will you settle for me holding you all night?"

"For now, Reed," she answers with that sadness I hate so much. Especially knowing I'm the one that put it there.

We'll get there, though, her and I. Soon, we'll find that place of understanding and trust. Of absolute certainty that it's us, forever.

14

REED

"Do you remember the conversation I had with you when June was in the hospital?" I ask Larry.

It's Thanksgiving and we've all gathered at June and Drew's house here in New Orleans. My mother arrived on Monday. Larry, Leighton's father, arrived yesterday. Luckily, Drew isn't playing today and was able to fly in with June.

Mom, as always, is in the kitchen preparing all the food. She loves a reason to cook for people and you can't trust June to do it anyway. We actively keep her away from cooking anything. She's that awful at it.

This year feels the way it's supposed to, with all of us together. June and Leighton inside with Mom, pretending to help, but more like keeping her company while they keep her wine glass full. And Larry, Drew, and I sitting out in the backyard with beers while talking sports.

There's a more important subject on my mind, though.

"I do," he says, leaning forward and resting his elbows on his knees. "Has that changed?"

"I wouldn't say changed, but it's grown over the years. It's more now," I say. Since our first time Saturday night after her date, I've spent two more nights in her bed. The other two nights were pure fucking torture. I'm not trying to invade every part of her world, even if I hate not having her wrapped in my arms as we sleep.

I've even tried to keep out of her way at the office the past few days. That's been easy since we've been so busy with the startup. It's much harder to keep a distance when we're home and she's so relaxed and looking like she wants to be fucked into an exhaustive sleep.

"Are you asking for her hand in marriage, son?" Larry asks.

"You and I both know she'd string both of us up by our manhood if we thought she needed your permission on who to marry." I laugh.

"Good answer. But be specific in what you are telling me."

"I do want to marry her, Larry. I'd do it right here and now, if she was ready. She's close, we're close, but I don't think she trusts it yet," I say. "I want you to know that I'm here for good. I'll take care of her, and I'll make sure she's happy."

Larry sits back in his chair, letting it all sink in as he stares me down, assessing my sincerity.

"I believe that, Reed. You've loved her for a long time, I've seen it. I know what your intentions have been, even if sometimes, they are misguided. And that you've tried to let her soar on her own terms. None of us have been blind to that, except her. But you might have a struggle on your hands, you understand?"

Don't I fucking know it.

Leighton didn't grow up with a strong relationship to learn from. Larry is her only family. Because of that and her mother's abandonment, she doesn't trust romantic love. I'm sure Connor leaving so quickly didn't help that situation.

"I'm up to the challenge since she'll be the one waiting on the other side of it. Your daughter is worth that and so much more."

"Yes, she is," he says. "If she agrees, are you all right with a hyphenated name? She's expressed several times that she wants to keep Ward."

"I've heard her say it. You're the most important person in her life, and she wants to honor you. I want what makes her happy. I'd never ask her to do something that didn't do that. I'd take Ward as my own last name if she asked."

"She just may." He laughs, and I join in, because it's not a lie. But neither was my answer. I want Leighton—whatever that looks like. "And if she doesn't choose to be with you?"

Drew softly groans next to me. We've not discussed Leighton or my feelings toward her. Drew's tried to pry, but I've kept those cards close to my chest.

"If I'm not who makes her happy, I'll step back. But I won't leave. I'm never leaving again."

"Fair enough, Reed. I'll back whatever decision my daughter makes, but I'll also offer my thanks since you're treating her like family and caring for her like you do. It means the world to me," Larry says, emotion bleeding through.

"She is family, Larry," Drew confirms. "As are you. That won't ever change, regardless of what happens with this blockhead." He pats me on the shoulder.

"I love her, Larry. She's my light, my heart. I've been an idiot about it for too long," I tell him. "But I'd burn the world to keep her safe."

Larry clears his throat again, trying to rein in his emotions. He once told me he believes he only exists because he was Leighton's father. Every decision he's made since she was born has been with her benefit in mind.

"It gives me a great sense of peace to know she'll never be alone. You can't possibly know," he finally gets out.

"Never, Larry."

Drew reinforces that just as June and Leighton step out the backdoor with fresh beers. Leighton looks at him curiously, but he brushes it off saying he will head inside to see if my mom needs any help. June immediately heads to curl up in Drew's lap, and Leighton moves to take the seat her father vacated.

I reach out, taking her hand in mine, and tug her onto my lap. She's surprised, but willingly lets me place her where I want her. Where I can bury my face in her hair and smell along her neck.

"Are you smelling me again, you creeper?"

"It's not where I want my face buried, but it will do until we have some privacy."

"Oh my god, eww," June squeals.

"Baby girl, I've spent far too long listening to my best friend coo over you. You don't get to be offended that I'm vocal about how damn sexy your BFF is," I tell my sister and watch Leighton blush as she analyzes me. These displays are new for her and me, but also for our family. Maybe she thought that I'd keep the same distance I always do. "What?"

"It's just different," Leighton says, shyly. It makes me hard because she's only ever like this with me.

"Different bad or different good?"

"Different good," she answers, and June gives a happy little sigh next to us. There is little she'd like more in the world than for Leighton to be her sister by law and choice.

"You ready to give it a title?" I ask and I know the answer immediately by the panic that flashes over her. So, I say the words to put her back at ease. "Don't worry about it, Love. We'll take it as slow as you need."

She'll get there when she gets there, and I won't bitch because I know she's worth it. She isn't hesitant because she doesn't want me. If I know her as well as I think I do, then I know it's because she still fears abandonment by those she loves. She's not at fault for that and I can't expect her to have that sort of faith in me. Yet.

"Did you call Noah?" Leighton turns the conversation away from us.

"I did, this morning. I wished him a happy turkey day and said that Drew and I would like to attend the wedding," June answers. Drew presses a kiss to the side of her mouth. He's not very vocal about, well, anything, honestly. He keeps most things close to his chest. It's how he got away with cheating on my sister for as long as he did, how she didn't know about his sexual preferences, or the full extent of the trauma his father inflicted on him when he was young. It's why I didn't know those things either.

"I'm sure that pleased him," I tell her.

"I think he was holding back tears," she responds, small drops welling in her own eyes.

"It means a lot to him that you don't shut him out, Junie."

"He doesn't want you to shut him out either, Drew. I think he loves working out with you more than he likes working with me."

"Bullshit, you're his best friend. I'm just the guy he has to put up with to have you in his life."

"It's more than that and you know it," she says, pressing a kiss to his forehead.

"Whatever I am to him, I know he'll be thrilled to have you there. And if it's too much, we can sneak out quietly."

"I was invited. If I go, I will happily cause a scene if you need to make a break for it," Leighton says, and I stiffen.

"You were invited?" I ask.

"As a plus one, not directly," she answers as if it means nothing.

"Connor?" June asks, eyeing me warily. Leighton nods, affirming that he did ask her.

"When did he ask you?" I ask, becoming increasingly more uncomfortable.

"The other day when he called."

"Did you tell him you'd go?"

"No, I said I'd consider it. It's still ten weeks away."

And she doesn't know if she'll be committed by then. *Fucking hell.* I have more work ahead of me than I expected.

Mom pokes her head out the backdoor to tell us dinner is ready, essentially killing any more conversation about Connor. For now, anyway.

Dinner, as always, is delicious, and I'm careful not to let my annoyance invade the rest of the evening. It's my fucking fault anyhow. I own that.

After dessert, Larry and Mom go for a walk. Larry takes one every day without fail and Mom is happy to tag along and let us 'kids' clean up after the feast. Which we do, each taking a task and completing it quickly until June's home is as clean as it was before we all invaded it. Drew takes the trash out as we're finishing up.

"Reed? There aren't any more trash bags under here," June says, her head shoved under the kitchen sink. "Can you see if there are any in the storage closet? I'll grab beers and meet you back outside."

"Sure thing," I say, heading down the hall to the closet. This house is a monstrosity and still needs a load of improvements. But June's done well in the time she's had with it. She's made it not only livable, but homey. Most importantly, she's made it *her* home, one she can grow old in happily. With Drew at her side.

My sister has a shopping problem, though. Evident by how stuffed this storage closet is. I'm sure she's the sole reason there was a toilet paper shortage back during the pandemic. Because it's here. All of it.

One side of the room is lined floor-to-ceiling with shelves. The other side is a large bank of lower cabinetry with a pristine white stone counter atop it. It's bare, but the shelves are overstuffed.

With toilet paper.

What I don't see at first glance are garbage bags. Pushing items aside, I look in every corner of every shelf from the top down. I'm crouched on the floor looking over a bottom shelf when Leighton finds me.

"Are you searching for the clitoris?" she whispers. "Because if yes, you're way off."

"How do you know with all this bath tissue in the way?"

"Oh honey, I know." She laughs, deep and throaty.

"I like it when you call me that," I tell her, standing and crowding her space. I reach behind her to push the door shut only to back her up against it.

"Do you?"

"I do. How much time do you think we have before our parents are back from their walk?"

"Not long."

"Better make this quick then."

"Make what quick?" she teases.

"Your orgasm, Love. You're going to give me one right now."

"I'm going to give you one of my orgasms?" She asks as if I make little sense, all the while she's pulling her dress up her legs inch by inch.

"Yes, it's my Thanksgiving gift from you." I unbutton my jeans and her eyes follow my hand movement.

"What do I get?"

"What do you want?"

Her gaze snaps to my mouth, and damnit, I want to give her that. But only a couple of hours ago she was telling me she was considering being Connor's date.

"If you want me to kiss you, you know how to get that," I say. "I'll keep giving you my cock, my fingers, my tongue in your cunt. You want that kiss? You tell me you're mine."

Leighton's dress is up above her hips now. Luckily, she isn't wearing anything underneath, giving me full access to her bare pussy. Pushing my jeans down far enough to pull my dick out, I take the last step to her.

"This spot right here," I say, pressing a finger between her breasts. "It's my favorite part of you to smell. I'd pick it over your hair or your pussy any day of the week."

"Have you always had such a dirty mouth?"

"Only with you." I drag my finger down her body until I can grab one of her thighs and hitch it up over my hip. It grants me the position I need, the entrance I want. "Hands around my neck, Love. Hang on, this is going to be fast. And hard."

I shove inside her on my last word and revel in the gasp she releases on a heavy exhale. It's the most exquisite sound. Barely letting her finish that breath, I pull out and thrust back in again. And again, and again, and again because I can't get enough. And if I have my way, she'll never go a day wanting to come and not being able to.

Every demon that follows her, I'll slay. Any dark spot in her life, I'll battle through to shine a light. When she's sad, I'll hold her hand until she's on the other side. I don't even need all that in return. All I want is for her to be as confident as I am in the idea that we're fucking fated to be together.

It's very little to ask.

"Reed." Her voice shakes on my name.

"Yes, Love?"

"I'm so close." Her hands come up to my cheeks as I slam her back into the door on one hard thrust.

I know she is. Closer to more than creaming over my dick, but that's all I need to be concerned with just now.

"Eyes open, Leighton," I say, resting my nose against hers. "See me. Here with you, right now. Falling apart together."

"Oh, fuck."

I grind my hips, giving her clit the friction it needs. Yeah, I know exactly where the fuck the clitoris is and what to do with hers.

"Oh fuck, Reed! Fuck," she shouts through her climax, taking me along with her. Her light eyes shimmer under her fluttering eyelids, but she's good at not looking away.

"My favorite thing in the world is your cunt quivering around my cock while you stare up at me. I'm not giving this up Leighton, I'll fight for it."

My dick slides out of her, and I replace it with my fingers, massaging our fluids into the sensitive skin of her labia and her thighs.

"What are you up to now?"

"Still savoring, just differently. It's probably good for your skin or something. Just roll with it."

Her head falls to my shoulder as she laughs. "You're lucky I love weird shit, Turner."

I almost come again at the word *love*. I'm all too eager to hear her say it for real.

"Stay put," I tell her, then turn to grab one of the many rolls of toilet paper. After cleaning us both up, I pull her dress back down and lead her out back, stopping in the bathroom to flush the evidence of our closet copulation.

We find June and Drew in the same position as earlier, her curled up in his burly arms. Thankfully, Mom and Larry aren't back yet. Larry loves me, but that doesn't mean he wants to know how I defile his daughter every chance I get.

"Oh fuck, Reed," June mimics as we walk out. I grin, because fuck it, I don't care if she heard me shag her friend.

"Shut it, June. Or I'm taking all the toys I've bought you back." Leighton laughs at her.

"Why? Doesn't sound like you'll need them with my brother living next door."

Damn fucking straight.

15

LEIGHTON

My dad flew home last night, and like every time we part ways, a familiar unease settles in my heart. There's always that wonder if it will be the last time I see him. He's willing to visit me more now that I have a home and he has a room of his own, but it's not the same as being close enough to see him regularly. Dad refuses to move though; he loves Southern California and the friends he's made in his retirement community. I don't want him to sacrifice that for me, and he doesn't want me to sacrifice my love for New Orleans for him.

So, sadness it is. It won't last long. I'll miss him for a few days before I'm back to normal. I've learned to embrace my melancholy because I know it's fleeting.

What helped most was finding Reed asleep on my couch again when I arrived home. It's been easy to get used to him being around. And if I'm honest, I was close to telling him what he wanted to hear last night. Only, I'm still not sure it's real. The sex is real and fucking amazing. Fantastic sex isn't what you build a loving, trusting relationship on though. Not that I know what you build it on since there aren't many great examples in my life. But I know it takes more than animal attraction and explosive orgasms.

Reed and I have those things. We don't have trust. I don't know that he'd never leave me, and he doesn't trust I have the same feelings for him he professes to have for me. So, what's my next step? If I jump in feet first, tell him I'm his, will the faith I need come? I don't know, and I'm terrified about that uncertainty.

As a child, I only loved two people and one of them left me. As an adult, I've been cautious about who I give that gift to because my odds of it being returned are shitty.

I'm a wuss.

Or very good at preserving the protections I placed around my heart at an early age. It's difficult to watch a parent walk out on you. It's even harder to watch your remaining parent, heartbroken and confused, suffer from that decision. I'll go all in with a man when I know without a doubt they won't make me promises they don't plan to keep.

I'd love that to be Reed, my heart wants it to be him. It's my head that's still very unsure, even as I stumble downstairs to the smell of bacon guiding my way. Reed is still here, cooking me breakfast with food he must have gone next door to his place to get, since I sure as hell didn't have this in my fridge.

Alongside the bacon is French toast sprinkled with powdered sugar and a large side of bright strawberries. Gooey cinnamon rolls may be my favorite breakfast food, but this runs close second. I've always had a sweet tooth first thing in the morning.

"Good morning," Reed says, voice still raspy from sleep. It's sexy and I want to forgo food and drag him back to bed. But we have work today and I'm not sure Reed is capable of quickies when we're in a house alone.

"Hi. You didn't have to do this," I tell him even as I grab the plate he pushes my way.

"If I hadn't, you'd have had nothing but an extra-large coffee for breakfast," he says, pressing a kiss to the side of my head as he passes me to sit at the table. I follow and sit across from him.

"Well, I might have grabbed a granola bar or something, too," I say in my defense. It's not true.

"You might have thought about it, but you wouldn't have done it. Even if you tried, you'd fail, because there aren't any in your kitchen, Love."

"Not the point, Turner. How'd you learn how to cook?"

"My mom. She taught me and June. I could follow along, I guess. You know how it turned out with June."

"Do I ever." I love her, but she is the absolute worst cook. "Did you know she tried to make ramen the first week of college? She fell asleep while the water was boiling and woke up to the smell of the bottom of the pan burning to the hot plate. I threw away all the cooking utensils after that."

"She's never told me that story."

"You'd never let her live it down."

"True," he admits.

"Don't tell her I told you. She'll think my loyalties have shifted."

Reed eyes me curiously but says nothing. Once again, like so many times before, I'm suspicious about what he's thinking.

"It will be our secret," he finally says. We finish eating and he stands to take both our plates back to the kitchen. "He'll be back in a few weeks, and that time will fly by."

"I know." I sigh and try to shake off whatever gives away my melancholy so easily. "Thank you for reminding me."

"Of course. Go get ready, we can ride together to the office, if you want."

"We can ride together but only if you want to come with me to karaoke night after work."

"Oh god," he groans. "All right, I'll take you."

A huge smile takes over my face as I rush upstairs to shower and dress.

"Okay, people. Pitch," Fran says when all the reporters have shuffled into the conference room. There aren't many of us. Two of us in senior positions, Veronica and myself. Veronica moved here from Memphis for this position. She's of similar age to me but with a wildly different background, having grown up in a large family here in the South. I like her immensely already, though. She's spunky and has a takes-no-shit vibe about her. Honestly, she reminds me of a younger version of Fran.

With us are four junior journalists. Adam, Jenna, Roland, and Sebastian. All four are in their early twenties, barely out of college but hungry for experience and to start a name for themselves. We spent time together every day last week, before the holiday weekend. Fran wanted us to get to know each other, and I've determined I like them all quite a lot, further solidifying that taking this job was the right decision.

"What about an event calendar in every issue for upcoming festivals? We could list many, but feature one or two of them every issue," Roland suggests.

"Work up a list of some of the more intriguing ones throughout the year and we'll revisit next Monday. I like the idea, but I want the list to be worthy."

"Absolutely," Roland says with a nod.

"There's a teacher in Baton Rouge, where my cousin attends high school. The students love him, he uses hip-hop, social media, and pop culture in the classroom. Also, he set up his own charity to make sure every student at the school has a backpack and necessary supplies each year. I'd like to go interview him." This comes from Jenna.

"That sounds promising. Go," Fran tells her.

We circle around a dozen more ideas. Some Fran shoots down outright, some she gives immediate approval, others she wants more information on.

"One thing I'd like to dig into is a new art installation being proposed in Nashville," I say.

"What type of installation?"

"Something similar to the street art in Bushwick, New York. An artist coalition introduced the idea to the city council and the mayor approved allocation of four city blocks in a part of town that has seen better times."

"Yes," Fran exclaims with a clap of her hands. "Perfect. Go dig up more details."

Though I've lived in New Orleans for several years now and Nashville isn't that far of a drive, I've never been there. If it's anything like Bushwick, it's bound to be amazing, and I'd love to follow the progression.

After making a few more plans, we break for lunch and spend the second half of the day researching and coordinating travel for those of us with out-of-town leads. By the time 2 rolls around, I'm dragging. I rarely get tired during the day, but it was a long week last week, added to by the holiday. And Reed. He wears me out in the most exquisite ways, which makes up for the lack of sleep. But coffee is needed if I'm going to make it through the next few hours of work and a night with my karaoke crew.

Reed and I have passed by each other several times today, exchanging niceties along with heated looks. At this rate, the whole damn staff will know how much his mere presence makes me blush.

"Coffee?"

"Yeah, I'm a tad low on energy it seems. Why do you think that is?" I ask, turning to Reed as he walks further into the employee lounge.

"It's not my fault if you get a good fuck when you come to bed looking truly fuckable."

"I was in pajamas printed with Santa hat wearing flamingos," I counter.

"Your clothes, or lack thereof, aren't what make you sexy, Leighton. They're just window dressing."

His words are so casually sure. As if it's a given I am desirable by being alive. Good and bad, Reed treats me differently than any man I've been with before. He's been sweet the past couple of weeks though. Only sweet, not showing any of that bitterness he's let shine since June's attack.

I spent so long believing he hated me, blamed me, or simply didn't like me around. Because it's hard for me to trust, it's supremely difficult to believe this version of Reed will stick. I'd sure like it if he would.

"When did you get to be so sweet?"

"I've always been, I just hid it well," he says. "Will you go on a date with me this weekend?"

"Um, yeah. But are you only asking me because you already know I'm a sure thing?"

"Of course." He laughs. "It's something I've been thinking about. We've just been busy. Wherever you want to go, even if it involves karaoke."

"Ooh, you must really like me, Reed Turner."

"Something like that, Leighton Ward," Reed whispers into my hair before he presses a kiss to my crown. "Have a good rest of your afternoon."

I have a great afternoon; thanks to caffeine, it flies by and before I know it, Reed is packing me up into his car to escort me to karaoke night. It's something I do regularly when I can round up the right friends. June is still here in New Orleans filming with Noah this week, though Drew has flown back to Seattle for his upcoming game.

That means June's cameramen and producer are here, too. All of whom love to come out with June and me. Sally, Phil, and young Mark are always a lot of fun. As has become a habit, we start the night at a classier joint down the street. It started as Noah's requirement. He would hang out with us, drinking out of plastic cups, only after we fed him a 'meal appropriate to his station'. While we all tease him endlessly over it, none of us complain about having good food. Our karaoke bar is top notch for just that... karaoke. Nothing else.

Noah isn't at the table when Reed and I work our way through the restaurant. The others are, and June stands to give her brother and me hugs.

"Hello, big brother," she greets Reed, amusement playing in her eyes. We text each other throughout the day, every day. So she already knew he was tagging along tonight, but she's still surprised that he agreed so easily.

"Hello, little sister." He hugs her before he pulls the chair out next to hers for me to sit in.

"Thank you," I say to him, and he smiles that sexy smile he only gives to me. He's flirted with women in front of me before, many times. But I've never seen him look at anyone the way he does me. It makes my pulse race.

The server comes by for orders and when he comes back with our first round of drinks, I turn to June.

"No Noah tonight?"

"He'll join us later, after he has dinner with the family. He makes a point to eat with Olivia when he's in town," Sally answers. Noah has a special relationship with Olivia, Lorelai's young sister, and he dotes on the child according to everything I've heard. It's sweet, really. While

Noah is kind, sweet isn't a descriptor I'd use for him often. Some men are fathers though, and Noah is one of them. My father is one, too.

I didn't have the opportunity to know Reed and June's father for long before he died, but he was a great dad. I'd know that by the way his children love and miss him like they do. If children are in my future, I want that for them.

Conversation flows easily. Reed and Mark talk football, while Sally and June speak quietly about her decision to go to Noah and Lorelai's wedding. Sally has become friends with Noah's fiancée. Turns out she likes Lorelai very much. Phil and I converse about film. He's a movie buff, mysteries to be specific, which I love too.

The server returns with our meals, placing my soup and salad in front of me, then moving around the table.

"I'm heading to Nashville at the end of the week," I tell June. "That art installation is almost off the ground and Fran gave me the go ahead."

"Oh, that's going to be a fun story to watch over the next couple of years. And you'll love Nashville, make sure you plan some time to roam the city."

"Will do. I'll keep an eye out for any old, haunted houses," I say to her, but movement on my other side catches my eye. Reed is slicing pieces of his steak and placing them on my side salad. "What are you doing?"

"Feeding you."

"I have my own food."

"You ordered food that wouldn't satisfy a rabbit. When you lot sing karaoke, you drink. Therefore, real food is necessary," he states as he also places a dinner roll on my plate.

"You can be so overbearing, Turner," I say with a heavy sigh.

"Overbearing is not always a bad thing," June singsongs next to me.

"How would you know? I wouldn't call Drew overbearing."

"He is at the right times," she says with a cheeky grin.

"Shut up, dear sister," Reed says, leaning forward to see her around me. June sticks her tongue out at him. "I'm just looking out for you, babe. Eat now. Please," he adds the last word like it pains him to say it, and I want to laugh but try, unsuccessfully, to tamp that down. He's ridiculous, and I don't hate it.

He's also not wrong, which is irritating but also endearing if you like that alpha male bravado. I don't always, but sometimes it is nice to have somebody else decide for you when you know their intentions are good.

"I don't plan to drink much tonight, it's a school night after all."

"Still," he says, his hand reaching under the table to rub along my thigh. "I'd feel better if you had more than broth and weeds."

"I need to watch my weight," I say.

"Fuck that. You don't need to be camera ready all the time anymore and you'd be just as brilliant and beautiful at any weight."

Reed renders me speechless for a moment with the conviction of his words. It's habit, these urges to 'look the part' all the time. I'll break it eventually, but I'll never tire of hearing him tell me nice things.

"I'm only doing it because that steak looks delicious."

"Okay," he says with a sly smile that tells me he doesn't care about the reason, as long as I comply.

By the time we walk into the karaoke bar, I'm giddy. This is one of my favorite things. I love to sing, to entertain, to get a little attention on my own terms. Especially with this group of people. Sally turns karaoke into a competition and we're always trying to one up each other. All in good fun.

First things first, though, I need to have a moment with my best friend. Grabbing June's hand in mine, I drag her along with me into the restroom.

"I need to tell you something."

"What's up?" she asks.

"I'm, like, seventy-five percent certain I'm falling in love with your stupid brother."

June bursts into tears immediately. I nearly panic, but she wears a huge smile under her watery eyes, so I know it's a happy cry.

"Oh my god," she wails. "I've waited so long for this." She throws her arms around my shoulders and pulls me close.

"You're okay with it?"

"I'm thrilled with it. But I've known for years. You're both shit at hiding it."

"I haven't been in love with him for years," I say, pulling back away so I can see her face.

She snickers, rolling her eyes.

"I haven't," I protest. "I've had a crush at times when he hasn't been a total ass to me. But that's all."

"Okay, Love," she placates. "I don't care about the past, just the future. Does he know?"

"I haven't told him."

"You should."

16
REED

Leighton's never more gorgeous than when she sings. She probably could have made a career of it, but one time I heard her say it would have taken all the fun out of it if singing was a job. Selfishly, I like I don't have to share this part of her with the whole world. But if it was what she wanted, I'd support it. Because, damn, her voice is amazing and the smile she wears while singing some poppy love song is infectious.

I can't take my eyes off her, even as I'm aware that most of the other men here tonight can't either. They don't matter, because her eyes are mostly on me tonight, too. They often are, only tonight she isn't trying to hide it and neither am I.

"You moved here for her," June says next to me. I side-eye her briefly, nodding as I divert my attention back to Leighton. "Because Connor left?"

"Because it was time. Past time, really. I waited longer than I should have."

"To tell her you love her?"

"To let her see it's safe to love me."

I sense June blinking up at me, maybe not understanding me, or maybe it never dawned on her how much I understand about Leighton.

"So, you're done being a brat to her?" she finally asks.

"Not likely," I say with a half-smile. "She likes it when I'm a brat as much as I love it when she is. I am done being absent in her life, though."

"I'm glad," she says, stopping whatever else she may have said when Noah Anders walks up.

"Hey, Reed. It's good to see you finally decided to take my advice." Noah is an impressive figure in the room. He intends to be, but even if it wasn't intentional, I believe he would be. He's nearly as massive as Drew is. Unlike my best friend, who is casual to a fault, Noah dresses nearly exclusively in impeccable, somewhat flashy, suits.

Tonight is no exception. His tailored, Kelly Green ensemble would stand out in a five-star establishment. This karaoke bar is not that, causing most patrons to glance his way at least twice.

Women want Noah Anders, men want to be Noah Anders. We all know it.

"What advice?" June asks him.

"Do you not trust my sage wisdom, sweet June?"

"I'm not sure, honestly," June answers, the words false. If my sister were to list all the people she trusted, it would be short, but Noah would be near the top.

"I only suggested he waste no more time in expressing his intentions to that whirlwind you call a friend," Noah says after a short bark of laughter, waving a finger toward Leighton on the stage.

"His suggestion came shortly before opportunity arose and the stars aligned."

"Stars aligned?" June's voice goes dreamy, her romantic heart always clinging to anything my artistic side lets out.

"Yes, baby girl," I say, wrapping an arm around her shoulder and pulling her in for a hug. "Leighton and I were written in the stars a millennia ago. Every life, finding each other time and time again."

"She can't be my soulmate and yours." June's nose crinkles but her eyes betray her.

"Sure, she can, she's extraordinary that way. I think you're my family in every one of my lives, June, which means when Leighton finds one of us in a lifetime, she finds us both."

"Never pictured you as such a romantic, Reed," Noah says.

"Hard not to be with her so close all the time now," I say as Leighton steps down from the stage, only to be replaced by Sally, Phil, and Mark. She bounces over to us with giddiness she always has after performing.

"Hello, Mr. Anders," she says in a tone like the villain from the *Matrix* movies.

"Good evening, American psycho," he retorts to her laughter.

"You're one to throw that compliment around."

"Touché," Noah agrees.

"Are you finally going to sing with us tonight?"

"Fuck no," he says, and I send him a smile in shared camaraderie. Neither of us ever partake on nights like this, instead we show up for the fun, the show, and to support the women in our lives.

"Fine," June and Leighton chime simultaneously. Then she turns to me, those blue eyes pinning me.

"I have an idea," Leighton tells me after watching the trio on stage finish their latest song. She steps up so close in front of me that I can count the beating pulse in her neck. The throbbing vein right there, begging for me to lick and nip at it.

"What's that, Love?"

I run my thumb under her jaw, lifting her face to mine, bringing her even closer. Nearly lip to lip, but not.

"I'm leaving for Nashville Thursday morning, staying until Sunday."

"What for?"

"They're putting in a new street art installation, and I want to write a story on it."

"Sounds amazing. What's your idea?"

"That you should go with me." The hue of her cheeks deepens a few shades.

"Like on a date that lasts three nights?"

"You know art," she says with a shrug. "It makes sense."

"*We* make sense," I tell her.

Her lashes flutter and her lips part as if she's about to say something, but her name is called from the stage. It's her turn. Again. Instead of words, I get a big grin from her before she scampers back up to the stage.

Conversation around me rises in volume as Sally and the guys find us. It all fades to silence again when Leighton lets the first note of Lana

Del Rey's "Born to Die" out. It's a sultry song that lends well to her voice. She never veers from the stare I share with her.

I know what's coming. It's instinct, I'm as certain of it as I am my next inhalation and exhalation of air.

Love is ready.

She doesn't have to sing about telling me that you're mine or crossing the finishing line for me to clue in. All I needed was the expression she wears.

Hunger. For me. The same as I always wear for her. The room steeps in desire and anticipation when the song ends. I'm almost afraid for her to touch me. We may ignite, the fire decimating us to ash. What a shame that would be! I haven't had nearly enough time inside Leighton to die now.

Weaving through the crowd to get back, I track her like the stalker she teases me about being. In her case, she's right. I'd follow her anywhere to keep her safe. Call that whatever you'd like. She stops a few feet from me, freezes in place for me to peruse her. The slight haze curtaining her eyes, the twitch of her lip as she struggles not to bite it, the nervous tap of one finger against her thigh.

The ball is in her court and she's too terrified to shoot it.

"You have to say it, Leighton."

"Do I though?" she hedges.

"Yeah, baby, you do," I say with humor, cupping her cheeks to hold her face steady on mine. "Be precise and sure."

"I want to be yours, Reed."

"Do you?" I reach a thumb over her bottom lip, pretending I can taste it with only my touch.

"I do."

"You either are mine or you aren't, Love. What's it going to be?"

Leighton nods.

"The words, Love. Say the words. Are you mine?"

"I am yours, Reed Turner."

Fuck yes, she is.

"You've always been. In my heart, you've always been."

Her eyes are glassy as she moves her hands to my chest, rising on her toes to get closer.

"Kiss me now. I've waited long enough."

"And you'll have to wait a little longer."

"Not fair," she pouts.

"I'm not kissing you for the first time in a shitty bar with an audience. Climb on, we'll get out of here."

"That's dumb," she says even as her arms slide up around my neck and I lift her to wrap her legs around my hips.

"I'm going to pay a lot of attention to that mouth. I don't want to get arrested for doing it publicly."

"Okay," she says into my neck. It shoots chills down my spine. "But hurry."

"When I'm done kissing you, I want to see how big my cock looks in your mouth."

Leighton's mouth goes slack as I tug her along the walkway to her front door.

"Oh. Okay," she stumbles over the words.

I punch the code into the electronic lock, shuffle her inside, and kick the door shut behind me. We're both anxious, fingers flying to undress each other. But each time she moves her mouth to mine, I pull back. Her frustration grows with her anticipation. I want her to shake with the need for it. Naked.

"Come closer, rub all that skin on me."

"Kiss me."

"Is it time?"

"Mmhmm."

I pull the hair at the nape of her neck so her mouth opens again. Every urge I have is to shove my tongue in far and deep. Taste every part of her, feel her lips on mine.

Not yet.

For so long, this has been my end goal, the prize at the end of the marathon. Taking it for granted, or rushing it, isn't something I'm willing to do.

"Stick your tongue out. As far as you can." She does, letting it loll out over her bottom lip. Starting at the tip, I lick the length of hers with my own before I suck it between my lips. I almost let our lips touch but stop short. Simultaneously, I tickle my fingers at her cunt, until I can feel the uncontrolled shiver wracking her body.

"Reed," she whines.

"Remember this," I softly call over her lips before I touch them with mine. A gentle press, then another, then more. So much more as we devour one another. The slide of her tongue against mine is all it takes for me to grow hard. "I need every part of me inside every part of you."

Leighton whimpers against me, her whole body going slack in my arms. I've only seen her cry twice. When my sister was in the hospital, so close to death. And when my father died unexpectedly in an auto accident a handful of years ago. It's not lost on me that both those times, she was mourning for my family. Or that I've never seen her cry for herself.

Until now.

Tears trail from the corner of her eyes, silent paths of emotion, but not sadness. I recognize when she's sad, even though she fights hard to hide it. This isn't that.

"Don't be overwhelmed, Love. It's just me."

"No." She shakes her head. "It's us."

"Kiss me again, my Love." I lift her easily into my arms. I'd keep her there forever if that made any sense. She seals her lips to mine as I carry her over and deposit her bare ass on the edge of her dining table.

"Fuck me right now, Reed."

"Right now?" I tease.

"Right now. Shove that fat cock inside my tight cunt."

"Now, who's got a dirty mouth?"

"You could make it dirtier. You said you wanted to."

"I do, baby," I tell her. "But kissing you is enough to nearly make me blow like a virgin, and I really want to do that in your pussy right now."

She shivers but pulls one leg up to allow me better access for entry. I don't hesitate any longer. Grabbing my dick with one hand and cupping her chin with the other, I position myself and move in. It's not our first time together, but it feels almost as if it is. The intimacy of kissing her while I slide my dick in and out of her wet cunt makes a world of difference. This isn't just sex, it's something more important, it's special. Because she's more, or because we are.

"I'll never get enough of the way your body tightens around me when I pull out. It wants to keep me inside as much as I want to stay there."

"I'll never tell you to leave it," she says, gasping between the words.

"Might make work a bit awkward." She laughs until I pinch her nipple and it turns into a moan. "I want to come on this spot. Watch it drip down the side of your tit before I lick it up and feed it to you with my own tongue."

"Oh my fucking god," she cries. "That's so hot, but guys never taste their own cum."

"Never?" I ask before I swallow the answer she's about to deliver. It's hard not to kiss her now that I've started. While her mouth is occupied, I pull her other leg up, spreading her knees high and wide. The position gives me more room to grind my thighs against her sweet ass as I thrust deeper. I know she likes it because her kiss misses the rhythm we'd established. Seeing the obvious ways she's affected only makes my blood pump faster, turns me on more, and I know I won't last much longer.

It's almost embarrassing how easily she undoes me.

"I'm gonna come, but I'll make it up to you," I say against her lips, and they curve into a wide grin. She's proud of herself for making me lose my shit. And lose it I do, because she grabs onto my ass for dear life while also arching her perfect tits up into my chest as she writhes against me. I come hard, maybe harder than I ever have. "Lie back, Love. I'll show you that a real man isn't afraid of his own cum."

"Really?" She blinks up at me.

"Lie back."

She doesn't lie flat, but lowers from bracing herself with her hands to her elbows. She wants to see and I don't mind.

"I'm already leaking out of you," I say, scooping up the amount dripping down, transferring it to her lower belly where I spread it around while I move to my knees.

"Cheater."

"Hardly. I came a lot." The chill of my words against her cunt sends goosebumps along her legs. Starting at her clit, I lick in small circles around it, then dip into her hole. Her thighs tense and squeeze around my head and it spurs me on. Shoving my tongue in farther a few times, I then move back to the sensitive spot above.

"Reed," she whines again, thrusting her hips up so she can grind against my chin. "How do you taste?"

"You've swallowed me before, you know. So, tell me. How do I taste?" I ask before returning to the task of driving her crazy with my mouth and my now added fingers.

"Like the most delicious thing I've ever eaten. You're like a warm dessert after a long day. One you want to make last, savoring every bite. You taste like you, and it's fucking delicious."

Like that, my dick tents. I'll get to feed it to her. But first, I need to taste her mixed with me. When I double my efforts, she explodes within seconds. Thighs once again squeezing as she threads her fingers into my hair to move me how she wants me. She shouldn't worry; I'm not leaving my post until she's lax and spent.

As soon as she is, I trail kisses and licks over her mound, breathing in deep before I move to her stomach. There, I drag my tongue over where I spread my seed just moments ago. Leighton squirms and giggles when I nibble up to her nipple and along the line of her neck.

"Want to know what we taste like mixed together?"

"Yes, please."

I kiss her with everything I am. Which is her…

She's my world. *My everything*.

17

LEIGHTON

Reed picks me up off the table and sets me on my feet. I snuggle close to the front of his body, not ready to lose the warmth of his skin. So much bare skin over sharp-cut muscles. His body is beautiful, and I want to cry again at how right it feels to be with him like this. I guess I'm emotional because I never believed this would happen, no matter how long I pined for it. It's not like me to be so weepy, but he's not like any man I've been with before.

"Bed?" he asks.

"I'm not tired enough for sleep, yet."

"I'll wear you out by letting you eat my cock."

I laugh at his crude words, all the while nodding my head. Hell yes, I'll suck him off. I wasn't lying about the taste of him. It's something I've craved since that first time. Reed lifts me over his shoulder like a caveman hauling his hard-won trophy off to his cave. My hands reach down instinctually to feel the flex of his ass cheeks as he takes the stairs up to my room.

Except I can't appreciate it properly as my stomach turns. It's not a strong urge to vomit, but the nausea makes itself known. I groan with displeasure as we reach the top of the staircase.

"What's wrong?" Reed asks, cuing in immediately.

"I'm sure it's nothing," I tell him when he sets me on my feet inside my bedroom door.

"What's nothing?" His hands find my cheeks and he tips my face to his. "You're clammy, so tell me, what's wrong?"

"Just a little woozy."

"You ate a decent proportion and only had one drink at the bar. Are you coming down with something?" Reed asks, feeling my forehead for a temperature spike. While I think it's silly, it's also charming how worried he is about me. Which is also silly, because he's worried about a woman he cares about. When did I get so sentimental about little things?

"Maybe." I shrug. "I was pretty tired all day today."

"Climb in bed. I'll go make you some tea and we can watch an episode of *Killing Eve* while you drink it."

"You're bossy," I say with a feigned pout.

"When your health is involved, yes."

"Just then?"

His only answer is a grin, and the concern in his eyes is enough to let me know that I'm not getting a dick dessert tonight.

If I was coming down with a cold, Reed's tea must have cured it because the past few days, I've felt fine. More than. I've felt alive. Reed and I spent our time in Nashville working and playing with equal enthusiasm. I knew inviting him along was a great idea. He lit up while talking to the artists that will be first to paint murals. One is a young man, barely eighteen years old. His name is Raphael and we spoke to him at length about his background and what art means to him. He's as bright as he is talented. They traded numbers and plan on keeping in touch, as Raphael will be studying graphic design at a local community college. Like how Reed started after high school graduation.

Fran was more than accepting of Reed tagging along with me to research the story. She encouraged it. Secretly, I think it's only because she's rooting for me and Reed as a couple. Whatever the reason, I'm happy for it.

When not speaking to artists and organizers, we saw the sites, ate the food, and even stopped into a honkey-tonk or two.

Now, I'm waking up to our last morning here securely ensconced in his arms. My favorite place. Only, I'm nauseous again. It hits like a brick, making me scramble out of the bed, tripping on the sheet wrapped around my legs. I barely make it to the toilet before I'm vomiting up hardly anything more substantial than stomach bile.

"Love?" Reed calls after me. I can't answer as I heave but answering is unnecessary. He hears me and before I can even ask, a cool washcloth is being patted on my cheek. "I thought you'd been feeling better."

"I guess not," I say between retching. It eventually stops and other than the feeling of an empty stomach, my body goes back to normal.

"Come on," Reed says, helping me up. "We'll shower, find you some toast, then get on the road back home."

"Ugh, it's such a long drive."

"I know, but I'll feel better when I get you there."

"I'm sure it's just a lingering bug."

"Maybe," he says, thoughtfully and unconvinced.

Maybe.

CONNOR

Since you haven't responded to my last several texts, I assume you don't want me to stay with you. I booked a room at Henry Howard. I'd still like to see you.

I miss you.

It's not that I've been ignoring Connor's messages. Not exactly, anyway. I've been busy and not feeling my best. He hasn't been a priority and I haven't let myself feel badly about that because I wasn't a priority to him either.

ME

You can't stay here. I'm seeing someone.

We can meet for coffee. Platonically.

CONNOR

Who are you seeing?

CONNOR

Disregard that. It's not my business. I'll hold you
to that coffee.

For the third day in a row, I have woken up with an uncontrollable
urge to vomit. Since Reed spends more time on my side of our house
than his, he's aware of this. And despite it being four o'clock in the
morning, he's determined we discover what's wrong with me. *Right now.*

It's not a lingering bug. No matter how much I hope and pretend it is.

"It's not this serious," I argue as he climbs into the driver's seat of
his car.

"Leighton, you barely keep any food down, you're exhausted, and
most concerning… you have vertigo. I'm taking you to the emergency
room."

"One time. I had vertigo once. All of which should be addressed by
my primary care, not by emergency services."

"That one time was today and I'm not letting it happen again. What if
you'd been driving?"

"Good grief, Reed."

"I am not fucking around with your health, Ward."

"We could stop at CVS and pick up a pregnancy test."

He's silent now. So am I as I watch the path his car takes shift in a
different direction. Nothing is said when he parks at the CVS, or when
he walks around the car to my side and holds his hand out for me. Still
no words while he leads me to the proper aisle and picks seven
pregnancy tests.

"Reed?" I ask for his attention once we're back on our way home.

"It's going to be okay. Everything is going to be okay." His words
sound with a certainty I don't share.

"Okay."

An hour, seven tests, and one severely empty bladder later, it's clear.

"Shit," I say absently as I look at each one again and again. *Positive. All of them.* Without a doubt, one of my eggs has been fertilized by a super sperm that somehow got through my bullshit IUD defenses. "How?"

"No contraceptive is one hundred percent effective."

"Obviously," I say through tears forming in the back of my throat.

"Hey, Love. I told you it was going to be okay."

How? Questions race through my brain, like how? And why now? I landed a fun job already more fulfilling than the ones I've had before. And then, you know, how? Damn it.

The biggest question is what happens if it turns out to be Connor's baby?

"Call your doctor and make an appointment."

"It's not even six a.m."

"I meant when they open. Get in as soon as you can," he says.

"Yes, sir," I say, trying hard to keep the apprehension out of my voice.

"I like those words, but not the worry behind them," he says. "Do you want to call June?"

"Fuck, yes." I sigh. "So much."

"Call. She'll come right over. I'll make the coffee."

June comes right over, hearing the urgency in my voice. She didn't even bother getting dressed, only wrapped herself up in a blanket and bounded from her front door to mine.

"What's wrong?" she demands upon entering.

"Come with me." I lead her up to my bathroom where the seven pieces of evidence still lay. Silent proof that my fun, easy life is about to have its ass handed to it. I wave my hand over them like I'm Vanna White, and step back for her to investigate.

"What is this… Oh, fuck," she says, picking them up one at a time. "Oh, fuck. How?"

Exactly.

"I have the distinct pleasure of being one of the rare few whose IUDs fails epically, it seems."

"Not that rare, actually."

"Do not 'actually' me right now, June McKenna," I whisper-shout.

"Okay, yeah, sorry. That's not helpful." She drops the seventh stick back on the counter and turns. "What do you want to do?"

"I don't know," I say. No words I've ever spoken have been truer. "I didn't anticipate this, of course. It's not part of my plan."

"You've never had a plan, Love. Other than for your career, which is going exactly per plan."

"Is it though?"

"Yes," she reassures. "It is."

"Not if I have a baby."

"Why? You can do anything with a child that you can do without."

"Fuck, that was a really icky thing for me to say. Wasn't it?" Women can do anything as a mother. I know this, I'm a proponent of mothers having successful careers. "I'm a mess, June. How am I supposed to make decisions right now?"

June laughs lightly and, honestly, it's the most calming thing she could do for me. I may feel like my life is falling apart, but she's looking at it from a different perspective. And I trust her implicitly.

"Of course, you're a mess, Love. It's a surprise and it's a decision you didn't expect to have to make. But whatever that decision is, we'll get through it. As a family."

A knock sounds at the door. June opens it to Reed holding two mugs. He hands us each one.

"I googled it—pregnant people can have caffeine, but it should be limited," he says.

"I hadn't even thought of that," I say absently. "If I keep it, what if I don't think of everything? What if I hurt the kid because I suck at thinking of all the things?"

"Hey," he says. "Stop. You'd be a fantastic mother, if that's what you choose to be. And June is right; we'll get through it as a family. We'll always be there to help you out."

June wraps her arm around me, pulling me to her side and resting her head on my shoulder. A comfort for us both.

"Thanks, big brother."

"You got it," he says, pressing kisses to both our foreheads before leaving us be. It's sweet, but brotherly to us both. I don't want brotherly

Reed right now. Or ever again. It adds another layer of confusion I try not to pay attention to, because *holy fuck I'm PREGNANT.*

"I don't know what to do, June."

"You'll work through it and figure it out. I'll be there to hold your hand no matter what. Either to take care of you, or to take care of you and my future niece or nephew."

"Oh."

"I didn't say that to scare you, Love. Or to pressure you. I support any decision you make wholeheartedly."

"No, I know. I just…" I stammer. "What if it isn't Reed's?"

"Do you think it isn't?"

"I have no way to know right now, but it could be. I don't have regular periods with IUD, so I have no way to be sure. There was a gap between Connor leaving and Reed and I starting up whatever this is, but I don't know how far along I am."

"Whatever this is?"

"We haven't labeled it is all I mean. I told him that night I want to be his, but we didn't really discuss it."

"Because he hauled you off like a Neanderthal instead." She rolls her eyes, but I see the wistfulness there. She wants Reed and I to be together.

"And then this happened."

"And then this happened," she parrots. "Get in to see a doctor, get an ultrasound. Let's get the facts and work from there. It's what we do."

"Yeah, okay, I can do this."

"Yes, you can, Leighton."

18

LEIGHTON

Eight days. Eight of the longest days of my life I've waited for this appointment. I almost had to beg my doctor to agree to the dating scan. She only caved because I can go months with no period and because I'm showing a handful of pregnancy symptoms. Symptoms… like it's an illness. Which, I suppose for some, it is.

I've had eight days to think about what I want. The news has been kept to Reed and June, only. Well, I'm sure she told Drew, and that's fine. I'd never ask her to keep a secret from her husband. But nobody else knows, not even my dad. We talk every few days, and it's been so hard not to tell him. Especially because he knows me so well and can sense something is wrong. He's not pushing for information yet, only because he'll be here before too long as he's spending Christmas with me. There will be nowhere for me to hide from him then.

Dad will support whatever decision I make, of that I'm certain. He won't approve that I didn't inform him of the pregnancy when I knew. But I'm not ready. I want to have decided before I tell him. Gathering all the information before publishing the story is what I do. This situation isn't any different.

I've made up my mind. One direction is pulling me harder than the other. That, too, is a secret. One I've kept only to myself.

So, as I lie here, listening to the tech point out things on the screen next to me, I can't help the tears that leak out of my eyes. The swooshing sounds echo the waves of emotion wracking my body. I was so close to having everything I wanted. Now, everything I want has changed. And I don't know if it's possible to have it all. I feel like I'm back at the start. Only of a new journey.

It's terrifying, but I know what I want. I want this baby. But it's clearly not Reed's. I'm too far along for that to be the case. The mix of feelings is overwhelming, and I wish June hadn't flown out to be with Drew. As selfish as that is, I wish my best friend was here. She would have stayed, she said so, but I told her no.

This baby has only one guarantee, and that's me always being here for it.

June is the first one I call when I leave my OBGYN's office.

"How did it go?" she answers on the first ring. All it takes is her voice and I'm in tears all over again.

"Umm, it went okay."

"Love. If it went okay, you wouldn't be sobbing on the phone," she says, tears clogging her own voice.

"It did go okay, I promise. I'm healthy, the baby is healthy. We're okay. It's just…"

"What, Leighton?"

"They estimate me to be thirteen weeks pregnant." No way it's Reed's. No way I'm making her a blood auntie, or her mom a grandmother. Something I know they'd both love dearly, especially since June and Drew won't be having children of their own.

It's a heavy realization when I didn't know I wanted to be the one to give that to them. But I do, and I think I have wanted to for a long time. A desire buried somewhere deep inside me that wasn't ready to have light shine on it yet.

But there it is.

"Okay. Do you know what you want to do?"

"I'm going to keep it. I'm calling Connor and telling him I'm keeping it." The conviction is easily heard in my words. I'm more certain about this than I've been about anything in my life.

"You know, I'm going to spoil the ever-loving shit out of your child, right?" Happiness drenches her words, and it breaks through some of my melancholy.

"Even though it's not Reed's?"

"Love, it's yours. That's all it takes to make your child family."

"Fuck, I love you," I sob.

"I love you, too. I'm going to call you every morning and before I go to bed every night to check on you both. *You're* going to call me anytime something happens. No matter what! If you get heartburn, I want to know about it."

"You're psychotic." I laugh.

"Am not," she play-pouts, making me laugh harder.

I am going to be okay.

My appointment was late enough in the day that there wasn't a need to go back into the office. Instead, I opt for writing the piece I'm working on from home. Reed made good on his plans for the back patio space and has turned it into a cozy outdoor living space. I curl up on the double chaise with a blanket, my laptop, and a cup of lemon tea as I work on expanding a story that June and Noah brought some attention to last year. The abandoned amusement park outside of town. A huge eyesore to those that live in the area, and a wildly popular spot for both artists and urban explorers.

Ivy and Olive were both on their balcony when I came outside. We exchanged our usual warm greeting, but it has grown quiet next door with the darkening sky. Reed will be home soon. We've developed a routine which always entails him feeding me dinner and not leaving my house after. He sleeps in my bed, and strangely enough, I haven't even been inside his home. He says it's not furnished and that my house is more comfortable. I haven't argued because I don't care where we spend our time. Only that we spend it together.

Tonight, everything changes. For how long, I'm not sure.

Bile tries to force up my throat. Fighting it back, I take a few moments to steady myself for what is to come. For the things I must do, to say to the two men consuming so much of my attention. Connor was the call I made after speaking with June today. If I had an idea of how I thought the conversation would go, it wasn't what happened.

"There you are," Reed calls as he steps out of my back door. A small grin tries to form on my lips because he's once again barged into my personal space without any thought of boundaries. Sadness washes it away before it has a chance to live.

Reed and I haven't had a chance to love. Maybe previous years apart could be blamed on his actions, but now it will be my own. The heartbreak of it all is enough to swallow me completely.

I see the moment he recognizes something isn't right.

"How was your appointment? You didn't answer my call earlier." No, I didn't. This isn't a phone conversation. We need to see each other's faces for this.

"Good," I say, setting my laptop aside.

Reed flops down on the chaise next to me, wrapping a big arm around me to snuggle in. "Why didn't you call me?"

He also tried to go with me to my appointment. By try, I mean, demanded. That wasn't an option for me though, because I think I knew what would happen. And I didn't want him to discover that I was carrying another man's baby with an ultrasound technician in the room with us. Reed can react in several ways. Each one will cause a different reaction in me.

"I wanted to tell you in person," I say quietly.

"Why are you scared?" he asks, pulling me onto his lap. The position is so similar to how we fit together for that first kiss so, so long ago. "What's wrong?"

"Physically, nothing is wrong. I'm healthy. We're healthy," I clarify, looking up at him through eyelashes that feel heavy with tears that haven't yet been shed.

"You're keeping it?"

I nod as my eyes flick between his, trying so hard to read his mind through his expression.

"I'm thirteen weeks along. It's Connor's."

There's no hiding it… the pain that flashes in his vision. Even as it passes in a rush because he doesn't want me to see that he'd hoped it was his. Again, I feel like I'm failing his family, his beautiful family that has given me so much. I swallow back another choked sob. Crying seems my go-to today, but I guess I can blame hormones on a portion of that.

"That's okay, it's okay," Reed says, trying to reassure us both, if I had to guess.

"Connor's coming home early to talk about it. He'll be here the day after tomorrow."

"You told him already?" Reed asks, pulling back a few inches to see my face better. It lets me see the tightness around his eyes where tension is setting in.

"I called him earlier to let him know."

"You didn't answer my call." There isn't accusation in his voice, yet I feel it anyhow.

"Speaking in person seemed like a better idea," I say almost sheepishly. Reed sits up, gaining more distance from me.

"What conversation are we having here, exactly?"

"One where I ask if we can slow things down while I figure it out?"

"Was that a question? Is it an option for me to say fuck no, and then you agree to continue with how things have been these past couple weeks?"

"No, Reed," I say with a heavy heart. "We can't continue on the same way while I'm pregnant with another man's child."

"Why not?" he asks calmly when I want him to rage instead. I'm scared and frustrated and unreasonably, I want him to be, too.

"Because that isn't fair to Connor."

Reed stands abruptly, giving me what I only wished for.

"Connor isn't the one here every day making sure you eat, or that you get enough rest," he says with a tight jaw. "Connor isn't the man sleeping in your bed. Connor isn't here at all."

"That doesn't mean I shouldn't consider his feelings," I say defensively.

"Where the baby is concerned, yes. But what does that have to do with you and me?"

"Maybe everything. Maybe nothing at all."

The simple truth is that I don't know. Since the notion I could be pregnant entered my head, every thought has been muddled and fogged. All I want is time for it all to clear, for my life as a mother to come into focus. For all the facts to be present so I can make decisions based on those instead of emotion.

"Don't do this, Leighton," he whispers the words, and it's as if I'm conjuring them up in my head. Reed's back is turned. He can't face me and I'm not sure I blame him as he picks up a fretful pace in front of me.

"I have to, Reed. I need to know I'm not making impulsive decisions now that I have someone else to think about, too."

He stops his stride and shoots me a glance so full of incredulousness, I feel like the biggest villain to ever walk the Earth. But I'm not that.

"And you see us as that? Nothing more than impulsive?"

"No, Reed," I say, standing up now myself and moving in front of him. "I'm not saying that. I'm not saying anything except that I need time and space to figure out what being pregnant with Connor's baby means."

His hand comes up to fist in the hair at the side of my face, but he doesn't pull me closer. We stand like this, arm's length apart, for several moments as we stare each other down. Each waiting for the other to say more. When his eyes close and his head tips back, face to the sparkling night sky, I know he's almost ready to speak.

And I'm terrified of what words he may deliver.

"Okay. Goodnight, Leighton."

Then he's gone, and I'm alone. Chilled to my bones as the soft evening breeze sings at me to follow him, don't let him run away, never let him go. Not that I don't listen, I do. I hear it as loud as thunder. Sometimes in life, timing is everything. I need more of it.

Eventually, I follow the path Reed took through my backdoor. A part of me is hoping I'll find him in my kitchen, ignoring my wishes, being stubborn and domineering. He isn't here though. The only trace he was is a container of takeout from my favorite burger place.

A scribbled note on the wrapper reads, *Cook it WELL DONE or the guy who ordered it may murder me.*

Tears fall from my eyes as I eat it. They stream out again when I climb into my empty bed that feels too big. Then once again the following morning when I awake, still alone, except for the little bundle growing inside my body.

I'm so tired of the tears, but I know they are nowhere near done with me yet.

19

REED

Giving Leighton space is fucking hard. Harder than anything I've done before.

All I have to hold on to is the hope that it will get easier. It's been only two days. Two days of both being in the office together and me trying my damndest to pretend I'm okay and everything is fine. Most of our coworkers haven't noticed the change.

Holly has.

"Do you want to get out of here for lunch, Reed?" she asks when she pokes her head into my office for about the eighth time today. Each with a new question that doesn't need asking. I'm not mad about it; she cares about me and that's the working relationship I want with my assistant. One who gives a shit about the job and me, as I do her. I need to trust her and that's only accomplished if she trusts me in return.

"Hell, yes. Where are we going?"

"I was thinking black bean burgers at Bearcat."

"Perfect," I say, shutting down the graphic I've been fine-tuning for the past twenty minutes. "You ready now?"

"Sure am, boss man," she says with a small salute. She's made a habit of that, along with the name. I don't mind, it's silly, and silly in the workplace works for me just fine. Plus, it was a good catch that she'd relaxed into the position here. Her nerves are gone, replaced by the confidence she should have. She's talented. She should be doing greater things and I hope one day she gets that opportunity.

On our way out of the office, I overhear… or maybe I eavesdrop a little, Leighton speaking on the phone.

"Six is fine. I'll be home before then, Connor."

It's a fresh stab to the heart, but I don't let it show. Not here, especially not in front of her. I can't pretend to understand what she's going through. No man can. While trying to not be pissed off and heartbroken, I'm also trying hard to give her what she asked for. Space. But I'll also always support her.

Last night, I beat her home. Well, I made sure I beat her home, so I had time to sneak into her house and drop off some chicken noodle soup and a side salad for her dinner. I was out and back on my side of our shared house before she got home.

I would happily repeat the process tonight, except it sounds like Connor will be there. *Happily* is perhaps the incorrect sentiment. I'm happy about little of this current situation. How can I be? Happy would mean being with the woman I love. Taking care of her during her pregnancy while it ravages her body in new ways and her hormones go insane is what would make me *happy*.

She can do it by herself. She's strong enough for all that. But she wouldn't have to if she'd let us be together how we should be.

Fucking Connor Anders.

This is my fault. It goes back to me not letting her know that I was in love with her when I should have. But I'm not giving up. I'm never giving up.

"You here with me, Reed?" Holly asks, keeping her pace with me on the walk two blocks over to the restaurant.

"Yes, sorry," I say, smiling at her. She reminds me of June more and more. Quiet, a little shy, always concerned about others.

"No need to apologize. I just worry about you."

"No need to worry."

"I don't believe you," she says with a crinkled nose.

"Have I ever lied to you before?"

"How the hell do I know?"

Something else about Holly that reminds me of my sister—she has an uncanny way of making me lighter with humor. Today, I appreciate it more than she could know.

"I promise I have not and will not lie to you, Miss Holly."

"Thank you, Mister Reed. I'd have more faith in that if you smiled more."

"Oh my god." I laugh. "Did you just tell me to smile more?"

"Gross, I did! I guess now you know what women feel like."

We're both laughing when we get to the door of the café, but our entry is interrupted by Ivy Broussard heading in our direction on the sidewalk.

"Reed," she calls in that smokey voice of hers.

"Ivy," I say with a wave. "What are you doing wandering the streets of Uptown?"

"All the lawyers and bankers lurk around here, darling. I've just finished the most boring of my errands."

"Ah, I see. Ivy Broussard, this is my coworker, Holly Stoops. Holly, meet my incomparable neighbor, Ivy."

"It's nice to meet you, Ms. Broussard. We're just about to have lunch, if you'd like to join," Holly offers.

After looking at me for confirmation that the invite is welcome, Ivy accepts, and I find myself at a table with two of the most interesting women I've met in years. We speak of art almost exclusively. Ivy's knowledge is extensive; she speaks of techniques as if she's an artist herself. Holly is as enraptured at her first meeting of the woman.

It's difficult not to be enamored by Ivy Broussard. She looks like a 1940's Hollywood starlet, sounds like a 1980's phone sex worker, and is as knowledgeable as an art encyclopedia.

"Listen, my darlings. Olive and I are having a small collection of friends over tomorrow night. I'd very much love for you both to be there."

"Oh, I would hate to intrude," Holly says, her eyes betraying her. She's dying to go. I lean back in my chair and smile.

"Good gravy, sweet child. It would be anything but an intrusion. You two would be my stars."

"Are you certain?"

"I insist, Holly. In fact, if you don't show up, I'll send my troop of strongmen over to drag you there."

"You have a troop of strongmen?" I ask.

"Of course, what woman of my station doesn't? They're the very best drag queens this city has to offer and they all adore me as much as I adore them."

"Well, now. I may have to stay home just for the experience," Holly says.

"Oh, you'll have an experience all right, just attend my little brouhaha."

"Okay, I accept."

"As do I. But only because I don't have to drive there," I say.

"Cheeky shit," Ivy says with a sultry laugh.

The rest of my day is better, easier, because I'm not choking on all things Leighton Ward. Because I can fill my time while waiting for her by filling it with interesting people. And the conversation has spurred me to want to paint, something I've not done much of the past few weeks. Probably because I was so focused on love and Leighton. Maybe we both need some space.

No… fuck that. I want her around all the time. I want to suffocate on all things Leighton Ward.

I hope one day she feels the same. I'm confident she will. So, again, while I'm upset at the way things are going, I know they'll work out. Being bitter about it won't help anything.

Even if life requires me to watch Connor pull up to the curb at the same time I do.

"Hey, man," I call when I exit my vehicle. "How was your flight?"

"Long, but good. Nice to see you, Reed."

Sure it is, because he most likely doesn't know that I've been sleeping with Leighton.

"You too, Connor."

It's not, but that's not his fault. Connor is an okay guy, despite how he fled the States. I imagine he had his reasons, and if he's anything like his brother, those reasons would only get shared with a selected few.

To ease some of my ever-present frustration, I work out before showering and relaxing with my dinner. Considering I'm a grown adult,

I may eat my damn fried chicken in my outdoor bath. Because I fucking can. Leighton can add that to her list of serial killer type shit I do.

There isn't any gym equipment here. No reason to set up a home gym when I've seen the plans Drew has for his own next door. Instead, I rely on moves that use my own body weight. Being cut isn't my goal, never has been, but I like to burn off the bullshit I eat.

I'm halfway through and stripped down to only a pair of sweatpants when Leighton's back door opens, and she walks out with Connor in tow.

"Reed did all the work, but I get to enjoy it," she says, not noticing me right away as I hang from the rafter of the patio cover. I've made it my makeshift pullup bar. Not letting the intrusion stop me, I keep up a steady pace while I track the pair on the other side of the yard. "I made fun of him for the little tub pool, but I have to admit, it's been nice."

"He painted this?" Connor asks walking closer to the back fence line.

"Yep."

"I didn't realize he was an artist."

"He's modest about it, I guess. I knew he dabbled, but this was unexpected." There is something like awe in her voice. Something I want to hear more of when she's talking about me.

"It's nice, comforting. The colors feel like an extension of what you've done inside."

"Yes, it's quickly become my favorite place to be."

"That's nice to hear," I grunt out, while doing L-sit pullups. Beads of sweat roll down my chest, and I watch as Leighton's attention hits me and then them. Her lips parting tell me she's affected.

Good.

"Sorry," she stutters out. "We didn't mean to interrupt."

"You haven't," I say, not changing my pace. My ego is too big to show any struggle in front of Connor. My brain tells me he's not my competition, but my heart and body aren't convinced.

I call it a win when Leighton's cheeks brighten and her eyes flutter because they haven't left my body. Not even when Connor steps closer to her, his hand brushing hers.

"We should go, babe. They won't hold the reservation."

That riles me up.

"Have a nice dinner, *babe*," I say, pulling myself up one more time. Connor's head bounces between us for a moment.

"Sure. Give me a minute to lock up. I'll meet you out front," she tells him. I drop my feet on the ground when he disappears inside. "It's just dinner, Reed. So we can talk."

"Like a date?"

"No. It most certainly is not a date."

"Does he know that?"

"I can't pretend to know what Connor thinks."

"Do you know what I think?"

"I wish," she says, laughter in her voice… and fuck, I've missed that.

"Let me tell you, then." I step closer to her. Right up in her personal space. "I think that my rules still apply, even though I'm giving you space."

"I never agreed to those."

"Your agreement was implied when you'd come home after a date and let me make you come." I lean forward to whisper the words in her ear.

"I can't agree to no long-term plans with the father of my baby, Reed," she says, and I flinch.

"You think that's what I'm asking?"

"I don't know." Frustration burns through her words.

"All I'm asking," I say slowly, "is that you be as fair to me as you are being to him. Can you give me that much?"

"Yes," Leighton tells me, bringing a palm up to my cheek. "Of course, Reed."

The possessive asshole that lives inside me wants rage at her. To remind her again and again that she said she was mine. It doesn't matter that she's carrying Connor's baby. Leighton is mine and I don't know how to go back to a life where she isn't. That's not the life I want. But that choice is not mine to make. I don't deserve Leighton just because I want her.

I have to earn her, and I can only do that by listening to what she asks, to what she wants.

"I trust you," I say, bringing her hand from my cheek to my heart. "I trust you, Love."

"Thank you," she says with a smile that lies. A reminder she doesn't want to be in this situation any more than I do.

"How have you been feeling?"

"I'm okay. Still vomiting some mornings, though."

"It will pass," I reassure her, and she nods. "Go have a nice dinner."

"Okay," she says, and walks away. She stops before she disappears. "Thank you, Reed."

"For what?"

"For not being mad at me." That sadness that sometimes seeps into her heart and soul is there. I hate it. I want to conquer her sadness and destroy it.

"Never, Love. I could never."

20

LEIGHTON

A few months ago, if someone had told me I would be pregnant with Connor's child, I believe I would have thought we made it. As a couple and a family.

Connor has the relationship with both his parents I had always dreamed of having. They are tight, share everything, don't keep secrets. I have that with my dad and always have. But I wanted more. I wanted two parents at home every night, sitting in the uncomfortable chairs at my choir concerts, holding hands while they watched me open gifts Christmas morning. I wanted a mother to show up to the mother-daughter tea parties that my grade school had every spring when we lived in Mississippi for a few years.

There were kids with no daddies occasionally, but I never knew one without a mom.

I don't want my child, or children, to go without either. I'd sacrifice a lot for that. For them.

So why does Connor feel so wrong now, after only a short time apart?

Only a few weeks with Reed and my heart is turned inside out, leaving it vulnerable and fragile in ways it hasn't been my entire adult life. I worry that the newness has me enthralled. Reed and I may be a shiny relationship with the sweet butterflies of fresh love… with the potential to turn into bitter moths.

"Reed is who you've been seeing since I left." Connor waits to make the statement until we're seated at a semi-secluded table in an upscale restaurant.

"I dated around a little first," I say before realizing how that could be taken. "And if you're about to question the paternity, your fragile balls will be getting an up close and personal look at this tiny appetizer fork."

"I wouldn't dare question you, Leighton." He laughs, holding up his hands.

"Good answer," I tell him, a smile breaking out of my own. Something Connor and I never lacked. We had many good times and never fought.

"Is it serious? What you have with Reed?"

"It has the potential to be," I answer, the words burning my lips as I say them.

"So do we," he says. "Especially now."

"Because of a baby?"

"No, not just that. I'll admit it changes things, but I already told you I missed you. I've thought of you every day."

"Lamenting your mistakes, Connor?" I wink.

"Absolutely. I should have told you as soon as the job came up. Then I should have tried everything to get you to agree to go with me."

"And had I still declined?"

"I'm confident I could have sweetened the pot enough to get you to commit to two years there with me. The next stop could have been anywhere you wanted. Palm Springs with Larry, maybe."

The server comes by for orders, and when he leaves, we're quiet again for a few minutes. Each of us contemplating the situation, how we got here, where we go now. It's not lost on me that Connor underestimates my love for this city. It's also not lost on me that he's making an effort here.

"I spent the plane ride back preparing the perfect things to say to you," Connor says. "Now that I have the chance to say them, it seems they've left my brain outright."

He wrings his hands twice, his nerves showing. It's a new tell, one

I've never seen him do before. Connor Anders was never nervous around me before.

"Thailand isn't an option for me, Connor. That needs to be taken off the table immediately. Okay?"

"Yes, I expected as much," he says. "I'm in contract on this project, though. Seeing it finished is the best move for my career. After that, a lot more doors will open for me. A lot more money, too."

"You know that's never been important to me. Besides, I make more now, too."

"I know, Leighton. But that doesn't mean I don't want to provide you and my child with every opportunity I can. If we must be geographically separated for a couple of years, it sure as hell should be financially beneficial for us."

Separated. Us.

Connor is speaking as if we're still a couple. Or, as if it's a guarantee we will be again. A noble notion, but not one I've given him evidence to believe in.

"Connor, a pregnancy doesn't mean we're back together."

"No, of course not. I don't mean to imply that we are."

"What are you implying?"

"That I'm all in, Leighton. As a father, one thousand percent. But I want more. I want you."

It's a rush, hearing someone tell you they want you. That they want to be with you. Regardless of if it is reciprocated, it's flattering, special. I don't take it lightly.

For the same reasons I'm afraid of the rush of new feelings with Reed, I'm leery of the things I feel when Connor says things like that. It's hard to trust my heart when love is involved because I've never been in love. I've always relied on my brains and instinct, but hormones are a bitch, and I don't know if I can count on those either.

Whoever told women that pregnancy is all happy glowing sunshine is an asshole. They really ought to teach women the truth; it messes with every part of you and I'm only getting started.

"What happens if I can't give you that, Connor?"

"I won't be a deadbeat dad, if that's what you're asking."

"That's not a thought I've had. I know you well enough to know that.

What I need to know is if you'll be amicable while negotiating custody and support."

Connor sits back in his seat, and grabbing his drink, he swallows a large amount of the amber whiskey.

"You know me well enough to know I won't be a deadbeat, but not well enough to know that I wouldn't take our child away from you or cheat you out of support?"

"I didn't mean it to sound so bad, honestly. It seems everything these days makes me edgy and confused. I need clarity and reassurance. The idea of having to battle you on anything stresses me out, Connor."

"We'll work through it all, babe. You don't need to worry. Whether we're together or not, I'm not going to push for anything that isn't healthy for you or the child."

"Thank you," I say, relieved.

"I get that you don't have much faith in me, but damn, it's a slap in the face. One I deserve, of course."

"Yes, you do," I tell him with a tearful laugh. "You shouldn't have left the way you did. It really hurt my feelings."

"Sorry for that, Leighton. I really am," he says. "Relationships aren't exactly easy for me, either."

"Sure, because you're a commitment phobic man," I tease. "It's hardly the same thing."

I mean it playfully, but it's true regardless. Connor grew up with two loving parents. He had a great example to learn from. Not the absent mom and pining dad I had. The two types of love I learned from were damaged; one loved themselves too much, the other not enough.

Plus, I've spent years reporting on the horrors regular people do to the ones they supposedly love every day. While I crave real, healthy love, I'm also terrified that I can't recognize it. At least I'm self-aware enough to know that about myself. But what's Connor's excuse?

Or Reed's?

"Can't deny that, I suppose," Connor says as the server approaches our table with the meals we ordered.

"Have you told your family?"

"Yes. It took Noah and my dad's help to convince my mother not to run straight over to your house. She's overjoyed. I'll apologize in advance for anything and everything she's about to put you through."

"Grace is a sweetheart, I'm sure it won't be all bad."

"She wanted to be a grandmother since before she was even a mother. With both you and Lorelai pregnant, she's losing her mind with plans of spoiling both babies."

"Shit, I hadn't even thought about Lorelai and I being pregnant at the same time. I guess it will be nice for them to have a cousin the same age."

"It's literally the only thing my mother talks about," he says. "So, I guess I should ask you if you'll let her be involved. Regardless of what happens with us."

"Of course," I say, genuinely. "I have no clue what the hell I'm doing. I'd welcome her advice and help."

"Oh, she'll have plenty of that."

Conversation continues while we eat, but we don't revisit the subject of 'us'. Something I'm grateful for, as I have nothing to add just now. My life this last month has been a rush. I want time for it to settle and my thoughts to sort.

All my decisions need to be weighed differently now that the consequences of them are heavier.

Reed and Connor may not like that, but I'll put my foot down. I will never be as selfish as my own mother was, never be as negligent of my child as she was with me.

Connor drives me home, and as we exit his rental car, he receives a message from his mother.

"She wants to know if she can text you," he says almost sheepishly.

"Yes," I laugh. "That would be fine. I adore your mother; she won't bother me."

Connor walks me to my front door and pauses. Maybe he's waiting for an invite, but that's not on my agenda tonight.

"When is your next doctor's appointment?"

"Four weeks."

"Maybe I can video call in?"

"Sure," I say. I won't stop him from being as involved as he wants to be. If he stays friendly and plays by the rules I set, anyway.

"Can I see you again tomorrow? Maybe bring some dinner by here?"

"Okay, but this can't be a nightly thing, Connor. Even if you're only here for two weeks. I told you I need space to make some decisions."

"I know you did, Leighton," he says. "I'm not trying to push, but I'm not giving up either." He reaches down to squeeze my hand before he leaves, and I'm left wondering how someone like me ended up in a situation like this.

It's quiet next door, and there is no sign of Reed in the backyard. The urge to speak to someone about my conversation with Connor is strong and my instinct screams to call Reed, that he should be the person I discuss all things with.

I call his sister instead.

"Hey, Love," she answers right away. "How did it go?"

"Good, I think."

"What did he say?"

"He's committed to his project in Thailand, which should take two years. He understands that's not somewhere I'm willing to relocate to, but he wants to support us, regardless."

"Us?" she asks, and though I know she's trying to keep it out, her voice betrays her. I hear the worry. And I think it's as much for Reed as it is for me.

"He says he wants me back," I hedge.

"What do you want?"

"I'm not sure how to be sure of what I want," I say. "It's frightening."

"Which part?"

"All of it."

"I may not be physically right by your side, but I am with you every step of the way. You know that, right?"

I love my best friend. We've often joked that we're each other's soulmates, but it's not a joke . June is the first and only best friend I ever had. The only woman I've ever trusted fully. In the decade I've known her, we've never fought, never judged one another, never had to apologize because we don't do the other wrong.

In a world of catty women, we found our other halves and I'm never letting her go. I'm never letting her run.

"I know, Love," I tell June, using our shared nickname. I'm the only one that calls her that, but her entire family has adopted it for me. A strange thing to be called when it's the one emotion I find the most confounding, the one I spent so much of my life feeling like it was out of reach. "Grace is very excited, Connor says. Happy to be a grandmother twice over in the coming months."

"Oh, I bet. Noah has said she's always wanted to be a grandmother."

"Connor said the same," I confirm. June doesn't say that her mom has craved that same thing. She hasn't spoken on it since June's attack in college left her unable to carry children safely. But I once overheard her ask Reed if he planned on settling down with a family. He said yes, when the time is right. Their mother was delighted by his answer. "I'm scared to make the wrong decision, June."

"Do you mean between Connor and Reed?"

"Yes, among other things."

"You've already made the hard decision, maybe the hardest you'll ever have to make. There's time for the rest. Try not to get too anxious about it."

"Easier said."

"Than done," she finishes for me. "I know, but I believe it's all going to be okay. And if it isn't, I'll kidnap you and your baby and move you in with me. We'll be fine."

"I love you, June."

"I'm amazing, so who wouldn't love me?"

"You are. You're the most amazing."

"I love you," she says. "Call me with anything. Call me with everything."

"Will do. Have a good night, June."

After I hang up with her, I ready myself for another cold and lonely night of sleep. It's hard to sleep now without the comfort of a warm arm wrapped around me to help ward away the thoughts that plague my dreams.

21

REED

Olive and Ivy's collection of friends, as they call them, are the most eclectic bunch you could expect to find in this city. And hell, if that isn't saying a lot for New Orleans. For the fourth night in a week, Holly and I have been invited over dinner, drinks, or both.

A homebody by nature, I'd normally decline so many invitations. But my favorite pastime, Leighton, has been busy since Connor came back to town. He's been by the house a lot. His mother, too. It's been enough for me to keep my distance. Though, I do sneak over to her house every morning and leave breakfast on the counter while she's showering.

It's my way of giving her space and still fulfilling my need to take care of her. Of them. I'm gone before she comes downstairs, but she makes a point of thanking me during the day. Either by texting me or finding me in the office. It's all sweet and somehow awfully impersonal as well.

I hate it. But it's what she wants. I did what I wanted for too long to not give her what she's asking for now. Doesn't mean I don't regret the fuck out of it.

If I'd have followed her after she graduated college, claimed her then, things now would be different. Instead, I followed my best friend and sister. Not that I regret that part, but I might have merged it together somehow.

Also, had things gone differently, this baby wouldn't exist. And that would be a damn shame. Seeing the look on Connor's mother's face as she walks out Leighton's back door tells me this baby will be adored by his family.

Wanting to decompress, I grabbed a beer and escaped into the oasis I built in the backyard under the glow of festoon lighting. I'm expected at the Broussards' shortly, but the Anders family arriving at Leighton's derails my schedule.

Connor's whole family is here—his parents and Noah. Noah's fiancée Lorelai is even here, along with her toddler sister whose name escapes me.

The child runs toward me right away but stops in her tracks when her attention leaves the outdoor tub and focuses on me.

"Hello," I call to her.

Her blonde hair bounces on her shoulders when she does a quick spin to see that Noah and Lorelai are close by and have a keen eye on her.

"Are you a hero or a vanilla?" she asks me.

At first, I think she's talking about sub sandwiches and ice cream. Children are simple that way. But then I clue in and realize the question is not so simple. She's asking if I'm a good guy or a bad guy.

"I'm a hero, not a *villain*," I tell her. "My name is Reed. You've probably met my sister, June."

"Oh, yes. I like Miss June very much. I sometimes have lunch with her and the giant."

"The giant? Do you mean, Drew?"

"Yes." She giggles. "He's too big, it's funny."

"Maybe you are just too small," I tease.

"I don't think so. Noah calls me a bull, so I must be big."

"A bull in a China shop, Livi," Noah says, walking up behind her. "It means something a little different than big."

"I don't think so," she says, running back over to her sister. Leighton stands with Lorelai and Grace. The elder woman seems to measure the difference in belly size between the two expectant mothers. Leighton is not yet showing, but Lorelai has a sizable bump.

Connor stands in the space separating them and us, speaking on his phone.

"How are you, Reed?"

"I'm keeping it together, Noah. How are you?"

"The best I've ever been," he answers. "I'm sorry you can't say the same. This must be difficult."

"As long as she's healthy and happy, I'll be fine." It's a dirty lie. I won't be fine, but I'll pretend to be.

"She's special, that one. Like your sister, but with more attitude."

"That's the fucking truth." I laugh. "You should have seen her when they were in college. She was wild. Vivacious like I'd never seen a woman her age. Confident and sure."

"I can picture that," he says with a nod.

"Sorry, I'm musing. I do that sometimes." I do it when I've been painting a lot. Which I have been, since it is what calms me the most. Another large canvas sits in my studio, the paint slowly filling in the blank space since Leighton asked to slow things down. But that's not Noah's business. That's for me alone.

"It's all good, I understand."

"Understand what?" Connor asks, finally done with his call and walking toward us.

"How the past creeps up on us at odd times," Noah answers. "It's good to see you, Reed, I hope we can do it again now that you're living in my city."

Noah saunters back to the women, leaving me with his brother and I get the feeling this was an orchestrated event.

"What's on your mind, Connor?"

"All things Leighton Ward."

"A feeling I know well," I say.

"I figured as much. I've always suspected your feelings for her."

"And?"

"I'm not giving up without a fight. It's about family now," he says. "If she chooses me, I need to know you won't be a problem."

While I've never loved Connor dating Leighton, I haven't ever had a reason to think negatively of the man. Until right now.

"There will never be a day of my life that I don't love that woman, Connor. I've always supported her decisions. If she chooses you, that won't change. I won't be a problem unless a day comes that she changes her mind about you. I'll be there waiting," I say, then take a final drink of my beer. "This has *always* been about family for me."

Leaving, I send a small wave to Leighton because I know she's watching us, and I don't want her to worry. These past few days have been hell for me. I'm not sure what they've been like for her, but I imagine much the same. If she's going to have shit days, it won't be because I'm being a broody asshole.

Olive and Ivy, like they have each night, welcome me with a whiskey and yet another introduction. They have friends in every part of the entertainment circle, but it's the artistically related ones they push me toward. Tonight, it's Simone, a woman about my age, who owns an exclusive gallery here in New Orleans.

"Simone," Ivy introduces, "this is Reed Turner, the one I've been telling you about."

"Nice to meet you, Simone," I say, offering a hand to shake.

"You as well, Reed. The sisters tell me they've hired you for their special project."

"Did they now?" I laugh. They've offered Holly and I a commission to paint the ceiling of their ballroom. We haven't yet committed to the project, though we've been discussing doing it. Holly's been hesitant, only because of the topic.

They've basically asked us for a pornographic version of the Sistine Chapel. I find it both amusing and challenging, but my career isn't only getting started. Holly's is; she needs to weigh how such a project could affect her future. It's more daring than anything she's done before, but I think secretly she craves that. I won't push her either way, this decision is up to her.

I'm getting good at taking a back seat to the women in my life, it seems. Whether I enjoy it or not.

"I have faith," Ivy says before flitting away to another group of friends.

"Watch out for those two," Simone warns. "They can be a handful of trouble."

"A fact I caught on to quite quickly," I say.

"If you're talented enough for the likes of them to court you, I'd love to see some of your work."

Simone and I chat most of the evening out on the balcony where it's quieter. I bring Holly into the conversation too, both of us showing Simone some of the work we have saved on our phones. Simone spent her teenage years living in Europe with her mother and French grandparents, after the devastating divorce of her parents. She's well-traveled because of it and has seen many of the classic art world's most treasured pieces. Holly is in awe of her experiences. Simone doesn't mind the younger woman's fancy; she welcomes the attention. Not in a snobby or aloof way, of course. I've known enough artists to know it's rare to be as talented as my assistant is and not have either a cockiness about it or some sort of imposters syndrome.

After university, Simone came back to the States to reconnect with her father who was living here. She, like so many others, instantly fell in love with New Orleans' unique charm and decided to stay. Her gallery opened five years ago and is the most respected in the city with highly regarded clientele flying in for openings regularly.

Simone is an exceptional contact to have for any artist. I've never had much desire to sell my paintings or have a gallery opening, but the world is one I love. It feeds the creative part of me that my job doesn't.

Discussion with Simone and Holly is so captivating that I barely notice when the noise from my backyard next door dies down. But I see when Connor's family all leaves and he lingers longer. I notice how he stays as close to Leighton as possible and every time he casually touches her.

I notice she doesn't pull away.

"Fresh drink, my darling," Ivy says, handing me a new glass. It's bourbon, the same brand both her mother and grandmother drank. She calls it The Potion and swears it brings good luck. She's full of shit, but I play along because I like the sisters very much. "I was not terribly excited to see the blonde one return."

"Me, either," I say as we peer down at Leighton and Connor, aka the blonde one.

"Is he here to stay?"

"In one way or another, yes."

"She's different with you." Turning my head to her, I notice how she studies the people in the yard below. I know the sisters are Peeping Toms, but it's more than casual spying. They thoughtfully observe those in their space. "More relaxed. She feels safer with you than I've ever seen her with any other man, save that handsome father of hers."

"Have you seen someone hurt her?" I ask, jumping to the worst-case scenario.

"No, darling. Never." She places her hand to my shoulder to soothe my temper. "I only mean that you bring out an ease in her. The only other time I see it is when her father or your sister is there with her."

"Just how often do you spy on her, Ivy?"

"I don't spy, amou. I witness. I often witness," she says with a smile and a wink. "Enough to know it's not the blonde one's company she wants right now."

Looking back down, my eyes meet hers, and I know Ivy is right. Leighton isn't focused on the man standing next to her, her attention is on me. She's not being obvious about the sly looks she sneaks at me. Connor hasn't caught on, at least that's how it seems as he chats and smiles.

The next time she looks my way, I nod my head toward the front of our house, hoping she'll understand.

Get rid of him and I'll come home.

Within minutes, she's ushering him out.

"I do believe you'll be exiting my gathering early this evening, darling."

"You would be correct, it seems, Ivy. Thank you for another great evening."

"It's always my pleasure having you, Reed. I hope to have you here more and more, once I get that mouse of yours on board."

I laugh and wish her luck before taking my time to say good night to the others. Leighton has made me wait for days; she can wait a few minutes in return. By the time I get there, Connor is gone and Leighton leans on the jamb of her front door.

Waiting for me.

"Hi."

"Hi, Reed."

"What are you doing?"

"You know I'm waiting for you," she says, pulling part of her bottom lip into her mouth.

"Why?" I don't move closer; the tension between us is thick as hell already from several feet away. I might suffocate on it fully if I take another step. One side of her oversized sweater falls off a shoulder, her hair is pulled up off her long neck, and those damned rosy cheeks that belong only… it's enough to make me hard in an instant.

But that's not why she wants me here tonight.

"I've missed you."

There it is. I move now, closer to her, so close I can hear the small gasp she makes at my nearness.

"I've been here the entire time, Leighton."

"Not really."

No, not really. I hide, I check out, I pretend she isn't spending time with a man she may choose over me.

"I'm here now," I whisper. "What are you going to do with me?"

"You're going to think it's silly."

"Never," I tell her.

Her eyes flit between mine, weighing my answer.

"Can you watch *Killing Eve* with me? And maybe, just cuddle?" She looks down at her feet when she says it. I'd smile at her embarrassment but that sad tone I hate so much is present. I don't like to see her sad.

"Hey, look at me, Leighton," I say and wait for her to look back up. "It's not silly. It's my favorite thing in the world."

She smiles but I don't think she believes me. So, I take her hand and lead her inside, not saying anything until I have her curled up in my arms on her sofa, a throw blanket draped over us and Sandra Oh on the television.

"What's making you sad, Love?"

"I'm not," she says, burying herself further under the blanket.

"Please don't do that with me," I say the words with my lips pressing into the crown of her head. "Don't lie for my benefit."

"How do you know me so well?"

I almost counter her question with how Connor does not… but that wouldn't be helpful to her. Or me. I can't be the asshole where I'm already on the outskirts of it. Where I want to be is here, in the inner circle with Leighton in *my* arms.

"Years of observation. Now answer me."

"Are you being bossy, Reed?"

"Yes. But stop pretending you don't like it and answer my question."

"It's all overwhelming, you know? The pregnancy, Connor being back, his whole family showering me with support. Plus, the new job and…" she hesitates. "It's a lot."

"And what? Me? Am I adding to you being overwhelmed?"

"No. You not being around adds to it. Does that make sense?"

I think back on what Ivy said, and yeah, it all makes sense.

"It does. You know that if you need something from me, all you need to do is ask?"

"With how much time I've been spending with Connor, I didn't know if I could. Plus, I did ask you for space. Now here I am, asking you to be as close as possible," she tells me, sounding weary and tired.

"You're pregnant, Love. You're allowed to change your mind from one moment to the next. I'll do my best to keep up."

Leighton turns her body to face mine. Her wiggling against me drives me so crazy I must fight to keep control of myself.

"It's insane, Reed. Truly. I'm all over the place, emotionally and physically. If it's this bad now, how am I going to manage being elated one minute, pissed off the next, then horny as hell in a split second for the next handful of months? I'm going to lose my mind." Her nose crinkles in disgust and it only makes me want her more.

"Horny, huh?"

"The likes you cannot understand," she huffs.

"How have you been handling that?"

"I have more toys than any one woman should have, Mr. Turner. I know how to take care of myself," she tells me with narrowed eyes.

"It's not quite the same though, is it?"

"God, no." She laughs.

"All you need to do is ask, Love."

2 2

LEIGHTON

I t's not fair. None of this is. It's not fair to Reed that I realized I was pregnant so soon after we pursued a relationship. It isn't fair to Connor that every time he touches me, I crave for it to be someone else. It sure as fuck isn't fair to the future child that my love life is such a mess that I can't promise to be stable when it arrives.

It isn't fair that I must *ask* Reed to give me the spectacular orgasm he always delivers when it's only been days since I asked him to slow things down.

But I will ask. I'll beg if that's what it takes.

"Would you hate me if I asked you to make me come right now?"

"No," Reed answers, so casually. "In fact, there is little you could do to make me hate you."

"Really?" I eye him with suspicion.

"Really."

"Like, if I was a cannibal. Would you hate me, then?"

"That's hardly realistic." He laughs. "You don't even like eating meat off a bone."

"Well, yeah, because that's gross," I say, too quickly. My addled mind is not keeping up. "Oh, right. What about if you found out I was a serial killer? You'd hate me then for sure."

"Doubtful."

"What? How?"

"Do you hate Villanelle?" He gestures to the television.

"No, she does it because she was brainwashed and trained to assassinate. She doesn't know any better until she meets Eve. Then she tries to change."

"Right. So maybe you'd have your reasons, too."

"Oh my god, she's not real, Reed." I sit up, turning on his lap to face him, my knees on either side of his thighs. "You can't sympathize with real life serial killers."

"I can if that real life serial killer is you."

"You are so wrong."

"So are you. I guess, with us, two wrongs do make a right."

"You're kind of romantic sometimes, you know that?"

"Only with you, Love."

"What do we do now?" I ask, meaning more than this instance. Maybe he knows that, maybe he chooses to ignore everything outside of us. Outside of right now.

"I help you pull your dress up and you help me pull my pants down."

I bark out a burst of laughter. "And then what?"

"And then I shove my hard cock in whatever hole you want it in."

Oh. My laughter is wiped away by pure fucking desire. It's been only days, but it feels like a lifetime since Reed's naked body was pressed up against mine.

Pulling my dress up and over my head, I toss it to the floor behind me. Reed stays still, not moving an inch.

"Touch me."

"Are you sure this is what you want? If we do this, he may not forgive you."

"If we don't, I may not forgive myself." Deep down, I know who has my heart. Reed's always been the only man with the ability to hold it in its entirety. The only thing left for me to do is get over my hang ups regarding love, marriage, and family. "If there are consequences to come, I'll pay them."

"Is it that simple?"

"Not remotely. But I don't like all this time without you, Reed. I don't enjoy it." Teary-eyed, I deliver the last part. My whole life, I've never told a man how I've felt about them. The three words I'm so terrified of. He should understand that while my life is so muddy just now, my heart isn't.

I don't say them, though I hope he knows anyway.

"I'll take what I can get," he mumbles before he kisses me hard, his tongue diving in and stealing any more conversation. Expertly, he reaches behind me to unclasp my bra. It joins my dress on the floor, while I shove hands between us to undo his jeans.

When they're open enough for me, I push a hand in and grasp his erection and almost cry at how much I've missed the feel of it. Hard, silky, and full of promise. Reed grunts in pleasure when I shove my other hand down the back to grip his taut ass. It's my favorite part of his body. The short time we were together, I touched it as often as I could.

Reed maneuvers us around until I'm lying on my back, and he braces himself above me.

"You're going to have to let go long enough for me to get us both naked."

"Hurry up," I urge.

"I've been wondering something," he says as he pulls my panties off. I raise a brow for him to continue. "Every time I've tasted your cunt, you've been pregnant. I wonder what you taste like normally."

"You've thought about that?" I ask, astonished. "Just how obsessed with me are you?"

"You have no idea," he says as his pants vanish. "How do you want it?"

"Whatever way ends with me coming."

"If that's up to me, you'll be coming several times," Reed says, pulling my legs straight up in the air. "Can you hold them up? Tight together?"

"Okay."

"If anything gets uncomfortable, you tell me," he says sternly.

"I'm pregnant, Reed, not fragile. You won't break anything."

"Just throwing it out there."

I'm about to make a snappy comeback when a warm wetness hits my clit, then slides down my slit.

"Did you just spit on me?" I ask on a full body shiver.

"Yes, I guess it makes this is mine now." His thumb slides through my labia. It's torturous, so slow, and so arousing.

"Reed, don't play."

"You're that needy, baby?"

"Yes! More than you can know."

"So, you don't want any foreplay?"

"Reed," I grind out in frustration. "Am I wet?" His thumb finally, *fucking finally*, dips inside me.

"Yeah, Love. Very."

"Then, can you please fuck me?"

"Only because you asked me so nicely, Leighton."

With quick speed, Reed scoots closer to me, his knees on either side of my ass as he holds my thighs and pushes in. Deep. Oh my god, so deep. I almost explode from the slight grind of pubic bones and his balls slapping my ass.

Pregnancy has made me easy.

"I'm not going to last long," I gasp in time with Reed's thrusts.

"Then we'll count how many times you come before I'm spent, because my dick is nowhere near ready to leave your pussy."

Reed pulls my legs up higher, effectively raising my ass off the sofa. It changes the angle, making him slide up against my happy spot. My toes curl, and I clench on a long moan. I can't say if it's just pregnancy hormone sex or if it's because I missed Reed so much, but this all feels like… more.

It's Reed. I'm making up shit to shy away from all the things my heart is telling me. Because I am in love with Reed Turner and that knowledge makes him fucking me feel more intense. More important.

More powerful.

And so goddamned sexy when he spreads my legs apart, leaving one to hang off the sofa and the other to hang off the back. It's more intoxicating when he keeps eye contact with me as he sucks two fingers into his mouth until they're dripping with his saliva, only for him to slide them into me with his dick.

Its fullness is unlike anything I've felt before. Reed keeps them there for a moment or two, then moves them to gently feather over my clit. Barely a touch, barely anything. But just enough to rock my shoulders down into the sofa, throwing my head back and my ass up.

I see the entire universe mirrored back in Reed's eyes as my body evaporates into one sensation. Pure fucking ecstasy.

Reed's movement only slows when my erratic breathing does.

"Reed?"

"Yes, Love?"

"I'm having a craving," I whisper.

"What do you want?" He pulls out, ready to jump up and get me whatever I want. "Do you need some water or tea?"

"No, it's not that kind of craving." I sit up so I can press my hands to the hard lines of his chest. He worked up a sweat bringing me to a climax, the evidence coats my fingertips, and I press harder. Reed takes the hint and sits back against the far arm of the couch.

I crawl over his legs, dragging my face from his groin, then slowly up over his dewy chest. As I go strongly inhaling, his skin pulls and pebbles under my nose. There's no colorful description for how Reed smells. It's just *him*. I don't stop until we're resting cheek to cheek.

"Did you just sniff me, you creeper?"

"Yes," I admit and drag my tongue over his earlobe and back down the neck, taking my time over the pulsing vein.

"Is that what you're craving? My scent?"

"No. It's your taste I want. The smell of you is a bonus."

"You're going to fuck me with your mouth."

Statement. Fact.

"Better than you've ever had," I say as I work further down his body, teasing with small nips until his beautifully thick cock bounces against my lips. I dart my tongue out, lapping him up from sack to tip where I find a salty pearl already waiting for me.

It's divine but not enough. Not nearly enough. I want it to coat my throat until I'm choking on it.

So, I get to work easing my body over him, taking in as much as I can. Cradling his cock in the curve of my tongue on the way down and sucking on the way up. Again and again, and over again. His hands curl around my skull, his heels digging into the cushions so he can take control of the pace and depth. I let him find what he needs so I can get what I want.

The taste intensifies with more precum leaking from his dick. I hum from how satisfying it is.

"Fucking hell, Love. Fucking hell."

I reach a hand under his body and grasp the globe of his ass; it tightens with each upward motion, and I hum again.

"Goddamnit, just like that."

"Mmmhmm."

Reed spills in my mouth and I love it, but also, I overestimated what I can take right now. I swallow a mouthful and let the rest spurt over his chest, up to his neck, a drop on his chin. He doesn't seem to mind as he stares at me the entire time.

I stare back while I run my fingers through what my mouth couldn't take.

"You're a beautiful mess."

"Lay that gorgeous body atop mine and get beautifully messy, too," he tells me.

When I do, his arms wrap around me tightly and I lick the drop from the cleft in his chin.

"How have you been feeling?"

"Lonely," I say without thinking about it. Gut truths like this only happen when I'm talking to my dad or June. With anyone else, I calculate and overanalyze. Reed's getting a part of me rarely seen.

"You're with people all the time. What's making you feel lonely?"

"Big life decisions that I didn't expect to be making just yet. Pressure from every side, even when nobody's actually applying it. Sleeping by myself when I'd gotten used to you in my bed."

"All you need to do is ask," he says.

"I know. I'm just trying to be fair. To be sure."

"What are you scared of, Love?"

That.

Love.

Or the lack thereof. The absence of love. The loss of love and the hurt it leaves in its wake as it flees… that's what is most terrifying. But there's more…

"What if I can't give this baby the family it deserves? What if I end up like my mother?"

"That's what you're worried about?" Reed asks but it isn't judgmental, more like curious.

"Among the other three million issues that have crossed my mind, yeah?"

"You know, my sister was in the hospital for a very long time after her attack."

"I know." I nod, my cheek brushing against his slick chest. "I was there."

"Exactly my point. You were there every single day, without fail. You picked up any slack left by medical staff or our family. It was you that advocated for her to get the best care possible. You never let up until the day she was released."

"I love her."

"I know. You love her like she's your own sister. Even then, when you'd only known her for a few years. And you were so young, with so many other responsibilities. But you stuck with her. You sat in her room and studied for finals, hell, you slept there most nights."

"What's your point, Turner?" I ask, though I see the direction he's taking.

"That there is no way you could ever love your own child any less than how you love my sister. You'll show this baby that same devotion and it will be the luckiest kid in the world to have you as its mommy."

"I'm going to be a mommy," I say, tears welling in my eyes from how much faith Reed has in me.

"You're going to be the best mommy. And your baby is going to be surrounded by family that loves them, no matter what. Regardless of what you choose." He pauses, takes a deep affected breath, then continues, "Your baby is going to have our family and Connor's. It'll have me."

"Thank you, Reed," I tell him. He mumbles something but we both grow quiet for a few long moments. The big, bossy man that moved in during the dead of night just weeks ago isn't the man rubbing warm palms over my back to soothe my worry. Reed has adapted to be what I need him to be in this moment.

I realize he's always done that, and I wonder how much I didn't see. How much did I willfully ignore where Reed was involved?

"My dad gets in tomorrow," I say conversationally because I want to keep hearing his voice.

"I know. I spoke to him yesterday."

"You did?" I like they have a relationship outside of me. "What did you talk about?"

"I don't see how it's your business," he says. I hear the smile in his voice without having to tilt my head up to him.

"Connor is coming by for dinner. He has gifts he wants to deliver before he heads to Lafayette to spend Christmas at his parents'."

Reed doesn't reply to that, and that's okay. I've confused the situation enough for all of us these past few days, and I don't want to continue doing that. One last conversation with Connor and then I'll tell Reed that my mind is made up.

My heart and my future belong to him.

2 3

LEIGHTON

When I called my dad to tell him I was pregnant, he wanted to book himself on the next flight from Palm Springs to New Orleans. I refused to let him, telling him that if I was going to take care of another human being, I needed to start by taking care of myself.

He agreed. Begrudgingly.

Now, as I meet him at baggage claim, I see the toll it's taken on him. He scans every inch of me, making sure I look healthy, rested, happy.

I may be none of those things fully, but I'm getting there. A wide smile takes over me, and my dad's shoulders relax.

"Hey, sweetheart," he says when he wraps me into a big hug.

"Hi, Dad. How was your flight?"

"Worth every uncomfortable minute of it. How was work?"

"It's so great, Dad. I love the freedom Fran gives us. Only a few more weeks until the launch." That's all true, but honestly, I also love that Reed is there too. He keeps a constant watch on me, even when he thinks he's being sly about it. I've also noticed that he's become something like a big brother to many of the young staff. They all go to him for his opinions, even the ones not in the art department. They look up to him, they respect him.

Today, I paid more attention to how he handles each coworker and I noticed he does the same with them as he does with me. He adapts; he switches to the part of his personality that is most effective for the situation he's in.

My grumpy Reed Turner is a fixer, a situational shapeshifter. And for the first time, I get it—the reason he didn't pursue me when I was still so young. Then, I had a wild side. I didn't shy away from a dare, even if it sent me running across campus, nude.

That happened more than once.

Reed had started with a big tech company in Seattle when we shared that first kiss. He had goals he wanted to accomplish. As did I, as soon as I grew up enough to focus on them.

The timing wasn't right.

It is now. I know now it's time to tell Reed I love him.

"I'm glad, Leighton. And Fran knows about the baby?"

"She does, and she's supportive."

"That's great, too. Now, feed me, kid. I'm starved."

"Connor is bringing food over. He's meeting us at my house."

"Just Connor?"

"Yes, I need to talk to him," I say, no longer hesitant about my decision. "To tell him I want to be with Reed."

My dad stops his trek toward the parking area, turning to look at me.

"You don't say?" he asks, a wide smile brightening his face.

"You okay with that, old man?"

"I'm better than okay with that, kid," he says, wrapping an arm around my shoulder and squeezing. "If that's what has you smiling like you got away with murder, I'm better than okay with it."

"That was a creepy way to say it," I say with a laugh.

"Where the hell do you think you get it from?"

"I hear you've been talking to him."

"We've been talking for years; I consider him a friend." There's more there than friendship, I can hear that much. "My relationship with him shouldn't be something that plays into your decision, though."

"You'd be okay if I wanted to marry Connor?"

"Did Connor propose?" he asks, stopping again to look at my face.

"No, Dad. He said he wanted to be with me, but marriage didn't come up."

"Well, for the record, whatever you choose is your decision alone. I'll be there for you no matter what. I trust you to know where your heart is."

"You have more confidence in me than I have in myself."

"Don't let fear or the past get in the way, sweetheart. You'll be okay."

***

Connor shows up with sushi.

"I remembered after I picked this up that pregnancy and sushi don't mix or something. So, I picked up some gumbo and etouffee as well." He shifts from foot to foot. I've never seen such obvious nerves from him. The Anders brothers are always poised and confident.

Maybe it's intuition, and he knows tonight things between us will change.

"Thank you, Connor. Dad will probably want a little of everything," I tell him. "Come on in."

Dad entertains Connor while I set the table and place the food out. Their conversation keeps pace throughout the meal, and I appreciate that my dad is playing interference for now. It's hard for me to eat much with the turning of my stomach.

The last thing I want to be is a heartbreaker. I don't want to hurt good people, and Connor is good people.

But he left me and only said he wanted more with me after it was revealed I was pregnant. So, I'm not sure the feelings he's proclaiming for me are genuine. Maybe we're both in a state of delusion. With the way the news has affected me, it's unfair for me to think it wouldn't be affecting Connor as well.

He'd be feeling pressure too, even if the extent of it is different.

All evening, I've imagined how our conversation will go. Connor has never shown me he isn't reasonable. I have no reason to believe he wouldn't be now, too. Except that I will ask him to not stand in the way of letting Reed be a secondary father figure to our child.

That's what I want. It's clear as day now. Marrying Reed and raising a family with him is my endgame. Even if there is never another child, I want Reed to be a strong presence in the life of this one. As its protector, caregiver, and teacher.

All while not reducing the role of Connor as the father of the baby I'm now carrying.

"I'll clean up," Dad says when they're done eating and I'm done playing with my food. A clear directive for me to straighten my spine and deal with the difficult discussion.

"Will you come sit with me out back, Connor?"

He nods and follows me out. While he takes a seat on the chaise, I stay standing, pacing around him.

"Leighton?"

"I'm not in love with you, Connor," I blurt. "I'm sorry, but I don't think it's fair for you not to know. Of course, it's going to strain things in ways, but I promise not to stand in the way of you being a father. Or from your family being a part of the baby's life. I hope you know I'd never do that."

A handful of seconds is all it takes for the words to spill out and the tears to fall. It's horrific to have to tell someone they can't be with their child every night to tuck them in and every morning be there when they wake up. And that's exactly what I said to Connor.

I would, and will, sacrifice so much for the safety and happiness of my child. Entering a relationship that in my heart I know is not one that will make either of their parents happy isn't one of those sacrifices.

Connor says nothing; he sits still with a blank stare.

"We won't make each other happy, Connor. I think you know that. I think it's why you left the way you did," I say with tears clogging my throat. "It's why I'm telling you now. This baby can't be born into a home that's already unstable."

He finally moves, only to hang his head in his hands so I can't see his face.

"I hate this, Leighton," he says, his voice breaking. "All those times my mom asked when I was going to settle down and give her grandbabies, I always cringed. It wasn't something I thought I wanted. Then you called with the news, and it was as if my view shifted. Like the colors in my vision had been muted and suddenly became so vibrant."

"What does it look like now?"

"Somewhere in between," he says, and I answer with a small sob. "Come here. Sit with me, we'll talk it all out."

He holds a hand up to me, I take it, and let him pull me down to his side. The night is chilly, so he covers me with a blanket and pulls me to his side. We both need comfort to get through this.

"Don't cry, this isn't anything we can't get through."

"Seems I cry all the time these days. There's no helping it," I say.

"I'm sorry for that. And for adding any pressure to you, that was never my intention. Both of our worlds are forever changing but you have the added stress of growing a whole other life," he says, wrapping an arm around me, his thumb drawing circles on my shoulder. "I'll be more cautious of that going forward."

"You've been fine, Connor. It's new for us all."

"It's new for Noah, too, but you'd never know it by observing him with Lorelai. He's so in tune to everything that he sees her needs before she does. While I'll be a world away when you'll be here figuring it all out alone."

Not alone, but that's beside the point right now.

"Noah is a next level clinger, though. You shouldn't try to live up to that," I say, lightening the mood when Connor laughs.

"Fuck, he really is. You know how Drew always has to be touching June if she's near?" I nod because, yeah, it's a behavior that everyone who is around the two for more than five minutes catches on to. June loves it though, so I don't judge. "Noah's worse with Lore. At least since she's been pregnant. I wouldn't be surprised if he tried to carry her everywhere, so she'd have no chance at tripping over something."

"It can't be that bad."

"Yes, it can. He made steaks the other night for dinner and wouldn't let her cut it up herself. She's usually mostly vegetarian but the pregnancy has her craving red meat. Anyway, he said she was too ravenous and out of practice at eating steak. So, he cut it up the same size he cut up Olivia's."

"Seriously?"

"No lie. Lorelai just laughed it off, though. Told him she'd put up with his bullshit, but he'd be making up for it. She's not your favorite, I know, but she's good for him. I've never seen him so happy."

"I'm happy for him," I say with all truthfulness. No, Lorelai is not my favorite. But they clearly love each other, so that's all that matters.

"I want that, too. The easiness they have, the understanding. The family." Connor's head drops back to rest on the cushion, and I feel the sigh of breath leave his chest. "I thought we could get there."

"We can, Connor. Separately though. We're not meant to be together. What we had was casualness, not easiness. That's not the same."

"Do you think you have it with Reed?" he asks, a tinge of bitterness seeping in.

The answer is on my lips right away, but I wait for the images to filter through my mind. Reed knows me better than almost anyone. In some aspects, he knows me more than any other in my life. Small moments from the past few weeks move into place like puzzle pieces creating the bigger picture. I hadn't noticed all the ways he shows he's been paying attention over the years. Reed knows all my favorite restaurants, all my favorite foods. He knows I'll skip meals if it means I don't have to prepare anything for myself. He's intuitive to my mood swings, knowing when I'm sad and why, when I need him near, or when I need him to challenge me.

Or when I need him to push me away, so I don't rotate around him like he's my own personal sun.

An older memory comes to life now, one long, long forgotten.

The day June woke up in the hospital after her stalker attacked her, I told Reed I would never let her out of my sight again. If it meant I followed her around the world for the rest of her life, I'd never let her be that vulnerable again.

Reed said she would end up in Seattle for a long time and that I'd be miserable because I need sunshine in my life. He said it was his job and Drew's job to keep her safe, that they had it covered. And under no uncertain terms was I to make career decisions based on June's whereabouts if I had better offers in other parts of the country.

Now I see that even then, he was looking out for my best interests.

Reed and June aren't so different. Empathetic in so many ways, June is more obvious about it, while Reed is stealthier. Like a big, gorgeous, helpful ninja.

Maybe all the years I've said June and I are soulmates isn't because we are, but because her brother and I are. The two are so close. My soul recognized what my brain wouldn't.

"Reed is the only man I can have that with."

"Fuck, I guess I've always known that," Connor says. "At least I know he'll make a good stepdad."

"How do you know that?" I already know that, but Connor doesn't know Reed as well.

"I've watched him with June, his mom, Drew. He's a little like Superman, waiting in the wings and observing until the other shoe falls and he steps in to save the day. It's like a special sense he has that one of them needs a little support with something and he's right there to give it."

"You've noticed that?"

"He's always been my competition." He shrugs. "I noticed everything."

"I'm not a prize to be won," I say without bite.

"You are, Leighton. Don't sell yourself short," he says into the crown of my head. "Promise you'll video chat with me often while I'm in Thailand? I don't want to miss out on all the gross pregnancy moments."

"Will you try to come home around the birth?"

"Come hell or high water," he promises. "I'll come home as often as I can until the contract is done, then I'll find something back here. I won't fuck you over on financial support, either."

"I never expected you would, and we shouldn't need much."

"What you need isn't the point. Half the DNA is mine, you'll be carrying the brunt of the care. Therefore, more than half the expenses should be my responsibility."

"If only all men were as reasonable as you," I muse.

"I'm not going to fuck this up. Our child is going to be loved, cared for, and spoiled as fuck."

"With our families? Definitely."

I include Reed's family, because they're mine and I'm theirs. Hopefully soon, that will be solidified by marriage documents, but that's something like putting the cart before the horse.

"You're a good man, Connor. Someday, the right woman is going to breeze in, knock you on your ass, and haul you off to her cave so you can make lots of beautiful babies together."

"Ah fuck, now you sound like my mother. Gross, Leighton."

"I mean it," I say, looking up at his face. "You are a good man. Thank you for making this less scary for me."

"You're a good woman. Thank you for being the mother of my child, you're going to be great at it."

Connor leans down and a searing kiss to my lips. It's telling me thank you, it's telling me goodbye. But all I hear is my mind screaming no and Ivy's voice next door as she calls out, "Darling, wait."

24

REED

As soon as the flight landed in Atlanta, I turned on my phone to find a text from Leighton.

There is also one from Drew, the only person I told I was fleeing New Orleans for a couple of nights.

I send a quick reply to him to let him know I've landed and am on my way. Then I compose what I want to say to Leighton.

Holly decided she wants to work on the ballroom ceiling at the Broussards'. We met over there last night to collaborate and take pictures of the space so she can sketch out plans. As we always do, we ended up on the balcony for an evening drink. Though you can't clearly hear the words spoken from yard to yard without the voice being raised, I caught some of the light laughter coming from Leighton and Connor.

It was the kiss that bothered me. That caused my blood to heat and burn in my veins. Those lips are mine, and there Connor was, tasting them like he has a right to.

Fuck, maybe he does.

Except last night she was mine, body and fucking soul. I can't believe that's changed so quickly. Connor said he would fight for her. As will I, but I need to clear my head with the help of my sister and my best friend.

Drew and I have never spent so much time apart, not since we met at eight. This season, I've already missed a handful of his games. My only excuse is because I've been pursuing a woman pregnant with another man's child.

My obsession has made me a shit friend and a shit brother.

ME

Last-minute decision, I flew to Atlanta for Drew's game on Sunday.

I'll fly back with June on Monday.

Drew will be following behind us to spend Christmas in New Orleans.

LOVE

Okay. I'd like to talk when you get back.

Oh, there will be plenty of talking. I don't want her worrying or stressing out, so I keep my attitude to myself.

ME

I'll let you know when I'm home. It's late, get some sleep.

JUNE

Check in, then come to room 812.

If I had to guess, June has spoken to Leighton and knows more of the situation than I do. Within an hour, I'm at the hotel, checked in, refreshed, and knocking on the door to my sister's room.

"Hey, man," Drew answers with a look of warning.

Yep, June has talked to Leighton and I'm in trouble.

"Hey, buddy. You ready for the game?"

"You know I am. It will be nice having you in the suite watching though, asshole."

"Yeah, yeah," I say. "I'll make more of an effort. Shit's just been… a lot."

"Is that Reed?" June hollers from the other side of the suite.

"Yeah, Junie."

"What the fuck, Reed?" She comes bounding up to me, not stopping until she is a foot away, tight fists on her hips.

"What?"

"Don't give me that shit," she growls. "You didn't tell her you were leaving. She was worried."

"We aren't a couple. I don't tell her about every plan I make." Though I try to keep the hurt of seeing her kiss Connor out of my tone, I fail. I hear it, and so do June and Drew.

"What happened?" June asks, concerned for me now.

"Maybe I don't want to talk about this with you?"

"Fuck that, Reed," Drew chimes in, handing me a beer he pulled out of the mini bar. "You wouldn't have picked up and flew out here on a whim if you didn't want to talk to us."

"It's possible I just missed my nosey-as-hell family."

"You can't lie to us, Reed. We see right through it," he says, waving a hand for me to sit on the small sofa.

I sit on the far end, allowing room for him with June on his lap—her favorite spot.

"Spill it," she demands. "You're both upset about something. What happened?"

"What do you want me to say, baby girl? I am in fucking love with the woman I just saw kissing the father of her yet-to-be-born baby. It sucks, and I wasn't in the mood to stick around for more."

"She kissed him," June gasps.

"Yes."

"You saw it?"

"I saw it," I confirm. "The night before, she was in my arms. She promised me she'd try to be fair, respect what we had been building together before she found out about the pregnancy. Watching them kiss hardly feels fair."

"I'm not saying that it's okay they shared a kiss," June says. "But should we be asking if it's fair to Connor that she was in your arms last night?"

It's a valid question, one I feel like I've put plenty of thought into and still haven't come up with a good answer. Regardless of what she does, he'll at least be able to call himself the father of the baby of the greatest woman I've ever known.

That's more than I have. So maybe I'm feeling irrationally jealous. I don't know, but I can't apologize for feeling it.

"I don't fucking know. I just know I don't like her kissing anyone else."

"It was just a kiss, Reed. With someone who means a lot in her life right now."

"It's not just a kiss," Drew and I say in unison.

"What does that mean?"

"Kissing is… I don't know, personal," Drew answers. "Intimate."

"That," I agree, waving a finger at my best friend. "Not everyone thinks that way. But I do, and she knows it."

"Maybe it's not what you think?"

"You talked to her, what did she say?" I ask my sister.

"That she saw you drive off when Connor left, and you weren't answering her text. I said you were on your way here and she kind of freaked out."

"Freaked out how?" Now I feel like an asshole. And yeah, I am. But fuck, I'm also only human and I deserve to have some space when needed, too. Her being upset isn't my goal, and I probably would have handled things differently if Larry wasn't there with her. She's not alone; I would have never left her alone and in distress.

"She cried mostly. Which she can't seem to stop doing these days."

"Was she crying because I was gone or because she wants me gone?"

"Reed, she'd never want you gone," Drew says.

I want to believe that, but how much easier would it be for her and Connor to move on as a family if I weren't living next door to her.

"I don't know. Maybe I should move, give her more space."

"Maybe you should quit making decisions for her and talk to her instead."

June places a hand on Drew's cheek, turning his face to hers so she can kiss him. He's speaking from experience; he made so many decisions without talking to June, he almost lost her because of them. June has had a therapist since she was attacked in college. Drew's had one since June caught him cheating on her. Therapy has done them both good, but Drew's commitment to it is as intense as his commitment to football always has been.

He's determined to better himself and never fuck up again. To never hurt my sister again.

I don't want to hurt Leighton. I don't want Leighton to *be* hurting.

But I also don't want to be hurt by Leighton.

"You're right, I should. I will. A cool off period wasn't a bad idea, though. My temper was getting the better of me, I was debating between hauling Connor to the airport and seeing him back on a plane to Thailand. Or hauling Leighton off to a dungeon where I can keep her forever."

"She'd love that last option," Drew says. June nods in agreement.

Fucking psychos… the lot of us.

"Can't very well do that with her being pregnant."

"Does that bother you?" Drew asks.

"Which part?"

"Either. Her being pregnant at all, and Connor being the dad."

"No," I answer quickly and truthfully. "I've always wanted the possibility of having kids someday. I've always only wanted them with her. That child will be just as much of her as it is him. I wouldn't love her wholly if I didn't love everything that's a part of her."

"Oh," June coos.

"Don't get too sentimental, baby girl. She hasn't professed any love to me."

"She loves you, dude."

"Yes, she does," June agrees.

"Leighton has not said that to me."

"Have you said it to her?" June asks.

"I… okay, not in so many words." I'm a dumbass on top of being an asshole. With a solid combination like that, it's no wonder she isn't falling at my feet and professing her love.

"Reed Chandler Turner," she scolds.

"Fuck, June. Don't pull out the middle name." I've always hated it. She knows it and uses it to her advantage, the little shit.

"You deserve it! How can you sit here feeling sorry for yourself when you haven't even told her how you feel?"

"It's not as if I haven't shown her," I argue.

"How?"

For the next twenty minutes, I blabber on about all the things I've done or try to do for Leighton daily. Some things she hasn't even noticed, like that her downstairs toilet no longer runs longer than it should be. Her kitchen faucet doesn't drip, and her screen door doesn't squeak. They're small annoyances but they all add up and I've been putting them to rest one by one so she could live more comfortably. Not to mention the meals, and fuck… it's not enough.

"I guess I haven't done much at all. Maybe I need a grand gesture or some shit."

"Maybe you need to talk to her and tell her exactly how you feel," Drew says, eyes rolling.

25

LEIGHTON

Reed is mad. I know he is, and I don't blame him. I was angry, too, and let Connor know in no uncertain terms. He crossed a line and took advantage of my emotions. Though he profusely apologized, it doesn't change that Reed saw and doesn't understand that I wanted no part of it.

Dad is concerned about how upset I am. All he knows is that I told Connor we couldn't be together because I'm in love with Reed, but that Reed left town unexpectedly. I didn't tell him Connor kissed me. In large part, I am protecting Connor. Because he's the father of the baby I'm carrying, and I don't want my dad to instantly be on edge around him.

I need everyone to get along for the sake of this child. Connor's infraction pisses me off, but it wasn't malicious. Just stupid. I don't believe he'll try anything like that again, he felt bad when I broke down about it. Admittedly, I was hysterical, and he didn't know what to do to calm me down.

It felt like I broke a promise to Reed, even though I pushed Connor away when my dumb, numb brain caught up to what was happening. By the time I was done berating Connor and convincing him I was calm enough for him to leave, Reed was driving away.

He didn't answer my call and waited until he was in Atlanta to answer my text. Evidence that he's mad.

But I am, too. Not just because of the move Connor pulled. But because of the shit Reed is pulling. He didn't have to run off the other night. I'm sure he's been missing Drew and June; Atlanta is so close it makes sense for him to catch the game. Reed used to go to most games, despite their location. But him not telling me, or June, until he was about to board a last-minute flight tells me he was leaving to get away from *me*.

It's the worst feeling and I've had to constantly remind myself that Reed is not my mother, and he isn't gone for good.

For the past two days, I've sulked, I've cried, I've raged. Now… I'm taking a move from his playbook. I will be the overbearing asshole all up in his face. He doesn't get to skirt me today or go hide next door at Ivy and Olive's house. June told me what time their flight lands and I'll be waiting for him.

Dad left for a walk and some last-minute gift shopping. When I walked out to the front porch with him, I stayed back, sitting on the steps so Reed can't avoid me. Except, there's a breeze and I'm a little cold. If Reed was in my position, he'd just barge into my house to wait for me. Only I don't know his door code. Unless he never changed his code either.

When Drew bought this place for us, he programmed them both with the same numbers, Reed's dad's birthday.

Moving to his door, I tentatively type in the digits. Sure enough, the lock rotates, and I open the door.

Hah!

Should I feel bad that I'm sneaking into his house? Probably. Especially since I've never been here before.

His house looks like an artist's home. The furniture is sparse, but each piece is amazing. The small entry has a long, hand-painted console table covered in vivid dark plums and blues. A large mirror hangs above, also painted but in a contrasting color pallet. It doesn't clash, though, they complement each other wonderfully.

The further I wander in, the more similar pieces there are. He doesn't have a dining table, or a sofa, but there is a large, overstuffed chair in the living room along with a television. The kitchen is stocked, and the cabinets are full of colorful dishes.

Reed doesn't live in black and white.

I take the steps upstairs slowly, only feeling a little guilty that I'm snooping through his house. Reed has had full rein of my house multiple times; I want the same this once. Maybe I'll take a nap in his bed, which will smell like him, until he gets home.

He might be upset with my breaking and entering, but if we're going to be together, he needs to let me all the way in. The same goes for me. No more games, no more confusion. It's time to be up front and blunt.

His bedroom door is the one I push open first. Again, it's hardly furnished with little more than a bed really. It's neatly made with a simple charcoal gray quilt that I pull up at the corner and bury my face in the pillow below.

Sure enough, it smells how I expected. I'm not ready to stop exploring though, so instead of curling up in the warm scent, I pull the quilt off the bed, wrapping it around me like a security blanket.

I wonder what he did with the spare room, since his mother stays at June's house now when she visits. I expect a gym or some other manly setup. What I find is something much more unexpected.

It's a studio, painted canvases filling every space. They are hung on the walls, sitting on the floor, leaning against the walls. Stacks and stacks of them. A tingle starts in my belly and quickly spreads throughout my body.

There are a handful of abstract scenery paintings, but the large majority are portraits.

Of me.

Some depict me when I was younger, back in my college days. Others portray me much more recently. It's the one perched on the easel that holds my attention the longest.

In it, my hair is the color it is now, with the slight sheen of pink. Only in the portrait, the length is longer than how I wear it. That's likely because in the painting, which shows me bare from the waist up, I'm very swollen with pregnancy. It's not crude or lurid. He shows me demurely covering my chest with one arm while the other cradles my belly.

On my left hand, there's a brilliant solitary champagne diamond, cradled between two black gold bands filled with tiny diamonds.

It's beautiful, the ring and the painting both.

Blinking back tears, I carefully finger through the paintings stacked against the walls. I recognize some of the moments, the clothes I wear in them. Many are memories we shared that he must have immortalized on canvas later.

I don't know how much time has passed, being so lost in awe I don't hear him enter his house and come upstairs.

"I may be a bigger creeper than you thought."

A smile grows on my face, but I don't turn to him.

"I always suspected, but this surpasses anything my imagination conjured."

"What are you doing here?"

"Waiting for you." I pull the quilt tighter around me.

"Did you need to break into my house to do that?" he asks from the doorway.

"It's hardly B and E when you never changed the door code."

"Touché."

"I'm mad at you, you know," I say softly.

"I'm mad, too."

Temper flares in my blood before I register he didn't say he was mad *at me*.

"You ran away."

"You kissed him."

"No, Reed. He kissed me, in the middle of an emotionally wrought conversation. He kissed goodbye to any potential romantic relationship with me after I made it clear that was not in our future."

He steps up behind me, the heat of his next words raising the hairs on the back of my neck.

"Why is a romance with the blonde one not in your future?"

"The blonde one?"

"It's what the sisters call him. Answer the question, Love." That bite I love so much is back in his voice. I like it when he tries to be bossy because it means I get to be bratty, and lately, that leads to him fucking me.

"I don't love Connor. I care about him; I'll always care about him as the father of my first-born child. But I've never been in love with him, it's not something I'm capable of."

"Why, Leighton? Say it." It's command and plea all in one.

Spinning to look at him, I take in every detail. Try to see him from an artist's eye, like he must do with me. His burnished hair is messier than usual, longer too, as it falls over one eyebrow. Intense eyes stare back at me through dark lashes above his cheekbones that have always grabbed my attention. Defined, sharp, giving him an edgier vibe to his otherwise all-American looks.

"I wonder, if I was as talented, if I could paint you from memory," I say, dropping the quilt and raising a hand to drag a finger along his jawbone.

His eyes close, as if pained, but he leans into my touch all the same.

"Fucking say it."

"You fucking say it," I snap. "You've known for longer and you've been running from it for years. You say it first."

"You think I've been running from it?"

"You certainly haven't been chasing it all these years."

"Not directly no, but I have been letting it grow. I didn't smother it, or you. I let you accomplish everything I knew you wanted."

"I wanted you," I say, pain of my own bleeding through. "I could have grown at your side, Reed. I didn't have to do it by myself."

"Do you think I don't know that? That I'm not aware of all the things that could be different right now if I hadn't made decisions by myself? I've done little else the past few days but weigh it all. Over and over and wonder if all I did was fuck everything up by giving you so much room that you filled the space with another man."

"Did you never question it before the past few days?"

"Of course I did. Look around you, Leighton. I'm hyper obsessed with you, to the point that I'm sure it's not healthy. Stupidly, I thought I had time. I thought you needed time. Then you met Connor. When that seemed to have fallen apart, I was determined to never let you get away again. Then..."

"Then I found out I was having a baby," I finish for him. Reed has never acted like me having Connor's baby is a deal breaker for him. Is that what he's saying now? Has he decided it's too much? "Is… is it too much to ask? For you to be in my life when I'm having his baby."

"How could you think that, Leighton?" Reed takes both my hands in his. He brings them up to his mouth and rubs his lips against my knuckles.

"Because you ran away," I cry. "Do you know how that felt? You didn't give me a chance to explain what happened or to tell you that I choose you. That I will always choose you. I worried that…"

I grow quiet, except for the hiccupping breaths as I try to control my crying.

"Hey." He wraps his arms around me, pulling me into his chest. "I'm sorry I scared you. That wasn't my intention, and I didn't properly think it through. I'm not her, Love."

"How can I trust that?"

"You choose that too, choose to trust me. Have faith in the ghoulish compulsion I have to be all up in your business. It hasn't subsided, it's only grown." That gets the laugh he's looking for. I shake with it against him. "Eyes to me, Love."

I use his shirt to wipe my face first, making him laugh right along with me. When my face upturns, he takes in my red eyes, that have been slightly bloodshot for the past couple of days due to my shit sleep.

"I'm not leaving. Ever. I love you."

"You do?"

"Fuck, Leighton," he says, exaggerating his exasperation. "Baby, how can you still not believe it? You are Ariadne to my Dionysus. The constellations don't exist without you."

"You know Greek Mythology, too?"

"Too?"

"You're an amazingly wonderful artist, you're an exceptional caregiver, there is no man more handsome than you." I tick off my fingers with each attribute. "You don't only fuck me like I like, you surpass it and surprise me. And now you prove you're smart, too. What do I offer this partnership?"

"Don't do that, Leighton. You know your worth. I know it, too, and I'm never going to ask you to prove it to me."

My eyes flicker back and forth on him, but I'm not questioning my love for him. I'm letting it settle. My brain is filing away all the facts, all the details forming the bigger picture. When I see the same possibilities for our life that he does, he recognizes it, and a smile twitches to life on his mouth.

"I love you, Reed."

"Fuck yeah, you do, Love." He frames my head with his warm hands and kisses me like it's our first time all over again.

26

REED

I sent Leighton home soon after her proclamation. She's exhausted, worn to the bone.

Because of me.

So, I asked her to take a nap while I shower, change, and work up a plan for dinner for us and Larry. It takes longer than I expected, but a couple hours later, I'm at her place setting the table with her father while Mediterranean chicken and vegetables roast in the oven.

Connor Anders called me earlier. It's what delayed me.

The blonde one wants to meet. I'm not sure if it's the best decision for him to be coming straight to me instead of involving Leighton. She won't like that. While I agreed to the chat, I have no intention of disrespecting her that same way.

We'll be discussing it tonight, along with some other things.

"I'm glad you're back, son," Larry says, placing the last of the silverware and napkins.

"Me too, I'm sorry I worried her. I wasn't thinking clearly."

"She's more emotional than usual, and it's still so early."

"True. I'll do better," I promise.

"I will, too."

We hear her footfalls on the stairs before she comes into our view, looking refreshed.

"What smells so good?"

"Dinner," I say. "There's also some decaffeinated tea in the kettle."

"Thank you," she says, raising to her toes to press a kiss on my chin.

"What's this?" Larry asks, all his teeth showing under a wide smile.

"We're together, Dad. Reed loooooves me," she elongates the word in a singsong voice.

"No shit, kid. He told me that years ago. Glad you finally came around," Larry says with a wink.

"What do you mean he told you?" Her hands go to her hips as her head bounces between us.

"When June was in the hospital." He waves a hand dismissively. "Reed told me he was going to marry you someday, when the time was right for both of you."

"You what?" Leighton turns now with both a redness on her cheeks and water pooling in her eyes.

"Baby, don't cry. You already know I've been in love with you for ages. This isn't really new information."

"You told my dad before you told me," she playfully pouts.

"Couldn't be helped. It spilled out while I was waxing on about how perfect you are," I say to her now smiling face.

"You love me a lot, huh? If you were a vampire, you'd turn me to keep me forever."

"You are so weird." I laugh in time with Larry's chuckle. "But, yes."

"I knew it!"

"All right, you nutjobs, let's eat," Larry says, placing the baking dish on the trivet on the table.

Near the end of the meal, Leighton is tearing up again. Over asparagus. I can't explain.

"This is ridiculous," she whines. "It can't be normal to be crying because I'm going to have asparagus pee."

"It's not that abnormal. Your mother was the same way when she was pregnant with you," Larry says.

Everyone grows still and quiet.

Leighton's mother, Beth, is not a subject either of them talk about.

Ever. It's hard to expect what Leighton's reactions will be when she's in the middle of being distraught over a vegetable.

Okay, maybe not that hard.

"I am not like her." Her voice is steel.

"You are, though. In the good ways. You have the best parts of her, the ones that made me love her," Larry says. Maybe it's because love is in the air, or new life, but it seems Larry is feeling sentimental. He sounds a little sad and wistful.

I feel for him. He's loved no other woman than the one who left him. I couldn't imagine Leighton leaving, disappearing for good, with hardly a word. Larry once told me he knew she was alive and living a life somewhere else. Why, and how he knew, wasn't something he revealed. But I know he kept tabs for long enough to know she left by choice, not by foul play.

He tried telling Leighton once or twice when he thought she was old enough to understand, but she refused to hear anything about her mother. It's a bitter subject.

"Dad," she says, but stops herself.

"You can be mad at her, sweetheart, she's earned that. But you need to know that she wasn't all bad. I wouldn't have loved her if she was. Despite what decisions she made, you aren't bound to follow in her footsteps because you learned from her. You're bound to be better because you learned how not to be like her."

Reaching over, I grip her hand in mine and watch one tear spill out and race down her cheek.

"You're right," she says, resigned. "I'll be the best mommy. Until the day I die."

"You will be," he agrees.

"I'll clean up, you guys go relax," she says, rushing to stand and gather the plates. We let her; she needs the minute to gain her bearings.

I need the minute myself.

"Damn Beth," Larry says under his breath when we settle in the living room to wait for Leighton.

"We'll be okay, Larry," I tell him.

"I know, son. I know you will. You see her better than she sees herself. Take care of her, or I'll haunt you in this life and the fucking next." He turns showing me the fucking scariest smile creeping over him.

"Goddamn, you Wards are a strange bunch." I laugh, and he joins in.

"You fit right in."

Leighton wanders in a few minutes later, spying the small gift bag I set on her coffee table.

"What's that?" she asks, taking a seat between her father and I on the sofa.

"We'll get to that in a minute. First, I want to talk to you about something."

"What?" She turns toward me.

"Connor called me. He wants to meet up to talk."

"About?"

"I can't be sure. But if I had to guess, he wants to talk about you and your baby."

"Why just to you?"

"Don't know." I shrug. "I'll find out, but I won't keep you out of the loop. Okay?"

"Okay. Thank you." She looks confused, mixed with concern. I don't like the latter.

"Peek into the bag there, Love."

"Is this where you keep the locks of my hair you've secretly stashed away all these years?" she jokes.

"Something like that." I laugh lightly. "Open the damn bag, or are you too scared?"

"Hardly," she retorts, giving the word all the bravado she can muster. But I see the tremble of her fingers. "What is this?"

"Start with the red."

There are three small boxes in the bag. The red is the oldest. Well-worn from me rubbing it with my thumb for so many years. If she examines it for even the briefest time, she'll notice.

When she flips it open, she finds a single, modest solitary diamond set in a simple yellow gold band.

"I bought that one when I was first sure. You were twenty-three years old. I carried it with me anytime you and I were in the same city. Just in case the time felt right."

"First sure of what?" she asks, knowing but needing to hear me say it.

"That someday I'd ask you to spend the rest of your life as my wife. Open the blue next."

The middle box is the one from Tiffany's. Inside is a bright cushion cut diamond, as opposed to the round of the first ring. This one is set in platinum, and more than a couple of carats bigger.

"I upgraded around your twenty-sixth birthday. I could afford better, and that one was closer to what I had wanted to purchase for you originally." I lean forward and see her tears welling again. I pull her onto my lap and wrap my hands around to rest on her stomach. "Don't cry, Love. Open the last one."

Her hands tremble now that she puts the second box down and reaches for the third, already knowing what she'll find. The split lid pops open smoothly to reveal the same ring I painted on her finger in the portrait that sits on my easel.

"Reed," she gasps. It's more beautiful in real life. I'm good, but I couldn't get its brilliance right.

"This one I bought the day after your doctor confirmed your pregnancy. After I knew it was Connor's baby growing inside you. It has three bands because it wouldn't be just you and I heading up our family. Connor would always have a voice. I have no qualms about being a partner with him in parenting. I need you to know that, believe it."

"You've carried a ring around for five years? Without us ever even dating? You and Drew are too much alike."

"Yes. When you know, you know. I've known for a long time and have been waiting for you to catch up."

I rub circles on her stomach with one hand, and move up the other to land over her heart as I hold her back close to my front. She lets her head fall back to rest on my shoulder and take it all in. Giving herself the time to let all the years she's known me settle into a fresh view.

To let all the things she thought she knew warp into new meaning. It's like shining a light on all the dark spots and seeing them clearly for the first time.

"I'm still a little mad at you," she says. "For never talking to me about this. And for leaving the other night."

"You can be a little mad at me for the rest of our lives if you want. I'd just prefer you do it with one of those rings on your finger."

"Is that your idea of a happy ever after, Reed? Me being a little mad at you," she wonders aloud. It is, honestly. Not being mad but having the fun we have when I'm a bear and she's poking at me. Maybe that's not everyone's fantasy. It is mine.

"My idea of a happy ever after is loving you until the day I collapse, and you loving me back," I tell her, turning her in my arms so we can see each other's faces. "It's having the family you've always wanted. It's giving you, and whatever children are involved, security and happiness. It's being called son by Larry, and it having a greater meaning. Happy ever after is you and June being able to say you are sisters, and it, too, meaning something deeper. It's being able to tell you I love you every day for the rest of our lives and hearing you say it back."

"I do, you know?"

"I know, Love. You going to be mine now? For good?"

"For good."

"Then pick a ring, kid. Before I'm swimming in tears over here," Larry says, quickly wiping his eyes.

27

REED

She picked the third one. Leighton said she liked the meaning behind it. All three rings belong to her; she can rotate them around for all I care. Or not wear one at all. If we're committed to each other, I don't need proof of that sitting on our fingers.

The choice is hers.

We're back at my place now, she's sleeping here because I can't wait to sink into her and I'm not sure we'll be quiet enough. Larry loves us, but not that much.

"I'm sorry I left. A change of scenery with my best friend seemed like a good idea at the time."

"I understand needing some space to gain perspective," she says. "But you need to tell me if you need that."

"Agreed. It won't happen again," I promise her.

"Nor will a kiss with Connor."

"I know." Connor and I have much to talk about, that kiss is just one of them. "You're going to be my wife, Leighton."

As she blinks up at me, I unbutton the row of small pearls that fasten the front of her dress. One by one while she gathers herself. I can almost picture the scenes flashing in her mind.

Images of what our future may look like. When the dress is

unfastened and I'm dragging it over her shoulders, she still hasn't answered.

"I'm never leaving you, baby. It's you and me forever, no matter what. Do you hear me?"

"Yes," she whispers.

"Do you believe me? Do you trust me?"

"Yes."

"I'm going to be the best husband to you, the best stepdaddy to this baby, the best dad to any others that may come. Okay?"

Reaching around, I undo the clasp of her bra and drag it down as well. Then I kneel to help her out of her flats and the tiny panties she wears.

She nods.

"How have you been feeling the last couple of days?" I pull my clothes off, quickly dropping them onto the pile with hers.

"Good."

"That's great, Love," I say. "I'm going to fuck you against the wall. I want to make sure you can handle it." The things I want to do to this woman. So many things. I'll need the rest of our lives to accomplish it all.

I'm determined to have it.

"I'll handle whatever you throw at me."

"There's a long list, Love. After this baby is born and you're all healed, I'm going to fill your cunt with honey marinated fruit and eat it out of you. That's at the top of our future plans."

"What else is on your list, Turner?" she asks as her eyes curtain with lustful haze.

"I've never been in that juicy ass, so that's there of course. And I definitely want to paint you."

"Paint me?" She's confused because I have a room full of paintings of her.

"I want to paint your body, Love. And fuck you while it's still wet."

"That sounds messy," she says, wrapping her arms around my neck. I grasp her ass and lift her so her legs can encircle my hips.

"You're not afraid of messy," I say as I thrust up into Leighton's perfect heat.

"Fuck, you're so hard," she says as her voice hitches.

"I've been stone since you told me you love me. It's been a very uncomfortable night." I back up the couple of steps needed for Leighton's back to settle against the wall. I lean forward to kiss her, but she darts her head aside. Raising an eyebrow at her, I move in again. And again, she dodges it. "You're not going to let me kiss you?"

"You didn't give me any foreplay," she huffs.

"Because your pussy was dripping wetness onto the tip of my dick, baby. I knew you needed it as badly as me." I continue thrusting into her, slowly and sweetly proving my damn point when she clenches around my dick hard enough that I know she doesn't want to lose it. "Do you feel how hard you're squeezing me?"

"Yes."

"Your cunt loves my cock as much as I love you." Moving one hand, I weigh her heavy tit in my palm. Soon, they'll swell. "Fuck, I can't wait to see how your body is going to change."

"I'm going to get stretch marks." She laughs.

"That's sexy as hell, baby," I tell her. "It's just a mark of the power you hold to nurture life. Now fucking kiss me, Love."

Finally, she moves her mouth, licking a long stroke over my chin, then parting my lips with her tongue. I twirl my thumb over her hard nipple, keeping my pace as slow as the one I'm holding with my dick. She tastes like… life.

She's my future and though it makes no sense, I want to fuck that feeling into her.

Keeping one hand firmly gripped on her ass and the other tangling in the long champagne locks trailing down her back, I bounce her harder on my dick. Her hands come up to pull at my hair as she takes control of the kiss.

My dick grows slick from her own wetness, making me more comfortable pushing harder into her. So hard she gasps into my mouth.

"My cock is the last one you ever get to feel," I say against her mouth.

"It's the only one I've ever truly craved, so, okay."

"Good answer, baby."

"This cunt is the only one you get. You're okay with that?"

"Yes, there is none better," I punctuate it with another kiss. Slipping out of her and placing her feet on the floor, I spin her to face the wall. "On your toes, ass out, and arch that back for me."

Kneeling behind her and spreading her ass cheeks, I start as far forward as I can, then drag my tongue back. Feeling her shiver and squirm spur me on. Circling around her ring a few times, I work up her wildness before pushing the tip of my tongue in.

"Oh, fuck," she whispers and pushes her ass back further onto my tongue.

I hum at her eagerness, the vibration nearly making her lose balance. "Push your hands on the wall, baby, I won't let you fall. But I'm going to be busy eating your pussy until your cum drips from my chin."

"Jesus."

"Come as much and as often as you want, Love. I'll be here until you're too spent to stay upright, then I'll move you to the bed and fuck you all over again."

I make good on my promise and work her over with my tongue, lips, and fingers until she comes twice. When her clit is sensitive and pulsing, I drag a finger through her folds and pull her wetness to her pucker, pushing it in a few times.

"Oh, shit. Reed, I can't. I can't stand anymore."

Rising up behind her, I snuggle in close, pushing my dick into the crease of her ass and covering her breasts with my hands.

"You need a break, Love?" I ask in her ear.

"No, I need you inside me. I want you closer than ever before." Emotion spills out of her—love and passion. It's promise, though, that I hear most.

"Come on, then." Picking her up with the care she deserves, I move her to the bed. Leighton will always be precious, but when she's less fragile, we can have longer bouts of raw sex. She needs something different. "How do you want it, Love?"

"You on your knees. I want to watch you as you watch yourself slide in and out of me."

Fuck.

"Those are the sexiest words I've ever heard, Leighton."

She raises her knees, pulling them closer to her core. It allows me space and the view she wants me to have, her luscious pussy, slightly pinker than usual due to the work it has put in tonight. I rise up on my knees, too. Giving her a show as I dip my fingers into her to collect enough of her juices to coat my dick. Her eyes follow my hand as I massage it in, the blush usually only showing on her cheeks flushes down to her chest.

Her next orgasm won't take much, she's so worked up already.

"This what you want? This cock?"

"Yes, Reed," she says on a moan, her hands snaking over her body. One lands on a breast, propping it up as if on offer. The other moves to dip inside herself. "Right here."

Bending, I latch onto the hard nipple, sucking and pulling enough to make her writhe, her hips flinching up. She keeps her hand there, pushing her breast into my mouth. Her other hand gives herself pleasure below, and I can feel it against my stomach. Pushing her hand away with my dick, I use the tip to take up the rhythm her hand was making.

"Reed," she cries. "Fuck me."

Giving no warning, I thrust in.

"Thank you." She sighs, making me laugh. When I lift off her tit, her sight is already on me. I hold her gaze for a minute before moving it to where I shift inside her. My cock as swollen as her pussy… it's fucking beautiful. I may have to paint this someday. The sisters next door would probably pay a fortune for it, but I'm not sharing Leighton's body with anyone.

Increasing my speed slowly, I watch for every sign that she's close. Occasionally flicking my sight to her and seeing that she's still fixed on my face is about to make me blow. She loves looking at me, and it gives me a sense of pride that I'm the man she wants. The one she's chosen. The one that gets to spend the rest of her life with her. The only one that gets to be this close, this intimate with her.

"Love," I call in awe of this moment. It finally all feels real, her and I cemented for good. Forever.

"Come for me, Reed. Let me see. Let me feel it."

I won't fall apart alone. Sucking my thumb into my mouth, I wet it thoroughly, then spit down on to her clit. Rubbing it around with my thumb, I drive her crazy enough to hit another orgasm. This one pulling me over the edge with her. I spill inside her, then pull out to let some spread over her lower abdomen. My chest heaves in time with hers.

In sync.

Careful not to place my weight on her, I fall on top of her, my lips landing on hers. Keeping the kiss soft, I roll us over so Leighton can sprawl atop me. My hands roam her back, soothing as her heart rate calms.

"First night of the rest of our lives," Leighton muses. A sense of peace rushes through me, never having felt so content with life as I do right now.

"It's just the beginning," I tell her, pressing a kiss to the top of her head. "I love you."

Leighton stretches up, her elbows coming to rest on either side of my head.

"I love you, too," she says. There's no longer any fear or apprehension in either her eyes or her voice, only enhancing my contentment. "Thank you."

"For what?" I ask, confused.

"For so much, Reed. For being what I need, when I need it. For not giving up when we found out I was pregnant. For including my dad in our future. For wanting me to be a part of your family."

"You don't need to thank me for any of that."

"I think if you knew the caliber of most single men out there, you'd not be saying that." She grins.

"Most single men out there are fuckheads."

"Truth." Her gears are turning, and I wait them out. "You spend a lot of time next door."

"I do. Do you want to know why?"

"If you want to tell me."

"I want to tell you everything, Love," I tell her. "The sisters have adopted Holly and me, in a way. Introduced us to their artist friends. But they've also commissioned us to paint the ceiling in their ballroom."

"Really?" Her head pops up in surprise. "What are you painting?"

"An orgy."

"Oh my god, I should have guessed. Will you paint us into it?"

"You're a dirty girl, Leighton Ward."

28

LEIGHTON

Reed and I decided not to tell anyone but my dad about our relationship status until they made it here for Christmas. Now that we're all gathering at June and Drew's for an early Christmas Eve dinner, I'm oddly nervous about it.

There isn't a reason to be, this was my family before Reed and I were a couple. They'll be my family regardless.

June, Drew, and Janet, who is Reed and June's mother, all arrived late last night. I haven't seen any of them yet, so they haven't seen the substantial ring sitting on my finger. Not that they'll need to see that to know Reed and I are officially together. The biggest indicator is that he dotes on me. The past two days have been full of Reed tending to any need I have.

It's been glorious. He's even made a habit of rubbing my feet.

"You're growing a whole-ass human in there; the least I can do is try to ease some of the burden," he said last night.

The reassurance that I'm not on my own in this pregnancy is a relief. He says he's here for the duration, for life. More than anything, I want to trust that. And I do. But what if that changes? What if life gets in the way somehow? Like it did with my mother.

There's no room for that worry today, though. Reed reminds me by squeezing my hand and leading me through the front door of the McKenna's home.

Drew spots us first, a huge smile taking over when he notices our entwined fingers.

"It's about damn time, you two," he says before pressing a kiss to my cheek and doing that weird fist bump shit guys do with Reed. "Junie's going to freak out."

"About what?" June asks, walking up behind her husband. Reed raises our linked hands to her. "Oh my god! Really?"

Her eyes brighten but she hasn't seen the whole picture yet. She hasn't seen my other hand. Janet joins us in the foyer, hearing the squeals of excitement from her daughter.

"What's happening?" Janet asks my dad, who followed us inside.

"Our kids finally pulled their heads out of their assholes," he says with a smile.

"Oh, it's about time," she echoes Drew.

"Why does everyone keep saying that," Reed says with sarcasm.

"What is that?" Janet whispers, pointing to my other hand.

June grabs my hand, raising it to her face and instantly breaking out in tears.

"Damnit," I whine. "If you cry, I'll cry!"

"We're going to be sisters," June basically wails as she pulls me from Reed so she can wrap her arms around me. As expected, I cry right along with her. We aren't alone, Janet joins in, too.

"You're already sisters in the ways that matter," Reed reminds her.

"But it will be, like, legal now too."

After a few moments, we all calm down. The men break off to do manly talk, and us women make our way into the kitchen where Janet is finishing dinner.

"How have you been feeling, dear?"

"Better. The morning sickness isn't every day and settling things with Connor has helped ease some stress," I answer Janet.

"I'm sure," she says. "I can only imagine how hard it is to navigate the situation. Especially with geography in the way. I hope he knows we'll take good care of you and the babe."

"I'll make sure he knows," I say, voice a cloggy mess.

"I'm getting another daughter and a grandbaby."

"Oh, Mom," June soothes her with a hug.

The evening progresses like this. Dry eyes turning wet at the drop of a dime. It takes barely anything to bring on the waterworks, but they're all happy tears and I wonder what I was ever nervous about.

This is my family, and they hold me in their hearts as I hold them. Completely.

Walking back home for the night, I stop at the mailbox to grab today's delivery, only to find a thick envelope with a return address in Texas. The name I don't recognize is Temple Alderman.

Dear Leighton,

Writing you this letter is difficult. I beg you to bear with me.

I was raised by a single mother. A woman who struggled and with many issues. She was an addict for most of my life, and often fell into deep bouts of depression. Sometimes she'd ramble about things, people, I didn't know or understand.

Until now.

I apologize for delivering the news this way, it isn't ideal, but I didn't want to intrude on your life any more than what was necessary. My mother recently passed away in a car accident. A truth I need to share with you because I've found out that she was your mother, as well.

After her passing, I found a box I'd never seen before. In it were trinkets she placed in there for safekeeping over the years. As well as a journal. I've included it, as I believe it's meant for you. Again, I'll offer an apology because I read it. Twice. I thought it might help me gain some insight, and it has.

I hope you can gain some, too. She kept track of you over the years.

For all her faults, of which there were many, I think she loved us both in her way.

I'm not like her.

Take your time with it all, Leighton. And if you'd ever like to talk, or meet the brother you likely didn't know existed, I'll be here. But if you don't, I'll understand. No pressure.

With Care,

Temple

"Love, what is it?" Reed asks me. But it's my father I hand the letter to.

"I have a brother," I say weakly. "My mother is dead, and I have a brother."

Reed curses, low and deep. Neither of us take our eyes off my father. Bizarrely, the knowledge that she's died isn't as shocking as the idea that I have a brother in the world. He's not even that far away according to the return address in Beaumont.

Dad eventually passes the letter to Reed, who scans it quickly.

"You okay, sweetheart?"

"I think," I answer my father. "Are you?"

"It's something I've been expecting every day since she left. That was almost twenty-five years ago. It's oddly settling, as messed up as that sounds," he says. He's trying for stoic strength, but I hear the sadness there. "I won't have to guess anymore."

"Understandable," I say a little numbly.

"Do you want to read the journal?" Reed asks.

I pull it out of the large envelope, which he takes from me and sets aside. It's not anything fancy, a simple composition notebook with worn edges and frayed corners. I flip the pages, not reading anything but taking in that it's full of writing, doodles, paragraphs here and there that are scratched out.

The back cover has my address written on it underneath a newspaper clipping of my picture from years ago when I did some freelance work for a newspaper in Houston.

"I'm not sure. Maybe not just yet."

"It's your call, kiddo."

"Do you want to read it?" I ask my dad.

"It won't change anything," he says with a shrug. "But I wouldn't mind."

"You knew her," I say, handing the notebook to him without hesitation. "Maybe you'll be able to glean something out of it."

"Maybe," he muses. "I'll give it back to you when I'm done."

With that, he retires to his room for the night. I'm sure he wants to be alone to reconcile his feelings. I cannot imagine what he's feeling, or will feel reading through Beth's words.

"You okay, baby?"

"I think so." I turn my face up to Reed's so he can see the truth of my words. "I'm more worried about Dad. But hopefully, he finds some sort of peace hidden in those words."

"He might," Reed agrees.

"Does it make me a bad person that I'm not feeling mournful?"

"No, I think it makes you honest. You didn't know her. Maybe it would make sense to mourn the idea that you could have known her someday, but you never expected that to happen. Did you?"

"No. I broke up with that fantasy when I was nine." Truthfully, maybe it was around the age of eleven. But I was young, regardless, when I learned she was never coming back. Maybe it was intuition, maybe it was just self-preservation. Either way, I knew I needed to be done hoping for her return.

"And what about this brother?"

"I want to meet him."

"Yeah?"

"Yes. Of that, I'm sure. Will you go with me?"

"Of course, Love. Where you go, I go." It's a promise he seals with a long kiss.

29

REED

I t's almost New Year's when Connor and I meet. He's staying at Noah's house, and I agreed to go there as opposed to him coming to Leighton's or my house. Only because I can't expect how this conversation will go and I want to avoid upsetting her.

Lorelai opens the door. It's still a strain to be more than forcefully polite to her. I've come to learn more about her, and I know the affair she had with my brother-in-law was not only her fault, or even at her suggestion. The details don't make it easier to know how to interact with her.

"Hi, Reed," she greets, stepping aside for me to enter her home.

"Hey, Lorelai. How are you doing?" I gesture to her tummy.

"I'm good, a lot of fluttering in there today. It's not something I'm quite used to yet."

"Fluttering?"

"Mmhm, it feels like I swallowed a live butterfly. I don't know how else to explain it, really."

"It's all pretty fucking new to us all, isn't it?"

"Oh, that was a bad one! You should put lots of coins in the jar," Olivia scolds, poking her head around the wall from which she was hiding behind.

"Sorry," I say to Lorelai.

"It's fine, Reed," she says with a kind smile. "She's heard Noah say that one on more than a few occasions."

"It's his favorite," Olivia agrees. "You're Miss June's brover."

"Brother," Lorelai enunciates.

"Brothver," Olivia tries.

"That was closer," I tell the child. "And yes, I'm Miss June's brother. My name is Reed, remember?"

"Sure." She nods with such exaggeration it's reminiscent of a bobblehead. "I'm Olivia. But they call me Livi cuz I haven't grown into my name yet."

"What? Who told you that?" Lorelai asks with humor.

"Connor. He said I need a littler name because I'm a shrimp," she says, tiny fists moving to her hips. "Is it cuz I eat so many shrimps?"

"Nah, Livi. It just takes time to grow bigger. You'll get there. Someday you'll be as big as your sister."

"Cool! Thanks, Miss June's brothver."

"You're welcome, shrimps Livi." She smiles wide with her overly large front teeth before running off.

"Follow me," Lorelai says. "We'll find Connor."

We do, in a small library with large windows overlooking a lush lotus pond outside.

"Thank you, Lorelai," I say as she leaves us alone. She smiles warmly but I see the bit of guilt she still carries. It's not so easy for her to be around me, either. Something we'll both work through for the child Leighton carries.

"Thanks for coming, Reed," Connor says, reaching a hand for me to shake. It's formal and weird, but I'll play along.

"No problem. What did you need?" I follow him to two overstuffed chairs set by the windows, both of us taking a seat.

"It's important to me that we're all dealing with the situation like adults, with proper respect for both Leighton and the baby. I don't want pettiness or bullshit to get in the way," he says. If Connor was like his brother, this could come across as a pompous directive. But Connor isn't as stuffy as Noah; he's reserved, for sure, but he doesn't carry the same aloofness as the elder Anders brother.

"That's important to me, too."

"You love her. Truly?" They don't say that the eyes are the window to the soul for nothing. If you're paying enough attention, you can read so much more from a look than from words. Connor knows the answer to the question he asked. What he's asking is something deeper.

I trust he cares for Leighton as more than the mother of his child. He wants her to be loved and cared for, but he's not only asking about her. He's asking me if my love for Leighton transfers to her child.

"More than I love anyone, Connor. Leighton comes before anything right now. When your baby is born, they'll take that first spot. It wouldn't be love if I didn't make her priorities mine, if I didn't love who she loves most. And who she'll love most is your baby."

"I won't be home for close to two years. You understand?" He swallows hard, his index finger tapping an indistinguishable tempo on the arm of the chair. Clear nerves, though he doesn't break his eye contact.

"I understand. Completely. I'll take the best care of your baby, Connor. Treat it like my own, but I won't interfere in your relationship. I want to be a partner, not a replacement."

Connor's jaw relaxes, some of the tension melting away.

"I'm trusting you, Reed. To keep your word, and to keep them both safe and happy."

"I appreciate that, Connor. And I don't take it for granted."

"My family has discussed it. They'd like to get to know you better as well. They already adore Leighton, but as long as you're with her, they'll consider you family too," he says with serene sincerity.

"I am with her and I'm never going to give her a cause to change that," I say. "I've asked her to marry me."

"She said yes, of course?"

"She did."

"Good. I think she's wanted that for a long time."

"For what it's worth, I'm sorry. I made stupid decisions thinking I knew what was best for her. I didn't really take into consideration that there could be collateral damage." That's the truth of it. My selfishness in waiting and keeping quiet has caused real consequences that I'm not the one paying for. It's not fair to Connor that he loves a woman whose heart was already taken but not claimed. "I wouldn't change it, because it's a path that's bringing a new life into families that want to shower it with love. But I am sorry that the cards are falling the way they are."

"With me in Thailand for two fucking years, while my firstborn child is born here."

"Yes. I'll help any way I can to ease that for you. You know Leighton will, as well." What that entails, I don't yet know. Lots of video calls, I imagine. I hope Connor's work will let him come back often enough to not feel as if he's missing his baby's first year of life. It's not my burden to carry, but I feel the weight of it regardless.

"I know she will. I care about her, Reed. A lot. I know she wouldn't be with a man who isn't worthy of her. Knowing June, seeing you around this past year, I know you'll treat my child well," he says. "That being said, you hurt either one of them and I'll make it my life mission to end you."

This is the first time I've witnessed any real protectiveness from Connor Anders. All the time he and Leighton dated, he never gave off any possessiveness or jealousy. Any observer would have thought the two were dating casually. I only knew differently because I know Leighton.

"I'd expect nothing less," I tell him with a smile. "My sentiment would be no different if our places were reversed."

"Oddly, that makes me feel better." Maybe that's what Leighton saw in him, he's a little demented like us.

"We can be friends, Connor. I know that's not ideal for you, but we can give your child the best life. Together."

"Agreed," he says after a beat. "Thank you again, Reed."

"When do you fly back?"

"Tomorrow. I'll come home in February for the wedding. After that, I don't know." He looks distant, sad even.

"We'll work it out as best we can. When you're home in February, maybe we can get together with the families, have dinner," I suggest to make him feel hopeful in some small way.

"I'd like that, Reed."

"Just no more kissing my future wife," I tell him.

"Fuck, man. I'm sorry about that. It wasn't my best move."

"No, but we've both made shitty decisions where Leighton is concerned. Let's agree to do better and put the rest behind us," I suggest.

"Deal."

Just then, Noah strides into the room dressed in a flashy plaid, tailored suit. His hands are in his pockets as if he has no care in the world. Maybe, that's true.

"Everything good?" he asks us.

"You know it is, you overbearing prick," Connor teases. "I know you've been eavesdropping from the hallway."

"Guilty as charged," Noah says, raising his hands in the air. "Just being cautious."

"Nosey, Noah. It's called nosey," Lorelai says, also entering the room.

"Shouldn't you be with Olivia?" he asks her, playfully rolling his eyes at her.

"She's watching a movie with Delilah."

I recall June and Leighton mentioning Lorelai's cousin coming to live with them. Delilah, like both Olivia and Lorelai, escaped their family's polygamist compound. It's hard to imagine the life the girl has lived to this point. I don't know her, but I'm glad she has the Anders looking out for her.

"Would you like anything to drink, Reed?" Noah asks.

"No, thank you. I think I'll head out. Unless there's more you want to talk about, Connor?"

"No, we covered it. You'll keep me apprised of anything I need to be aware of?"

"Of course."

"Thank you," he says, once again shaking my hand. This time, he looks more at ease doing it.

"I'll walk you out," Noah offers, and I follow him out. "I thought all our lives were tangled together before, but you all had to add your own knots to the web, eh?"

"Seems fate wants us all connected no matter how hard we all fight it," I say.

"We're all good at fighting though, aren't we?"

"Some of us more than others, I'd say. Leighton and I don't fight. Not exactly, anyway."

"That's not true, my friend," Noah says. "You and Leighton fought against your destiny, and then you fought for it. Now you can retire your swords and bask in the treasures won."

"Good point, Noah. I guess I'll be seeing even more of you now."

"You can fucking count on it, Reed."

"Noah! Coins," Olivia yells from behind some door somewhere. I glance around but she's nowhere to be seen.

"She's a ninja one minute and a tornado the next." He laughs.

Smiling, I decide I'm looking forward to having one or two ninja tornadoes around the house myself. An idea forms in my head and I submerge myself in it on my walk home, stopping to pick up food since I haven't grocery shopped in too many days.

An hour later, Leighton finds me at my kitchen table, laptop open, and hanging up from a call with my sister.

"What's this?" she asks, looking at the screen of my computer.

"A house I want us to go look at."

"For what?"

"Love," I say as I pull her onto my lap. "We're going to have a baby soon, and maybe more in the near future. I love our duplex here, but it's not very big. We could renovate it, make it a single family. But then I thought what if we found a place of our own, big enough for whatever family we grow. That would free up this place to give Larry some privacy while he visits. And I thought my side could be a home base for Connor when he comes back to town. We could turn the studio into a room for the baby. At least until he moves back from Thailand. Then… I don't know. Maybe Lorelai will have another wayward family member that needs a safe place to stay."

"You've thought a lot about it already?"

"I'm obsessive, in case you haven't noticed," I tell her. "This one is only two blocks away, in between here and Noah's."

"It's pretty," she says, flipping through the pictures of the old, stately four bedroom. It's already been renovated and is ready. There would be nothing to do but furnish it. "But pricey. How can we afford that?"

"By painting an orgy on the ceiling of two extremely eccentric sisters who live next door."

"How much are they paying you?" she asks, shocked. She's been in their home several times; she knows their ballroom isn't all that large. Though it will take Holly and I months and months of free time to complete it, I have the money stashed away. Perks of your best friend slash brother-in-law being filthy rich. He pays way more than his share and I've been able to save up between that and living frugally, in general. Buying this house, or one like it, will wipe out those savings as a down payment, but it's worth it and the Broussards' commission will pay it back.

"A lot, Love. Enough to get us into a home where we can raise a family."

"I'm going to have to stop calling you Grumpy Reed now, aren't I?"

"Is that what you call me?" I laugh.

"In my head, yeah." She shrugs.

"Do you know what I call you in my head?"

"What?" she asks, crinkling her nose as if she's afraid to know.

"Mine."

EPILOGUE 1. LEIGHTON

"I'm nervous."

"That's understandable, but I'm right here with you," Reed says as we walk into the coffee shop in Beaumont, Texas.

Two weeks after I received Temple's letter, I wrote him one of my own. We kept it in the pen pal stage for a month, until I was ready for more. Which wasn't until after I was ready to read my mother's journal.

Reed was by my side every step of the way. He'd hold me in his arms while I flipped through the pages. If I found something confusing, he'd read it with me and try to see it from a different perspective or help me decipher the rambling scrawl. It was harder in the beginning pages, when her mind was addled from her addictions. There were pages filled with only my name written repeatedly.

Then there was scribbling that made little sense. I imagine those were written during a good high. The pages that describe how she hated herself and wanted it all to end likely were the days she was crashing down. Back and forth they'd go until slowly the words became clearer. They became more like letters written to me. Or, to the girl she imagined I was as a child.

She said I was better off without her. Because she wasn't clean, and she wasn't good. The sweet words didn't last all that long before they'd turn back to dark and ugly. It was written over years and years, and it doesn't appear she was ever sober for long. That's something I hope Temple can clear up for me.

There were a lot of apologies on the pages. Both for me and my father. All ring hollow when there was never follow through on making her mistakes right.

There were also pages where she blamed me, or rather being pregnant with me, for her state of mind.

I haven't forgiven her, and I don't think I ever can. Feeling sorry for her illness is another matter, but there was never anything I could do to help her with that. Dad and I discussed it when I finished reading the journal, and I'm certain he tried everything he could to help her.

My mother is behind me now. My own motherhood is what I am focused on, and I'll be a damn good one. With people who I trust by my side to help me if I stumble in ways she did. Reed will battle any demons that rear their heads with me. He won't leave my side; I know that now.

I have faith in him and in us.

"There he is," Reed says, nodding his head to a table in the back of the café.

"How do you know?" I whisper.

"Love. He looks just like you. Same eyes, same freckles."

The stranger stares at me while I stare back at him. There is no question. The man must be Temple. By the looks of him, he's as nervous about this meeting as I am. We've written back and forth a few times, but we never wrote anything too important. All the letters were little more than pleasantries and details of this meetup.

Reed was adamant I was not to give Temple too many of my personal details until we met him in person. We'd love to take him at face value, but we don't want to be stupid either. Especially with the baby on the way.

"Leighton?" he asks, standing from his chair. He rakes the blonde curls back off his forehead with his left hand. It's a longer, shaggier cut. One that's more popular with the younger crowd. Temple is less than five years younger than me, but that still only makes him twenty-four.

"Yes, hi. You must be Temple," I answer, a tear trying to leak out of one eye. Reed notices and swipes it away before it falls.

"Hi, yeah," he says with a wide grin. "Just so you know, I'm kind of a crier. If you go there, I go with you."

"Ah, hell. I didn't bring enough tissues for the both of you," Reed teases. "I'm Reed, Leighton's fiancé."

"Nice to meet you both. The pregnancy making you cry a lot?" Temple asks.

"You have no idea." I take a seat in the chair Reed pulls out for me, the one directly across from my brother.

Holy shit, I have a brother.

"I'm a labor and delivery nurse," he says. "I have a decent idea."

"Oh. You said you worked in the medical field, but I wouldn't have guessed that."

"I knew at an early age it was the field I wanted to be in. Big dreams of being a doctor and saving everyone's lives, and all that. I was able to get scholarships to get me through nursing school, and I figured medical school could come later," he says. Reed tenses beside me, his palm stretching out over my thigh. We discussed the possibility that Temple could be after money, that he could be an addict like she was. "Honestly, though? I love what I do. This job started out as a temporary step in the right direction. But I love it too much to leave it now. And in a way, it feels like I'm helping mothers because I couldn't help mine."

"Can I ask what happened to your dad?"

Temple looks down at his coffee for a moment before he answers, swirling a finger in caramel colored liquid, then sucking it clean.

"My dad was her dealer. Maybe you guessed that already. He stuck around for about six years, but they weren't good years. When they were high, they were nice, but were never hungry and would forget to feed me. When they weren't high, well, things were violent. But at least there would be some groceries around, you know?" He stops because I cannot stave off the crying now. I've known him all of three minutes and I'm so mad on behalf of the little boy he was. "Hey, Leighton, no. It's fine, I'm fine now. I'm not trying to upset you, I just… I just want to know you and I want you to know me."

"I'm sorry," I cry. "Ignore me, keep going." Reed hands me a tissue and gives a nod to Temple for him to continue.

"Eventually the drugs started to dry up, for one reason or another. He was gone more and more, and Mom had her first experience with being clean. She kicked him out, though he continually tried to come back. Until one day he didn't. She thought he'd left for good, but he'd been killed in a deal gone bad. The day after we found out, she scored and stayed high for days because she blamed herself for his death."

"Fuck, man. I'm sorry," Reed says.

"It's fine." Temple shrugs. "Things weren't good after he died, but they were better than they'd been with him there."

We talk more about his childhood, mostly the depressing details of how she'd turned to sex work to pay the bills and provide meager sustenance. Temple is smart though; he hasn't let the circumstances of his childhood hold him back. He's used them to fuel his ambitions.

He has a girlfriend, a fellow nurse. They've been together for two years. Isabelle is her name, and she wanted to come along today but she's working, and Temple didn't want to overwhelm me.

By the time our three-hour coffee date is winding down, it's clear that he isn't fishing for anything from me. He's sweet as pie, and has cried with me no less than four times.

"I wish we had more time, but I have a shift in an hour," he says. "Can we do this again? Would that be okay with you?"

Temple blushes, and Reed laughs lightly under his breath.

"Temple, you're not getting rid of us now that we're in your life," my fiancé tells him.

"Yeah? It's not too much having a long-lost brother?" His eyes dart between us.

"No, it's actually kind of the greatest thing ever," I say on a sob and drag him into my arms for a hug. "I always wanted one."

"Thank fuck." He sighs into my shoulder. "I always wanted a family, too."

EPILOGUE 2. REED

"Fuuuuuuucccccckkkkk! Is it supposed to hurt this bad? This can't be normal," Leighton cries. "Something's wrong, Connor. Reed, fix it!"

Connor and I share a glance over her hospital bed, his wide eyes telling me he's feeling the same thing I am.

Terrified.

Not because anything is wrong with the baby. According to the doctor and the crew of nurses on duty, we're moving along exactly how we're supposed to be. The estimated guess is that the baby will be here within the next couple of hours.

No, we're terrified of Leighton. She's been possessed by a demon, if the words being spewed out of her mouth today are any indication, anyway.

Leighton has a dirty mouth at the right moment, but she's never been foul. Today, she's used every curse word you can think of and some I'm sure she's made up on the spot. They come out of her in long streams of creative combinations. And they're nearly always directed at Connor and me.

Though I don't know what the fuck I've done.

"Love, I can't fix it. Unless you've changed your mind about an epidural. Do you want one now?" I bring the cool washcloth back to her face to wipe the fresh wave of painful tears. Leighton was adamant she did not want a 'huge-ass motherfucking needle' shoved in her. She's doing this drug free. And no amount of reason has changed her mind.

"No. Why do you keep asking me that? Do you hate me? Did I fuck your husband or something?" she yells through another wave of pain.

I burst out laughing. Though I try to turn away from her to hide it, there's no way to mask the loud guffaw. Worse, Connor and June join in.

"It's not funny." Now she's whining. "None of this is humorous. I'm dying over here, and you three are fucking laughing at me."

"Ah, Leighton. You're not dying, you're having your beautiful baby today." June steps in to ease the situation, knowing she is the one getting the least wrath coming from my wife today.

Yeah… wife. We're all official as of only two weeks ago. That wasn't the plan. We hadn't come up with much of a plan. There didn't seem to be a rush. Until one day Leighton woke me up at three in the morning and said we had to get married right away. She was suddenly very concerned about being in the hospital and the staff not letting me into the room because I wasn't her husband or some such shit. It was all dramatic but there was no settling her down about it. Once I agreed that we could get married whenever and however she wanted, she stilled and fell back to sleep.

I expected her to forget by morning, but she didn't. Within days, she had us set up with a Justice of the Peace and our family all flown in to be witnesses.

I'm now Reed Ward-Turner, legally. Though, that is because of my own lunatic ramblings. She didn't ask me to do it. But here's how I see it —the baby she's about to deliver will be a Ward-Anders. It will only carry half her last name and none of mine. I get it, but I don't love the idea that any babies Leighton and I have carry both her last names and only one of mine. It's an insanely trivial thing, but those are my specialty. Like the whole kissing thing.

This way, our future children will have the same last names as both their parents. And I'll have a connection with this one in the name Ward.

The process here in Louisiana was a tad daunting, but worth it when

I saw the look on Leighton's face when it became official. That family connection means more to her than she likes to let on.

Maybe it's dumb, but I don't give a shit. I like it; Leighton and Larry loved it. That's all that matters. Everyone else can fuck right off. Nothing about our family, including its extended members, is conventional. We're a messed up, twisted bunch who's making their own set of rules in life.

"It hurts, June. Get the doctor, please! There's something else in there with the baby. Babies are cute and slobbery and would never cause this much pain. It has got to be something else. Like an alien. I think I have a Xenomorph in me." Her face is red as she rides out this long contraction.

"Our baby is not an alien, Leighton," Connor braves the words through another bout of laughter.

"Fuck you, Connor Anders! This is really why you fled to Thailand, isn't it? Because you knew what you put inside me. It's probably hereditary. I always said Noah couldn't possibly be human."

"Yes, sweetheart. It's all part of the Anders' master plan of populating the world. One cyborg at a time," he says with a snort.

"Okay, okay," I butt in. "Can you two give me a few minutes with my wife?" I direct the question to Connor and my sister. Leighton needs something like a touch grass moment. A little grounding right now will go a long way. At least, I hope.

After the two leave the room and Leighton's contraction subsides, I sit on the side of the bed, letting her curl into my chest while I run my hands over her head. She's slick with perspiration and a slight tremble still rocks her body.

"Reed, this is so hard."

"I know, my Love." I cup the back of her head and make her look up at me. "There's nothing I can do to help you with the pain, and I hate that so much. But you can do this, and on the other end of it is going to be the most perfect little human waiting to be cuddled and loved by its mommy. Who cannot be throwing ridiculous or mean words at every person that walks through that door."

I keep it light; I'm not scolding her or telling her how to deal with the situation. I'm trying to get her to calm down, she's far too agitated. Her body is going through some shit right now.

"Am I being mean?" she asks, tears welling in her eyes.

"Not so much, but you have told Connor to fuck off twelve times in the last twenty minutes. And I think you made one of the nurses cry earlier. Maybe we can tone some of that down?"

"Oh, no," she says, embarrassed. "Am I losing my mind?"

"No, sweetheart. You're in labor. It's a lot. You need to decide if you have it in you to go a little longer or if you want the doctor to help with the pain."

"I don't want needles, Reed."

"Okay, so how can I help?"

"This helps. You touching me and talking to me," she says, wrapping her arms around me to pull me closer.

We haven't spent any time apart since she put that ring on her finger. Every night ends this way, her body spread over mine. Though the sex has slowed the closer the due date came, the intimacy we share hasn't been curbed. One of my favorite things is massaging lotion into her tired skin after a long day. She hasn't slowed down with work, and I'm glad because she's finding so much fulfillment in it.

Fran suggested Leighton write a feature every issue for pregnant women that will morph into new motherhood when she returns to work after having the baby. Leighton embraced it wholeheartedly and has even become a champion of sorts for a mommy-to-be group of low-income and single mothers by hooking them up with resources around the city they weren't aware of.

She's taking her pregnancy in stride, even though the crying never went away. She still does that at the drop of a dime.

Connor set up a schedule that worked for everyone and he's been able to be involved. I would go to her appointments with her and video chat with him, so he felt present. We did the same thing during her baby shower, and when we set up the nursery at both our new house and my duplex.

Connor and I have become friends. There isn't any animosity between us. The more he saw of Leighton and I together, the more he understood the love we have for each other. He admitted that he couldn't give her that, and that maybe the baby confused things for him. Maybe that's the truth of it, I don't know, but I know that I like we've found a place where we can be honest and work together for the family we're building.

"I'll keep touching you through it all," I tell her, rubbing my nose against hers. "And in a couple of months, I'm going to show your poor battered body how much I appreciate all the work it's doing right now."

"A couple of months feels so far away." She sighs heavily.

"It does right now, but it's going to fly by. And I want you nicely healed before I shove my cock and tongue back in your pretty cunt." A shiver runs down her spine and it's the response I want. The one that says she's feeling languid and gooey… at least a little bit for a moment or two before the next contraction hits. "I still can't wait to know what you'll taste like without all the added hormones or whatever."

"Do you think it will be that different?'

"I don't know." I shrug. "But I have this flavor committed to memory and am excited to add another to my pallet."

"You are so obsessed with me, weirdo."

"I am. I always will be," I confirm.

The next few hours are about the same. Her enduring all the pain and me occasionally kicking everyone out so I have a few minutes to help her relax between them.

Until it's time and the doctor comes into the room to deliver our son.

Orion Frey Ward-Anders.

Leighton and Connor made a deal that she could pick the first name if he could pick the middle. She chose Orion because the constellations have bigger meaning to her now since I told her they don't exist for me without her. She may be feisty on the outside, but she's a mushy romantic at heart. That suits me fine, because I am one, too.

Frey has a Norse meaning of prosperity and fertility. Which fits, since this child fought strong odds to be conceived, and it will be prosperous with the abundance of family. An indication of that is shown on the faces of everyone in the hospital with us.

My family is here; June and my mother sobbing in Drew's arms. Larry is here holding Leighton's hand while the baby is passed around to be cooed at. Connor's family all stopped in, too. Including Noah's wife and their newborn, who have been sitting patiently in the waiting room. Lorelai, being a new mother herself, even dropped off a gift basket full of self-care products for Leighton. It was sweet, and the more we're around her, the more we understand why Noah loves her so much.

We may be one of the most oddly entwined of families and we may shun many of societies' norms. But there is no lack of love or support. What Noah told me that night replays in my mind often. We're good fighters, this lot. We fight for one another; we fight through whatever comes our way. We fight for love, and in the end, that's always worth it.

ABOUT THE AUTHOR

Alison lives somewhere in the shadow of a Pacific Northwest Mountain, bordered by the Puget Sound, and not too far from the country roads she grew up on.

When she's not writing, she can be found avidly reading, traveling with youthful wanderlust, or slowly turning the inside of her home into her own personal houseplant jungle.

MORE FROM AUTHOR ALISON RHYMES

Subscribe to Alison's Newsletter for Early News and Bonus Scenes

Broken Play

They have ties that bind.

June grew up in the shadow of her brother and his best friend, Drew McKenna. She stood back while Drew dated his way through high school and college, watching and waiting. Waiting for him to realize he loved her as much as she loved him.

When he did, it was the happiest she'd ever been. Until she found him with another woman only five years after their marriage.

Leaving her husband was a simple decision, but there was no easy way to cut him out of her family.

When June receives a fresh start to her career, she also finds what could be a new lease on love. Reality hits Drew with a vengeance.

He wants her back.

She wants to make him suffer.

Brutal Play

Mistress.

Whore.

Lorelai has been called every name in the book. Except for the ones she's always dreamed of.

My love.

Mine.

Noah Anders is the only man to have ever owned her heart. But it's her soul he wants.

Theirs is a battle of wills, tempers, ego, friendship, and loyalty.

He wants retribution.

She just wants to survive.

www.ingramcontent.com/pod-product-compliance
Lightning Source LLC
Chambersburg PA
CBHW061251310726
48971CB00007B/2310